In the Name of the Father

IN THE NAME OF THE
FATHER

An Essay on Quebec Nationalism

DANIEL POLIQUIN

Translated by Don Winkler

Douglas & McIntyre
Vancouver / Toronto

01 02 03 04 05 / 5 4 3 2 1

Douglas & McIntyre Ltd.
2323 Quebec Street, Suite 201
Vancouver, British Columbia V5T 4S7

National Library of Canada Cataloguing in Publication Data
Poliquin, Daniel
    In the name of the father

    Translation of: Le roman colonial.
    ISBN 1-55054-858-1
    1. Nationalism—Quebec (Province). 2. Canadians, French-speaking—
Quebec (Province). 3. Quebec (Province)—History—Autonomy and
independence movements. I. Winkler, Donald. II. Title.
FC2926.9.N3P6413 2001   320.54'09714   C2001-910233-X
F1053.2.P6413 2001

We gratefully acknowledge the financial support of the Canada Council for
the Arts, the British Columbia Ministry of Tourism, Small Business and
Culture, and the Government of Canada through the Book Publishing
Industry Development Program (BPIDP) for our publishing activities.

Copy editing by Robin Van Heck
Cover design by Gordon Robertson
Front cover caricatures by Michael Darmanin
Front cover photograph by David Laurence
Text design and typesetting by Julie Cochrane
Printed and bound in Canada by Friesens
Printed on acid-free paper

Contents

~

To my friend André Binette,
who'll vote yes, no matter what.

～ Foreword

I SOMETIMES HAVE the feeling that our history is an unending novel about a colony. And so I thought I'd have a go at writing my own chapter. As things now stand . . .

～ Reader, My Mirror-Image, My Kin

NOVEMBER, ST. DENIS Street, Montreal.

As he does every Friday, Charles-Olivier Lesieur, book-lover and nationalist, is browsing in his favourite bookstore. On the shelf of new arrivals my book is staring him in the face. He's heard about it. It's my colonial novel, *In the Name of the Father,* and he will avoid it like the plague. He won't read it, and he certainly won't buy it. Tempted nevertheless to pick up a copy just to dog-ear it a bit before tossing it back, he gives it a quick glance.

Then another gentleman comes in, well-dressed, and in a loud voice asks for my book. A young salesman points him in the right direction. The gentleman makes an obvious point of picking it off the shelf, and says to the petite woman at the cash: "I know nothing about politics, it's a gift." The little cashier gives him a neutral smile. The gentleman leaves.

Charles-Olivier watches him go, outraged to see this stranger buying, right under his nose, a book that he sees as pernicious. He decides that his day will not be complete if he can't deliver a little moral lesson. Since he has to address it to someone, he picks on the young salesman. "Aren't you ashamed to be selling books like that, published by turncoats who take money from the Canada Council for the Arts? It's disgraceful!" The young salesman, who's had a long day, musters a tolerant expression. "Well, I'll have no part of it! You can fleece the taxpayer, maybe, but not the consumer. I'll be back once you've taken that book off your shelves. Good day!" The other customers trade knowing glances. They've seen it all before . . .

The bookstore returns to its library-like state of tranquillity. Making a show of being busy, the salesman goes to the counter with a few sale books and dawdles long enough to ask the girl at the cash if she's free after work. With a quick look, she makes it clear that the answer is yes. He smiles. She smiles.

OUR FRIEND LESIEUR is proud of himself, and with reason. It's not every day one does a good deed and saves money at the same time. And so he goes over in his mind what he'll tell his buddies at the office. "They wanted me to buy a copy, they almost twisted my arm! I told them where to go and walked out! You should have seen their faces!" His colleague at the next desk, who reads all the book reviews but never the books because she doesn't have the time, will inevitably say that she's seen some parts of it, and yes, it is unsavoury. Which will take some of the lustre off Lesieur's coup.

No, better say nothing. Especially since someone in the department might ask them both if in fact they've read the book. A little upstart, new on the job, had pulled that stunt when Mordecai Richler launched the literary torpedo about which all right-thinking Quebeckers had an opinion even if they'd never laid eyes on it. "I read some passages," Lesieur and his colleague had replied in unison. "So your opinion is worthless," the newcomer had shot back. "To have read some passages of Proust is not to have read *Remembrance of Things Past,*

2

I'm sorry." Lesieur doesn't much like this former neophyte who has since become his boss. And so he decides to obey his first impulse: lips sealed!

On the other hand, he could use the anecdote to get under the skin of his regular bridge partner. He's a person of independent means who always votes no, doubtless because of his money. Those with possessions are possessed by what they possess, said Charles de Gaulle to explain why the French bourgeois rallied to the Vichy regime. "What the hell," he thinks, "with this story I'll get a rise out of my rich friend, and that will make me feel better. Too bad he's so deaf."

As this is in fact his bridge night he hastens his steps, looking forward to a change of scene — and who would blame him?

HE ARRIVES AT HIS club, shakes a few hands, and settles in at his usual table. The hostess, a charming woman that he's had his eye on for a while now, tells him that his usual partner, the hard-of-hearing man of affluence, is under the weather. As a matter of fact, the poor fellow is bedridden. She has, however, found someone to take his place, none other than the well-dressed gentleman earlier encountered. Just his luck, one Canadian is filling in for another.

Lesieur rises to greet him, a bit ill at ease, but determined at the first opportunity to put him in his place. But the other doesn't recognize him, doesn't seem even to have noticed him at the bookstore, preoccupied as he was with his ideological purchase. A bit wounded in his self-esteem, Charles-Olivier is consoled by the thought that at least he can get on with his game.

As the evening unfolds he studies his new partner, who it's clear is none the wiser. He watches for anglicisms in his speech that would betray his inferior education and his status as a colonized individual wanting in memory. But in vain. The gentleman speaks as well as he dresses, talks less loudly than in the bookstore, and even gets off a few well-turned phrases for the benefit of the charming hostess. Lesieur is disappointed. He would have preferred the man to be something of a fool. He's not, and what's more, he's a good card player, which is particularly irritating. At the break, the two men get to know each other a little. They are surprised to discover that they went to the same school, and that they liked the same film in the same year, *My Uncle Benjamin,* with Jacques Brel, who for once gave a good performance. Decidedly, this well-dressed gentleman is hard to dislike.

Together they beat the pants off the opposition, Madame Laramée and Mademoiselle Laplante. They even rack up the best score in the club. Then comes the party. Tea is served, and nibblies, and polite conversation ensues.

Everyone heads home, but Charles-Olivier lingers awhile to pay court to his charming hostess, who is a McGill graduate and newly divorced, or so it is rumoured. Suddenly, on an empty chair, a bag from the bookstore catches his eye. But the well-dressed man has already left. As no one is around, Charles-Olivier opens the bag and sees inside, of course, the book he didn't want. The gentleman, too cavalier perhaps, must have left it behind. Deftly he slips the bag into his jacket pocket, fully intending to return it the following month to this partner who, when you come down to it, is not so bad after all.

On his way home in the bus, Charles-Olivier, unsettled a bit by his dubious acquisition, forgets for a moment the lovely eyes of the charming hostess, and wonders whether he shouldn't at least peek at the book. He will be careful, of course, to turn the pages gently so as to leave no trace of his having perused it. What counts in the end is to be frank while remaining civil, and if you can save a little money in the process, where's the harm? The opportunity is too good to let pass. And so he will read the enemy, determined in advance to be bored, and that will give him a perfect chance to nail his boss to the wall, telling him yes, he's actually read this dangerous book, and he knows whereof he speaks! That will also silence his colleague at the next desk, the tiresome lady who reads all the professional critics . . . "And anyway I don't have to read it to the very end, I'll just say I decided to stop, it was too revolting, simple as that."

He picks up the book, opens it.

WHAT IS THE well-dressed gentleman doing all this time? Well, believe it or not, he has wangled a rendezvous with the charming hostess and is waiting for her in a small quiet bar. No way to know more than that. What I do know, on the other hand, and this from a reliable source, is that the young salesman and the little cashier have made great strides: the lucky boy and girl are coupling vigorously. It was bound to happen, it was in the stars.

And what of us, in all that? Not much. Like Monsieur Lesieur, we are looking forward to the upcoming pages of this long colonial novel which was begun centuries ago and which, chances are, has a long future still ahead of it.

I
The Language of
Our Fathers

~

∼ The Man of Faith

CHARLES-OLIVIER LESIEUR: a pretty name, it even has a noble ring to it. Of course it's not exactly his, I've altered it somewhat to avoid legal complications. It's the sort of ruse that commonly serves to spare the feelings of whomever. After all, I certainly wouldn't want to open a book and see myself named and described from head to toe, my most intimate thoughts revealed. It would be enough to give one a persecution complex, something that for a straight-arrow nationalist like our friend would be most superfluous. And so Lesieur.

(You will have noted here, I hope, a certain delicacy on my part. I could have saddled him with a name that would make you smile. Labine, for example. Let's not stop there: Frank Labine. But such mockery would be too facile, and dishonest as well, because my reader-hero is not a caricature with a human face such as you find in summer theatres or Quebec films. No, he's all nuance. Like the rest of us. In fact, there are no nationalists free of secret or avowed contradictions, just as there are no Canadians free of paradox. These subtleties will perhaps irk dyed-in-the-wool ideologues more at home with easy targets, but that's their problem. And don't go looking either for any high-mindedness in what I've done. No, it's just that the name Frank Labine was already taken—it belongs to the well-dressed gentleman, the bridge whiz.)

A word on his first name. It really is Charles, but his godfather's first name was Émile, and on his baptismal record there is no hyphen. Charles Émile looks old-fashioned, and besides, you'd think it were the name of a Quebec horse. And so all through his youth Lesieur had himself called Charlie, just like all the other Charleses.

Once in university he found himself with four other Charleses in his sociology class—the Quebec family is so small that fashionable Christian names spread like weeds. You want proof? The Michels and Dianes of yesteryear are today called Mathieu and Stéphanie. In the 1960s, when the cult of the 1837 Patriotes was revived, our Charlie fell in love with their beautiful double-barrelled names, Denis-Benjamin Viger, George-Étienne Cartier (ah yes . . .), and he made his first nationalist profession of faith by dubbing himself Olivier. The ennobling hyphen came later. When old friends hailed him with a "Hey, Charlie!" that to his ears was too loud, he let them know in no uncertain terms that he had decolonized himself. Even today, he fumes if someone resurrects his English diminutive.

The only problem is that he never let the registry office in on his patriotic flirtation, and that has caused him all sorts of problems with the Quebec taxman, who doesn't take it lightly when people fool with their identity. And some people may get a bit of a shock when they discover his actual first name on the day the bell tolls for him at last and his obituary appears. But Charles-Olivier never thinks about his own death, only the death of his people, and that one he has determined to ward off by voting yes in all the referendums. Or almost all.

Everyone knows a Charles-Olivier Lesieur. A good man

that can be found, happily, in the millions. Nothing in his nature is liable to win him either public regard or public censure. Born in Kamouraska in 1948, he is my contemporary, although older by six years. His father was a general storekeeper, town councillor, Knight of Columbus, and from time to time organizer for the Union Nationale party. His mother was a teacher before she married. He has four brothers and three sisters, a large family today, then one of normal size. He did well in primary school, fairly well at high school in Ste. Anne de la Pocatière. He is of the last generation to have studied a little Greek and much Latin, learning that he detested then and is inordinately proud of now. Finally, he received a bachelor's degree at Laval and a master's in library science from the University of Montreal.

After his studies he was tempted briefly by the thought of teaching in those countries piously referred to as Developing, but his fiancée at the time insisted that his health was not sufficiently robust, which was the truth, and he has never forgiven her. "Were it not for you I would have known adventure, distant perfumed lands. Our children would have grown up differently, they would have met interesting people, but you never wanted that . . . ."

And so Charles-Olivier started out and ended up as a librarian in the Montreal civic administration. For a while he had his eye on Ottawa, where there were better-paying jobs in his field, but he would have had to learn English and distance himself from his little world. The grapes were unripe, he decided, and he never risked applying. A few years later, when nationalist protests were at their height, he began telling those around him that he had deliberately turned his back on that corrupting civil service because he had refused to pledge allegiance to the Queen of England. As no one congratulated him, he stopped talking about it. Once, however, he tried resurrecting this image-enhancing legend to impress his children, but his wife laughed in his face in the presence of his offspring, and this affront too he has never forgiven her. That's not all. In contradicting him, she'd even had the gall to say, "Come on, *Charlie!*" How low can you stoop?

It's disconcerting to see one's heroic halo tarnished, even if it's a bogus one. In this respect Charles-Olivier would have done better to settle in Ottawa, he would have been in good company. I myself, who studied at the local bilingual university, have lost track of the number of Québécois who claimed they were there because their political activities led the provincial authorities to bar them from all the Quebec colleges. Separatists exiled to Ottawa, that didn't quite hold water. My predecessors, for their part, had met those who said they'd fled the Duplessis regime. Each Ottawa generation has had its own wave of phony Quebec refugees. Lesieur would have been right at home. You can become an instant hero there with no trouble at all.

He had two children. Scrimping and saving, he bought himself a little house on Gohier Island. But as he wouldn't stop cheating on his wife with his colleague at the next desk, the reader of reviews, one fine day Madame left him there with the children and returned to Sherbrooke. Poor him. He paid dearly for his dalliance. For three long years he was saddled with child care on top of his work, until his wife finished training as a nurse and took the children back. It was a hard grind, and as the concept of leave for work-related stress had not yet been hatched, his bosses and workmates offered him no sympathy. Nor did his adjacent colleague. Times were hard, and to safeguard his health he treated himself to a little jaunt in Italy, thereby missing the 1980 referendum. But no one needs to know that, and besides, it's the thought that counts . . .

He saw little of his children after that, and ended up selling the house on Gohier Island, but that suited him rather well even if he dared not show it too clearly. Charles-Olivier moved back to Montreal, into a studio worthy of an indigent student. He returned to the carefree life of his youth, dutifully paying support money to his ungrateful ex and blowing the rest of his income on fine books and good restaurant meals. An unexceptional destiny for a man who does no one any harm and, despite what he tells the women he is courting, does not suffer unduly. Like many other men he imagines that the sins he ascribes to his former spouse will incite his future conquests to compensate him for his unhappiness.

His children are no longer children. They didn't go far in their studies, something he never fails to reproach them for—them and their mother—but he is wrong in that. They earn their living honourably, the elder as a laboratory technician and the younger as a teacher in a daycare. Charles-Olivier rarely sees them but there seems to be no animosity on either side. Things are all right, in other words. He's not yet a grandfather, which makes him feel rueful and relieved at the same time.

Professionally he's achieved, to say the least, nothing spectacular, but he's never complained either. He didn't feel he was suited for upper management, and he never blamed anyone for his lack of advancement. He was active in the union at one point but drifted away when the Parti Québécois, in 1981, divested its loyal servants of their pre-referendum bribes. Bad years. Ever since he's refused, haughtily, to be a member of the party even if it's the only one he'd ever vote for. National solidarity will have its due.

Now he's very much focussed on one thing. In 2003 he will have completed thirty-three years of service, which will entitle him to an almost full pension. If his calculations are accurate, and they generally are in such matters, the blessed day will fall on a Wednesday. He won't be living extravagantly, he's put almost nothing aside because he has a stubbornly aristocratic contempt for money. He's decided not to do volunteer work, nor to travel. He will cash in his RRSP savings, will go to the movies often, and will take advantage of all the reductions afforded the elderly. He does intend to join those associations that encourage repertory theatre and symphony orchestras, as one must do one's bit in life to support high culture. And that way he will meet people — women especially.

Speaking of women. We are aware of no frequentations on his part at present, nor does he seem to be going out of his way to seek them. For a long time he favoured married women, more accommodating than those who wanted to settle down. Cruising the bars was not his style either. He much preferred an encounter at a concert or a theatre matinee, but for that you must be patient. Fortunately he is. He had recently taken up again with his colleague, but that went sour when she bought the building in which he lives. It was one thing for her to be his mistress but quite another for her to be his landlady — I don't know why, but it made him feel her inferior. They pass the time of day all the same when their paths cross, and it's perhaps her recollection of the good times they had that keeps her from raising his rent. Just as his feeling towards her stops him from giving her an earful every time she recites word for word what's in the cultural pages of papers he's already read.

In short, he's a good person with no serious flaws, other than his view of the opposite sex, which is marred by a sense of injustice and could do with some rethinking. You can always count on him when it's a question of recycling or collections at the office, and he never refuses to help out new colleagues. He's cultivated as well. He reads, and quite a lot; his tastes are eclectic, and you can't stump him when it comes to the literary scene.

He can tell you who owns what publishing house, which one a particular writer is with and why. But you'll never meet him at the Montreal Book Fair, with its panel discussions and its futile "signings." A vulgar spectacle.

This man has everything it takes to be happy. He sometimes fancies that when he retires — his retirement is a frequent preoccupation — he'll buy a condo with his savings and the small legacy he received from his parents, somewhere in that rural Quebec he pretends to love: Sorel or the Gaspé. But that he loves from a distance only. In fact this city mouse looks down on those villages, and rather unkindly deems them impervious to high culture.

He's no innocent, Charles-Olivier. He's seen a lot of Europe and, as is not uncommon, adores France but detests the French. For a while he studied German at the Goethe Institute, but the language quickly stymied him. He fell back on Spanish, which he thought would be easier, given its link to Latin, but here again he was disappointed. He gets along in English, reads it easily in any case. He's never been to Florida, something of which he is proud, as he finds the Québécois who live there too common for his taste. He prefers Spain. Italy isn't bad either.

HE'S A NATIONALIST, he'll say so himself. But he doesn't like the word taken alone. He always appends the adjectives "open" and "modern," like all those who read *Time,* go to Costa Rica in winter, and eat at a Chinese restaurant at least once a year, with chopsticks, of course.

When told that nationalism in France is Le Pen, and in Russia Zhirinovsky, he climbs the walls. One mustn't say that, it's not fair, Bouchard has nothing in common with Milosevic (which is true). And moreover, it shows a shocking ignorance of

the Quebec reality. Here nationalism is free of suspect frater-
nizations and will never lead to gas chambers or serial rapes.
Elsewhere is elsewhere and here it's not the same. The logic is
irrefutable.

He shudders when you mention Camus, who said he loved
his country too well to be a nationalist. He replies that if Camus
had experienced the monstrous injustice of Canada . . . You
wound him also when you remind him of General de Gaulle's
pronouncement: "Nationalists are those who exploit the nation
to the detriment of others." He says that the quotation has been
taken out of context, and besides, de Gaulle supported Quebec's
aspirations for independence. Don't worry, he has an answer for
everything.

But Charles-Olivier could not tell you just when he felt the
call. Was it during the "McGill français" demonstrations? No,
he wasn't there. His brother yes, but not him. Was it a book that
marked him, or a professor? No, not really. De Gaulle on the
City Hall balcony, July 28, 1967? Not that either. He was astonished at the time, but there was no feeling of pride. Perhaps his
family. His father voted blue, his mother red, nothing very remarkable there. He never heard Canon Groulx's name spoken
in the house. Perhaps, then, the October Crisis? In retrospect,
he would love to be able to say yes, but his wife had just given
birth and he had other concerns.

Try as he will, he can't find the moment. His memory seems
to be failing him. And by the way, what is the name of the charming hostess at the bridge club who has a degree from McGill, a
round bottom, and a lovely smile, and who is unattached? A
pharmacist to boot, a fine match for a fellow like himself. And
who doesn't smoke. But good God, what is her name? He was
introduced to her, after all. For the moment he can only recall
the face of his new partner, Frank Labine. Age, really . . .

Charles-Olivier does remember, however, when he bought his membership card for Pierre Bourgault's Rassemblement pour l'indépendance nationale, the RIN. It was the first and last time he joined a political party, and it was just before the 1966 elections. He couldn't yet vote, but he was a supporter all the same. Proud of himself, he'd shown the card to the young woman who was to be the mother of his children. She'd only said, "Ah yes . . ." That was all. Can you imagine that? It's unthinkable, it's appalling! You're there wanting to liberate your country, and she says, "Ah, yes . . ." Mind you, in her family no one had anything to do with politics, it was considered good only for profiteers and dreamers. That's what discouraged Charles-Olivier from ever following through on his beautiful gesture. Always her. He told her that she was colonized! It was the first time he used that word to insult someone, and he's used it often since. She didn't even react, she just went off shopping with her mother. He was so put off that he didn't phone her for two days.

When the question is asked, he says he's always been a nationalist. He secretly envies those who can boast of a long-standing commitment, like Michel Chartrand, who was an activist in the 1930s and whose marriage was performed by Lionel Groulx himself. Charles-Olivier can't point to a single moment of truth. He is a nationalist because.

In truth, Monsieur Lesieur is a believer. Only that, but that above all. His is the serene and simple faith that knows no doubts. Which is perfect, as nationalism is a religion, with its dogmas, its crusaders, its priests, and its heretics.

A few dogmas. English Canada is not a real country, and the only culture here worthy of the name is French. The English hate us. The Night of the Long Knives is a fact. Quebec is a country that was conquered in 1760, the Québécois are a conquered people. Whoever does not agree with this is colonized, whoever agrees has discovered freedom, individual freedom that will one day be followed by collective freedom. Hydro-Québec is ours. The Jews are against us because they are with the English, and when Mordecai Richler brings up the anti-Semitic statements made by some pillars of the independence movement, it's to damage us in foreign eyes.

What else? Oh yes. Sovereignty-association is feasible, and the day after a yes in the referendum we will at last be able to negotiate people to people! Lucien Bouchard said so. Independence is the only way to ensure linguistic and cultural security for Quebec, and without it the Québécois will disappear, to the very last person. The French minorities in the English provinces have all been massacred. Pierre Bourgault said so. We've been good to the Indians, those ingrates. We've been generous to the English, who are racists. All those who are assimilated are traitors or sad souls. All Franco-Ontarians are assimilated or will be soon. One day no one will speak French any more on the island of Montreal. The individual rights we enjoy in Canada are all very well, but as Canada refuses to recognize our collective rights, they're worthless. Lionel Groulx was a great man, never mind what they say. Pierre Falardeau has talent. Josée Legault writes well. The constitutional status quo is unacceptable. Lise Bissonnette said so. Jean Chrétien is an embarrassment to us abroad. Hydro-Québec is ours, you can't say it often enough.

Rock-solid certainties. He'll die as he has lived, a believer. I always tell those of my friends who work hard to make Canada loved that they're wasting their time with Monsieur Lesieur. Not because he is stupid or ignorant. On the contrary. But as I just said, he's a believer! He's sure that he is being lied to when he's presented with arguments—however well supported by the evidence — that run counter to his own ideas. Repeat in his presence a declaration of Lionel Groulx that reeks of anti-Semitism, and it's as though you were sullying the name of Mohammed in front of a Muslim. You could tie him to a chair and recite the whole gamut of arguments, as reasonable and generous as can be, proving the need for a federative bond, and he won't retain a single one. In *Remembrance of Things Past,* Proust rightly says: "Facts have no access to the world where our beliefs reside." That's the way it is.

I hold that Monsieur Lesieur's ideas are to be respected. Just as we respect the Jehovah's Witnesses who do not celebrate Christmas, the Jews who won't eat shellfish, or the Catholics who believe in the Virgin Mary. Don't think I consider myself more intelligent than he is, or that I imagine myself free of irrational or unfounded beliefs, that's far from the case. The author's no better than his reader.

∼ The Man of Little Faith

A LESIEUR DOESN'T like a Labine. "With a name like that he must be Franco-Ontarian," says the first of the second. Colonized, in any case. And those nouveau-riche, elegant airs! Look at his scarf, the same colour as his jacket lining. You see that everywhere now. And he had the nerve to make eyes at the charming hostess at the bridge club, that's really a bit much! But good God, what is her name?

He ransacks his memory in vain, and that depresses him all over again. He really does feel he's getting old. This intimation of impending decline only adds to his pain. Soon we will all be old or dead. He suddenly remembers that Pierre Bourgault, who in his youth held him spellbound with his fiery speeches, is now sixty-six years old. Jacques Parizeau is almost seventy, Pierre Vadeboncoeur almost eighty. Not counting all those stout militants now deceased, Camille Laurin or Pierre Vallières. Even Lucien Bouchard is sixty-two, four years younger than Jean Chrétien. At least Monsieur Bouchard has young children, that's some consolation. But the others? Old men and old women.

In Quebec, say the nationalists, all the real patriots have

white hair. (It's true. I once attended a debate between sover-eigntist writers, which was more like a round table, and the average age of the participants was unsettling.) Monsieur Lesieur is right to contend that sovereignty must come quickly, other-wise Quebec will soon be no more than a separatist graveyard.

"What good are we after all," he muses. "We'll all die with-out realizing our dreams. Quebec will not be a country any more than I will have held in my arms the charming hostess." It's not a laughing matter.

And all this time, the Frank Labines eat heartily, drink good wine, read bad books and steal the wives of those worthier than themselves. "Damn it to hell, what is her name? Next bridge game I'll give him an earful, this Labine, I'll tell him what I think of those useless Francos, those sellouts, that rabble! I'll tell him everything!"

His anger quickly dissipates. "Ariane. Yes, that's it, Ariane. It's just come to me, I heard someone call her by her first name. Ariane, it's beautiful, Theseus, the Minotaur, the Labyrinth . . . She has every virtue an aesthete could wish for: she's well-spoken, she's educated, she has a career, she has excellent taste in clothes, and she must have money. If she were to place a per-sonal ad in *Le Devoir,* she'd get a reply from Outremont the very next morning. Her last name is coming back to me too, I can feel it. Yes! Claveau . . . Daviault . . . something like that! In any case I'm not far off the mark, and I know her last name harmo-nizes with her first. 'Ariane Daviault, you with all your class, would you have a soft spot in your heart for me, who's not a bad catch either? Unlike that asshole Franco-Ontarian, Frank Labine!'"

Bad news for Monsieur Lesieur: Frank Labine isn't even Franco-Ontarian. He'll have to find some other reason to hate him, but that shouldn't be too hard a task.

Frank Labine was born in Métabetchouan, in the region of Lac Saint-Jean. To this may be attributed his straightforward way of expressing himself. His father, who died young, was a farmer, and his mother, a housewife. The couple had six children, and François is the youngest. He's the only one in the family to have received a classical education, part in Jonquière, the rest at La Pocatière. He's two years older than Charles-Olivier.

Having completed his studies, he hesitated between becoming a notary or a civil servant. He opted for the private sector. An uncle who had an insurance agency in Quebec City offered to train him in the business. One year later, tired of the office routine, his uncle's laziness, and the narrow streets of Quebec that he had found so charming in summer, he was ready for a change of scene. A large company courted him. He'd already learned quite a bit of English at his aunt's in New Hampshire (like everyone else he had his Aunt-Rita-in-the-States), and he had a basic but practical knowledge which, supplemented by some private lessons in conversation from an elderly lady in the Upper Town, qualified him for a training course in Hartford, Connecticut, followed by a posting to Toronto. The great adventure had begun.

Three years in Toronto, three years in Sudbury. He returned to Quebec, having acquired a wife but not a country. Her name was Cheryl, and she came from a good family of Lithuanian miners. They had met through a choir (yes, he's a music lover) for which she was, in the evening, the designated pianist. During the day she was a secretary in a large insurance company, a happy coincidence. Monsieur and Madame Labine settled in Saint-Laurent. He became an office manager and she, a mother. Two children, a boy and a girl, who went to French school. Both attended university in Ontario, where they now live. Today they work, they have children of their own, and

Monsieur Labine is a doting grandfather who spoils his grand-children rotten.

He too is a good man. His hair is white. He wears dark suits, the gold watch he was given by his company, and a signet ring on his right hand. To see him in conversation you would think he was a municipal councillor on his way out of mass. But only if you were unaware of his disdain for politics. He votes, but with no great conviction, and the insurance business has taught him not to discuss politics with his clients. First, because there's nothing to be gained, and second, because you never know who you're going to be talking to. Selling insurance to a New Democrat pays just as well as selling to a Conservative, so why make enemies? He prefers to talk about hockey or opera.

We should therefore be wary of the thoughtful mask he puts on when in his presence the conversation turns to serious matters. His fixed expression seems to imply that his brain is a hothouse of intense deliberation. But it's more than likely that he's thinking of something quite irrelevant, or nothing at all. This apolitical animal cares as little about the Constitution as about his first long-ago drunken spree. And he's not one of those who thinks only about money: "All that matters in life is a job, okay? Bread and butter on the table!" No, it's not that at all. He's given due thought to the constitutional question, as an informed individual who browses through the newspaper every Saturday, reads a few books each year, listens to Radio-Canada, and never misses the television news at ten o'clock.

Over and over he's heard talk of Pierre Trudeau's constitu-tional power play, the yoke of Ottawa, the Canadian prison, Lise Bissonnette's shameful status quo, Pierre Falardeau's Vichy regime. And one fine day he asked himself the only question that counts: "Am I unhappy in this country? Or even, should I be?" The reply came back in the negative, with the rider that if there were beggars on every corner of St. Denis Street, it wasn't because of the Constitution. That day he turned the page for good.

He has to admit that he even likes the Charter of Rights and Freedoms. Deep down inside, he knows that a new Roncarelli Affair is impossible, the Jehovah's Witnesses will never again be persecuted, and that there will be no more Padlock Law, either. If he is sometimes ashamed of Canadian history, it's because he's been reminded that Native people did not get the vote until 1960. And when he thinks of his First Nations fellow citizens holed up on their reserves, he tells himself that we could have done a lot better in this regard, and that frankly it's about time we did. He blushes also reading the book by Irving Abella and Harold Troper, *None Is Too Many,* concerning Ottawa's anti-Semitic immigration policy during the Second World War. He gets angry when he thinks about Frederick Johnson, author of the directive that condemned thousands of innocent people to the Nazi abattoirs. He also remembers the thousands of Québécois who signed the St. Jean Baptiste Society petition against Jewish immigration. In such moments he is not proud of his country, but he does like what it has become. Not all the time, but still . . .

And so he tells himself that the Parti Québécois government can play the martyr to its heart's content, or the Quebec Liberal Party can play the nationalist game, he no longer cares either way. He's shut the door on all those outmoded or imaginary grievances. In fact, he doesn't even think about them, no more than he thinks about the Conquest or those hanged in 1837. He's at peace with himself and that's the way it is.

But he's not a Liberal. He even voted PQ in 1976 to teach Robert Bourassa a lesson for taking it for granted that the Quebec electorate was in thrall to the Liberal Party. He didn't turn out for the 1980 referendum, but in 1995 he voted yes. Not that he gave credence to the PQ line guaranteeing everyone a pie in the sky. But he was one of those strategic voters who thought they were slyer than everyone else, and believed that a strong yes vote would be good for Quebec's future, would give it more bargaining power.

But he had the scare of his life when he saw that the PQ fraud had almost worked, and he swore that he wouldn't be caught napping again. And then there was the sad pronouncement on the ethnic vote by Jacques Parizeau, this personage whom he had once respected. He was expecting de Gaulle and Le Pen turned up. It broke his heart that night to see what an imposture was this nationalism that claimed to be open and modern. Next time he would vote no with both hands.

And yet there were still days when he saw himself as a nationalist. I can understand why. To him the word means patriot, someone who loves his own people, simple as that. I love my country and those who live there, and I want the best for them with all my heart.

Ah yes, Frank. He hadn't acquired this diminutive in Ontario, it had been his since he was a child, just as his brother, whose real name was Thomas, had been Tom. The dog on the family farm was called Jim. The horses too had English names — it's an old Quebec tradition that goes back to when all the horses arrived from the West already baptized and trained with English words like *back up, whoa,* and all the rest. I'm not inventing this. Marcel Trudel explains it better than I do in his memoirs, and François Hertel tells the same story. There's nothing colonized in this bestial onomastics, it's just the natural consequence of economic and cultural coexistence.

There are lots of Franks in Quebec. And Toms, Gerrys, Johnnys, Pits, Moes, Rons, Bobs, and Bernies. They don't all speak English, some of them speak not a word. We'd be wrong to make anything of that. We're also familiar with Bob Morane, Jack Lang, Eddy Mitchell, and Johnny Halliday, who as good Frenchmen in France can't very well be called colonized.

Frank Labine, in Sudbury, did not develop a disdain for Franco-Ontarians. On the contrary. Lesieur would claim that it was professional cunning and self-interest that made that impossible. He'd be wrong. Every time Frank met a French-speaker in Ontario, he immediately felt a kinship. No one ever told him he had so much family out there, and he has always reproached his teachers for having not been aware of it. It was always a pleasant surprise, and he was happy to offer his new friends services in their own language. He followed their school conflicts from afar, but as I said, politics didn't interest him very much. On the other hand, he loved getting together with them at their bingo games, at mass, at their parties. There he made clients and friends, in that order.

A Gilles Archambault, and along with him three-quarters of the nationalist intellectuals, would say with contempt that Frank Labine is only a French Canadian. Not even a Québécois. There was a time not so long ago when the former term was the standard one, and the latter a daring coinage. Now the new has supplanted the old. It's not the end of the world, it's a fact of life, and perfectly natural besides.

When you come down to it, what does he believe in, Frank Labine? Not a whole lot, it would appear. In any case, you won't see him defending Canada tooth and nail against a fervent Lesieur. He'll let the latter talk, and pretend dutifully to be listening, a bit like one lets a sports fan ramble on on the subject of a sport one knows nothing about. One remains polite, doesn't interrupt, and changes the subject at the first opportunity. That doesn't make him, either, into the French Canadian whose mythic spinelessness excites the disgust of Gilles Archambault. No, he has his convictions, quiet ones, but convictions all the same.

For instance, he is immune to the alarmist argument on the federal side that seeks to prove that an independent Quebec would instantly head down the road of underdevelopment, as de Gaulle said in reference to an independent Algeria. Nor does he swallow the sovereigntist line proclaiming that only an independent Quebec can prosper with dignity. For Labine, only two things count: first, that the Québécois are no less capable than anyone else, and can make their own way; second, that if Quebec independence were such a great deal, separation would have been a fait accompli long ago. And since that's not the case, it must mean that . . .

And don't go to him singing the praises of "our beautiful Rockies." He's never seen them (neither have I, for that matter). If this argument held water, Canada would long ago have annexed the Alps too, according to Pierre Bourgault, who for once has something of a case. On the other hand, Labine has lived and travelled enough to turn his back on those, such as Jean Larose, who hate Canada, or others, like Pierre Vadeboncoeur, who are militantly indifferent to it.

As for the French language and Quebec culture, he's for them a hundred per cent—on that point Monsieur Lesieur could never fault him. He senses that if nationalism has known such success, it's in reaction to the palpable injustice of the 1960s and before, when French, the majority language, was subordinate to English in all economic sectors. This was the happily long-ago time when Gaston Miron was right in saying that "bilingualism is the other's unilingualism."

And so Frank applauded Bill 101, and still supports it, even if he dislikes its letter-measuring bureaucrats. He no longer believes that French is on the verge of extinction, he has no truck with such apocalyptic views. He would prefer to see Madame Beaudoin's henchmen go after certain Radio-Canada journalists and political commentators who do violence to the French language in utter impunity; at least there they would be providing a useful service, and they'd have their work cut out for them for the next twenty years.

One last thing. There was a time when Frank Labine had warm feelings for the State. He believed in the mythology that exalted the Quebec State's appropriation of what it required to promote the public good. He was proud of his compatriots who had become engineers, financiers, entrepreneurs, thanks to government incentives. He's still proud of them. But he has become wary. The civil service of today is but a unionized bourgeoisie jealous of its prerogatives. The revenue ministry is a bottomless well, and its gluttonous levies no longer finance ambitious projects, as once they did.

His greatest disappointment: Hydro-Québec, which is nothing more for him now than an arm of the tax-hungry State, with its complaisant consultants and its legion of overpaid vice-presidents that elaborate public inquiries continue to absolve. It's a soulless enterprise that muzzles all criticism with the State's complicity and uses emotional blackmail and intimidation to cynically manipulate the national psyche. Labine opted out when he saw Hydro-Québec enlist the arbitrary powers of the cabinet to despoil the St. François Valley, flying in the face of fundamental civil rights. And what is more, if you complain you're told to keep quiet because Hydro-Québec, after all, is ours. No, he's no longer playing that game, he's dropped out of it for good.

Beyond that, nothing special. His nationalist allegiance finds expression primarily through his interest in hockey.

While he's a Canadiens fan, he's always had a weakness for the French-language players on other teams, such as Gilbert Perrault and Marcel Dionne. Their goals are more beautiful than those of others, and he forgives them when they score on the Canadiens. His sports-oriented nationalism extends, as a matter of course, to other players who speak French, Dave Keon, Bobby Smith, Mike Bossy and the rest, whom he will allow to score against Gump Worsley or Patrick Roy.

But what he loves most is a pretty play, and a goal scored, whether by a Mario Tremblay or a Bob Gainey, still brings you a Stanley Cup. To understand the way he thinks we only have to take the Canada-Russia confrontations in the early 1990s. Gretzky and Lemieux led Canada to victory. Labine might have said: When Gretzky gets a goal, I rejoice, because we've scored, but when Lemieux gets a goal, I scream my head off, because *I've* scored. That's it in a nutshell.

In short, Monsieur Labine believes what he wants. He's a free man, like all those thousands of Québécois who are too independent to want the independence of Quebec.

~ The Heretic

Monsieur Lesieur would say that if I refuse to think the way he does it's because I'm Franco-Ontarian. He's wrong. That has nothing to do with it.

Sadly, Monsieur Lesieur is quick to denigrate French Canadians from elsewhere. In this he's following the example of a long line of nationalist curates. One need only recall novelist Yves Beauchemin's characterization of Franco-Ontarians as "still warm bodies." Beauchemin, himself an eminent curate, will never live down that text that he thought was witty, but that blew up in his face like a malodorous bomb. And how can we forget the filmmaker Pierre Falardeau, that other great victim of imaginary persecution, who declared on the eve of the last referendum that Franco-Ontarians are the doormats on which the English wipe their feet before they enter their houses. Very sweet, and thank you very much.

In the arsenal of reassuring truisms dear to a believer like Lesieur, there is one that describes a Franco-Ontarian like myself as someone who has been assimilated and so is colonized and so is a collaborator. He is no different from those Algerians who fought along with the French to keep their country in France, or those black slaves whom the Southern secessionists tried to enlist in their struggle against the liberator Lincoln. He's a kind of wimp, one who doesn't know where his best interests lie.

This is to forget that Quebec nationalism has found some of its most distinguished recruits beyond its frontiers. There's Jules-Paul Tardivel, for instance, the very archetype of a true believer, author of *For My Country,* Quebec's first novel of political fiction. Yes, the separatist ideology first saw the light in a novel, grew up there, and no doubt will die there.

Tardivel was born in the United States of a father from the Auvergne and a British mother. He grew up in Saint Louis, Missouri. He studied in Quebec, relearned his mother tongue, became a fervent adherent of a budding nationalism, founded a newspaper, *La Vérité* (The Truth — this was not a man who had second thoughts), and all his life lobbied for a French Catholic state in North America. His son-in-law was to be Omer Héroux of *Le Devoir.*

And so the first apostle of literary separatism had English for his mother tongue. Another more recent example is Charles Castonguay, the nationalists' favourite demographer, whose projections have been auguring for the last thirty years the imminent disappearance of French outside Quebec, and whose pronouncements have been seized on by right-thinking nationalists, such as Josée Legault, to lend credence to their apocalyptic theses.

There are other notable architects of separatist thought who fled one inhospitable country or another to man the nationalist barricades here. There's Robert Rumilly, the historian who was panicked by the prospect of French Indochina's collapse. And the FLQ member François Schirm, former paratrooper, French also despite his German name. There's also Guy Bouthillier, president of the Montreal St. Jean Baptiste

Society, who is Franco-American (like Jack Kerouac, the great American writer, and Willie Chrétien, father of Jean, but they were not believers . . .). And François Beaulne, PQ member of the National Assembly, who hails from Ottawa's Sandy Hill. Or the actor Jacques L'Heureux, who entertained my sons as Passe-Montagne on TV, and who attended the same high school as I did, in the next class. And then my friend André Binette, who listened to all my youthful confessions as I did his, and who today is a lawyer, the author of a book on the national question, and an associate of André Joli-Coeur, who defended Quebec's cause before the Supreme Court.

No, Monsieur Lesieur is wrong to castigate Franco-Ontarians. They're not all like me. Up until recently they could count among their number Jean Éthier-Blais, a native of Sturgeon Falls, who hid his origins successfully for a very long time. Today Lesieur has a staunch ally in Jean-Paul Marchand from Penetanguishine, Ontario, who is the Bloc Québécois member of Parliament for Quebec East and the author of a book in which he states flat out that the assimilation of French-speaking people in Canada is part of a sinister federal plot. This much is certain: if Quebec does not achieve independence, no one will be able to say that it's because of these ill-born Franco-Ontarians. On the contrary, they have served the cause well. And as for those who stayed home, they at least have the merit of never having voted in a referendum.

LIKE MY FRIEND Lesieur, I can't honestly say just when I lost my nationalist faith. There was a time in fact when he and I thought much the same, but in vastly different contexts.

On the other hand, I do clearly remember how the idea of Quebec independence first entered my life, never again to leave it. Naturally, it was thanks to television. It was 1963 and I was nine years old. People were talking a lot in those days about a certain Marcel Chaput, who, unhappy with the RIN, founded the Parti républicain du Québec, and who, to assure his movement's solvency, undertook a fundraising fast. His stomach empty, he hoped to influence people by imbuing them with a kind of Ghandian guilt. And he collected a lot of money. A few months later, broke again, he repeated the exercise. But there was no second miracle. He stepped down from the presidency of his party, and a fickle splinter group took the opportunity to dissolve it altogether. Ah yes.

These misfortunes were greeted with derision. That was unfair, because Monsieur Chaput had at the time written a courageous and lucid manifesto called *Why I Am a Separatist,* in which he had succinctly laid out his convictions. But the times were not ripe for forerunners. Almost all were considered harmless cranks.

Towards the end of my elementary school education, and later at high school, the secession of Quebec was a popular debating topic for students with speechifying ambitions. But it was only an idea, vague and preposterous, nothing more. Then came de Gaulle, but the General made little impact on Franco-Ontarians. There were a few separatists among my friends. Some were even members of the RIN in Hull. But as they tended to come from the bottom of the class, no one took them seriously. The FLQ was at work also, but far away. A couple of bums, we said, so few of them . . .

My nationalist sympathies were awakened by an injustice. I was fourteen. Up to then the bitter struggle for French schools in Ontario had had little impact on me — a child is not going to feel grateful to the people who send him to school. But at the beginning of Grade 9 I discovered that the mathematics teacher gave his class only in English. Why? His name was Lepage, just as mine was Poliquin. So? My older brother explained that the sciences were taught in English because of the departmental exams that used to be given. "Better get used to it, my boy."

"But there are no more provincial exams!"

"I know, but that's the way it's still done, too bad."

"Shit!"

The next year the math teacher, Monsieur Perron, proudly announced that he was now allowed to teach the subject in French in Ontario public schools. He began the course immediately, but then a hand went up, that of Bill, a little newcomer.

"I'm sorry sir, I don't understand a word," he explained. His parents had registered him at our school so he could learn French, but math was so important . . . Monsieur Perron didn't hesitate an instant. So that poor little Bill wouldn't fail his year, he would give the class in English. "Well, boys, the task at hand today . . ." *Maudite marde!*

Here Monsieur Lesieur and all the other nationalist believers would interject that Monsieur Perron was one of those colonized individuals who went down on their knees before the conqueror, in this case a thirteen-year-old boy called Bill, not a very threatening figure. The ancestral reflex of submission . . . a reading that's as false as it is unjust. Monsieur Perron was simply a citizen who respected the law. He had got into the habit of teaching science in English, especially since he himself had gone to a bilingual school where French was tolerated only in Religion, History, and, of course, French classes. He was used to teaching in English, and less sure of himself in French. Bill's arrival must have suited him fine. It meant a year of grace.

Monsieur Perron was no fearful coolie out of French Indochina. Someone who is really colonized is nothing, has nothing, has no existence of his own, kowtows at the slightest provocation. Monsieur Perron, however, existed. I knew him. He was a university-trained teacher, the head of a family, a property owner; he voted as he pleased, he even had opinions. But in this instance his behaviour was that of a member of a minority who defers in the name of a certain false politeness. Because the first thing you learn when you're part of a linguistic minority is invisibility. Since the colour of your skin isn't going to betray you, you can blend into the background by getting rid of your accent. Out of an ancient fear, perhaps, of being singled out, you go along with the crowd. From there to anglicizing your name and shifting allegiances for the sake of a marriage is only a small step that many take quite cheerfully.

Perron would doubtless have been amazed to find himself accused of knuckling under to a child. He would have replied that he was only thinking of the student, so seemingly defenseless in our midst, and besides you have to be courteous, we live in Canada after all. A sincere response, I'm sure. I've seen so many families that around the table on Christmas Eve will speak English because an anglophone has the good fortune to be present. When in the past I became indignant, I was put in my place and told that the poor visitor mustn't be led to think we're talking about him behind his back, he might feel slighted. An argument, by the way, that I've never endorsed.

But be careful! Before resorting to a simplistic colonial assessment of the situation, we must remember that someone in the minority doesn't necessarily dream of being part of the majority. He may even feel in the majority himself. By addressing his counterpart in his own language, he is showing him that he is his equal, if not his superior. No complexes for him, it's the other who ought to have a few, that's what he's saying between the lines when speaking English with such relish. These sociolinguistic situations are always murky, shot through with

35

complex motives that often have nothing to do with the false and summary explanations that demagogues devise and the gullible lap up.

The story had a happy ending all the same. Monsieur Perron had taken into consideration Bill's interests but not ours. A small delegation that included me sought Bill out and politely presented him with our problem: "Listen, you're a good guy, we like you fine, but you see, for once there's a math class in French, and we'd like to have it. We're already lousy in math, and when it's taught in English that just makes it worse. So should four or five of us suffer just because the teacher wants to be nice to you? Does that seem fair? Do you think in Vancouver the math teacher would start teaching in French just to make Shorty Goulet over there happy?" He was decent, Bill, he even came with us to tell the teacher it was okay, he'd registered in French school, and he'd make the best of it.

The next day the class resumed in French. Was I happy! Good old Bill, good old Perron, they'd understood what was fair. Good for us, who'd kept up our side! Mind you, that didn't do me much good in the long run. Hopeless as I was in mathematics, I still failed my year. Bill, for his part, passed. Two years later, at the Versailles college where my father had sent me, I was no less befuddled by the bathtub that fills with water in time for one to make the 2:15 train for Lyon. *Merde* . . .

THOSE WERE CRUCIAL years for the independence movement, and, of course, in Ottawa we were the last to know. After the General's cry to arms and René Lévesque's wrenching break with the Quebec Liberal Party, Pierre Elliott Trudeau assumed power at the federal level. On the fringes of these developments, the FLQ was gaining strength.

At this point in my life there was a two-year hiatus in Paris. My father, a journalist at Radio-Canada, had been posted to Paris and the family went along. Two wonderful years. We heard about Quebec, but from afar, and for me the only news worth noting was the eruption on the scene of Robert Charlebois. At last a real Québécois rock star, with enough talent to sing his own songs and not corny translations like his lamentable forerunners. And who, unlike Gilles Vigneault and so many others, didn't apologize because he had an accent. He was what he was, without compromise, and he succeeded like no one else. Franco-Ontarian friends told me later that it was Charlebois's shining example that deterred them forever from the comforts of assimilation. In him we found someone who spoke for us; he was on our wavelength, he made us dream.

Our family's return coincided with the October Crisis, an event that caused little anxiety among Ottawa youth. We found it amusing, all these olive-clad soldiers guarding ministers and ambassadors already half-comatose from boredom. The Parti Québécois existed, made respectable by René Lévesque. Something had changed though, at school; those who saw themselves as separatists were now at the head of the class. It was becoming serious.

It's then that I became a militant Franco-Ontarian. Some of my friends got me involved; they quickly lost interest, but I stayed on. Partly for the adventure, but for the sake of justice as well. Since I belonged to a generation that was changing the world, why not begin at home? In a Northern Ontario town a school board had refused a French school to a population that was eighty-five per cent francophone. The opportunity was there, and I jumped at it.

This was the crisis of Sturgeon Falls. Yes, the same Sturgeon Falls where Jean Éthier-Blais, who never gave a thought to his compatriots, was born. To be fair, it must be said that in the last years of his life he came clean about his origins, while mythologizing them to the limit, of course. (Well-intentioned flatterers even tried to portray him as the father of Franco-Ontarian literature. He knew it to be a fiction, but it pleased him nonetheless. No one should be surprised. Nothing is more typical of Quebec nationalism than the honouring or the rejection of fictive paternities. More on that later.)

My militancy was primarily literary. I wrote reports, preambles to petitions, letters of protest, speeches that others read or listened to. Three years of service. At the same time, I'd begun studying German. This never distracted me from my convictions, but it did help me find my vocation, which was in literature and nowhere else. I didn't do a lot, in other words, but I learned an enormous amount.

I also met people in Embrun, Niagara Falls, and Timmins for whom to live in French as a minority was normal and in no way glorious. Others, on the fringes, were full of passion, and like lay Jesuits talked endlessly about the Cause. Quietly, I gave them a wide berth. But I preferred them to those whose militancy served mainly as a political springboard. Mind you, both groups were useful. There were also those exemplary men and women whose commitment was totally disinterested. Ah yes, they do exist.

I was also aware of our struggle's limitations. At the time I was reading Julien Benda's *The Treason of the Intellectuals,* a book I only came to understand in the thick of the action. But Benda had shocked me in the beginning when he wrote that language was a relative value. That was heresy to the militant I dreamed of being. What? I'm manning the barricades for a value that is not absolute? Impossible!

A little while later I was sharing confidences with an old

war-horse who had lived through all our struggles. I'll give him the name Riverain, one of the many pseudonyms my father used when he published his tales and stories. Riverain remembered the time, not all that distant, when bank employees in Toronto could not speak French among themselves. It was the politics of homogenization at its most extreme, as practised everywhere then, in business and government alike. And what is most curious is that everyone thought they were doing the right thing in practising assimilation. His memories became mine and I reacted angrily. "Didn't you want to plant bombs under those bastards?"

"No," he answered calmly. "It made me furious, of course, but it was such an unfair policy that it gave me a thirst for justice that I have never lost. Since that time I fight not for the French language, but for justice. I speak French where I want, when I want, because it's just. To be a francophone in Ontario is to be on the side of freedom and justice, simple as that." I asked him if he'd read Benda. "Who? No, never heard of him."

Another time, he went further. "One of my sons married an Irish woman. They don't talk French in his home. My only grandson calls me *Granddaddy,* you see the problem? But they've learned French all the same, and I fight for their right to continue to do so. I have to admit that my activities keep me away from home, and that suits me because my wife gets on my nerves like you can't imagine." (You see why I've given him a false name.) "And I'll even tell you that if I had to choose between the life of my grandson, Michael, and his language, I'd choose his life. Imagine a doctor who told you, 'My dear sir, I'm giving you a choice. If I operate on your grandson, he will live to a good old age but he'll speak only English. If I don't operate, he'll speak French but he'll die young.' What would you do in my place? No, my boy, language is important, it's beautiful, but

39

it's life that counts." Today still, I'm convinced that Riverain had read Benda, or he would never have chosen justice and liberty over language and culture. Like Montesquieu, he considered himself human by destiny but French only by chance.

I STUDIED AT the University of Ottawa, in the company of students who were mostly from Quebec. A lot of good eggs, a few bad apples also. From them I suffered the worst affronts I'd ever had to endure since I'd begun to show my Franco-Ontarian colours. Their language was violent, and they would tolerate no differences. In their company you had better not be Jewish, Chinese, or whatever else. They held the high ground in the days when almost all young people were nationalists except for a few idealists and an even smaller number of opportunists who threw in their lot with the Young Liberals. (A wise decision for some, who are today members of Parliament, ministers, judges, etc.) Their hatred of the Franco-Ontarians was visceral. They resented our ease in English, emblematic of a successful colonization, they hated our friendships with other groups they judged hostile from the word go, and they despised our status as living examples of a federalism that worked.

Their denunciations are still seared into my psyche. "Eat shit, you goddam dirty Franco! You kiss English ass, for God's sake! And you, Poliquin, instead of going after schools that won't do anyone any good, you can come with us or you and your sluts can all croak together." It was charming, no question. Among the insulted and injured of whom I was only one, Paul, today a Quebec filmmaker, was so intimidated by the Québécois that he kept his mouth shut most of the time. There was also Claude, a brilliant fellow, who in their company spoke the broadest possible Québécois in order to show his allegiance. It should be said that with his Ottawa friends he spoke franglais, and if a Frenchman came to our table, hints of a Parisian accent rolled magically off his tongue. Not someone to be trusted. A real Franco, the spiteful would say. No, he was afraid, he wanted to please, that's all. I saw him recently. He's a university professor, has a family, is a far cry from the young, terrorized member of a minority I once knew.

We should pardon him his youthful irresolution. At the age we were, mimicry came easy. It's not for nothing that, even today, in the corridors of French schools in Ontario all you hear is English. It was the same thing in my time. Adolescence is the age when to stand out is to be harshly punished by one's peers, and salvation is to be found only in conforming to what already prevails. Sometimes I see my former classmates, once anglicized to the nth degree, now correcting the mistakes in French made by their children. They have matured, and they, too, are no longer afraid.

BUT IT'S NOT THE nationalist bullies who kept me in Ontario at that time. No, it's Hegel. That's right. With his *Dialectic of the Master and the Slave,* of all things. I had applied the principle to the Franco-Ontarian situation in an earnest essay. The master, who never has to reflect because all his desires are as good as orders, atrophies and dies; the slave, who always has to choose between punishment and reward, learns to think, and it is that ability to think that enables him one day to supplant the master. He who is in the majority does not choose his fate, but someone in a minority does, and this prepares him for reflection and for growth. QED.

My classmates in Phil 101 thought I was very funny, as you may well imagine. What? You mean the Québécois will one day get the best of the English, are you off your rocker? With all my wounded gravitas, I replied that that wasn't what I meant to say. What I wanted to say was that the Franco-Ontarian I would remain would always hold on to a certain nimbleness of thought and action, but the majority would not. The linguistic minority's ability to choose would guarantee them lifelong freedom. Don't you see? Oh, never mind . . .

All that remains to me of these adolescent arguments is the conviction that the one sad thing about assimilation is that the assimilated ceases to choose. But to think you can make a Monsieur Lesieur understand that is to dream in colour. For him, and he is not alone, the assimilated individual is a poor lost soul who wanders the surface of the earth bereft of identity, submissive, devoid of will and substance. I gladly pardon him the misplaced pity he feels for my fellows, because there was a time when I thought exactly the same way. Brainwashed by Lionel Groulx, I confounded language and faith, and considered assimilation to be a hell for traitors and cowards.

Until the day I met an assimilated gentleman who was in excellent health. A good father, an accomplished engineer, happy at home, he had lost his French as a child in Rochester, New York, where his father had gone to work as a researcher. Did he have regrets? None. His unilingualism was a minor matter for him. This meeting was for me a true epiphany. So there really were happy, endearing individuals, concerned about their fellow man, in short good people, who no longer spoke French? And who hadn't even read Benda! I couldn't get over it. He and his wife were, however, delighted to have me know that their daughter was in French immersion, and that she was their interpreter when they went camping in Quebec.

And so I was a bit ashamed of my erstwhile summary judgements. Since that day, I no longer feel I've the right to judge anyone: neither Pete Duquette, taxi driver, "I'm sorry, I don't speak French any more," nor François Olivares and Éliane Rehnquist, who speak not a word of Portuguese or Danish. All citizens have the right to become other, to switch majority, and no nationalist in the world has any business asking them for an accounting or showing them contempt.

The assimilated individual is not handicapped, whatever our believer Lesieur may think. For assimilation to be a defect, language would have to be considered an absolute value. But not everyone sees it that way, each person makes up his own mind, and we must respect his choice or his stance. And so I have friends who, fed up with being part of the Franco-Ontarian minority, have become Québécois. A decision that Monsieur Lesieur would applaud, despite the fact that he'll always be wary of those born elsewhere. I've seen others who, tired of all the interrogations surrounding identity, have gone over to the other side and don't speak a word of French to their children. They've all made a choice, they've exercised a fundamental right that deserves respect. And the only difference between my friend Lesieur and me is that he approves of the first and condemns the second. I think it's too bad that he thinks that way, but it's his point of view. End of discussion.

I'm not an apologist for assimilation. I just want to demystify it. I say this without the least feeling of shame: I myself do not speak the language of my ancestors, who were Breton. My name in Breton means "little white river," and my first name, derived from Hebrew, a language I also do not speak, means "God judges." Worse still, this dual patrimony, Celtic and Semitic, rarely even enters my mind.

"What are you going on about, then?" asks my friend Lesieur. "Why don't you just become English Canadian and have done with it? What's all this militant solidarity with your own people? Do you have nothing better to do?" Well, it's just that to my mind there is only one thing that counts, and that's to preserve the right to choose, to get the most out of a culture that has always enriched me and has never let me down. It's by choice and not from moral obligation that I'm determined to transmit this knowledge to my three sons. I still remember the reaction of my eldest when I took him to see *Cyrano de Bergerac,* with Gérard Depardieu, subtitled in English in an Ottawa cinema. After the film, dazzled as I was, he asked me: "The people who can't speak French, how can they ever appreciate a masterpiece like that?" I understood then that he was thanking us, his mother and me, for our vigilance. *That* Monsieur Lesieur can certainly understand.

I'd also like to say to Monsieur Lesieur that he needs me, that I will always be for him a convenient stooge. I still remember those university classmates who loudly proclaimed their dismay at the anglicized French my cohorts spoke, and who thought highly of their own linguistic prowess, even though, without knowing it, they hardly spoke any better. We, at least, were able to speak English, too.

Still, I could understand their being angry at the outright spinelessness of those who kept their language locked up inside them. Or worse, who felt only hatred for themselves. Yes, it's sad to say, but I also witnessed the kind of self-hatred on the part of the minority that makes assimilation seem a jolly romp by comparison and arouses active contempt in the larger community. I tried telling them that submissiveness can crop up in any milieu and that it's a matter more of personality than of culture, but there was nothing to be done: the mythic Franco-Ontarian was too central to their self-esteem.

In this game of unjust denigration and trumped up self-enhancement, the Franco-Ontarian represents for the nationalist an inferior, diminished being, whose example must not be followed. Look at what we'll become if . . . For Lionel Groulx, it was cultural bastards. Or it could be Cajuns, about whom nationalists have little good to say. "Quebec will not be a Louisiana of the north," stormed René Lévesque, remember?

We can easily see what's behind all those insults. In the case of Groulx, the answer is simple. The motto of his *Action française* was "Towards superiority." For him, the superiority of certain races, the French among them, was a self-evident fact. As it was for many of his contemporaries, who were often, it should be said, more hateful than him. Whoever spoke French badly was well and truly biologically inferior. That was the thinking of his time, and he and his successors, of which there are still a great number, have never had the savvy to discard that idea. As for Lévesque, he was just following the script of a nationalist politician brandishing the flag of a looming apocalypse for the French language.

I forgive Lionel Groulx, who read too much Barrès. I am less forgiving of Lévesque, who conveniently overlooked the fact that Cajun culture exists; its food and its music are known around the world. It's an authentic culture, unique, hybridized of course—that in fact is its genius—and it certainly doesn't deserve to be looked down upon. As for my university classmates, they were the rich who make fun of poor people's clothes; nothing much to admire in that.

But I stopped blaming them long ago. One has the right to have been young and to have made hasty judgements, and they have perhaps changed their attitude since then. Perhaps. But that's not the case for Monsieur Lesieur. As I've said, he is a believer. He has the unshakeable faith of a country priest. Of a priest for all seasons. Of a father, in fact.

~ The Faith of the Father

QUEBEC'S NATIONAL faith is very much bound up with the father. The father who browbeats his children so they'll defend their heritage, the son who avenges his humiliated progenitor or sacrifices his life to realize the dreams of those who came before. Seen from a novelistic point of view, this psychodrama would be fascinating were it not so repetitive.

Mère patrie: "Our mother the fatherland." It's a curiously androgynous turn of phrase, but in point of fact the second term always takes precedence over the first. Talk as much as you want about the mother tongue, this is still the land of our fathers. The mother's words, but the coin in the father's pocket. The nationalists go even further: Lionel Groulx and his spiritual son Yves Michaud talk of "the language of our fathers." The mother is nowhere to be seen. And General de Gaulle used exactly the same words.

They're not wrong. French is the language of Tardivel's father, of Charles Castonguay's father also, as I've said. Pierre Falardeau bears witness as well, when he recounts his nationalist epiphany. He was about fifteen years old and it was the middle of an election campaign. Jean Lesage was proposing to nationalize electricity. A public meeting was organized at an old theatre, the Monument-National in Montreal. "My father decided to take me. It was my first direct contact with politics." Falardeau was not alone in this. From Michel Chartrand to Lucien Bouchard, it was always the father who passed down the national faith. The father of FLQ member Jacques Lanctôt was a militant right-wing nationalist, and Alexis Cossette-Trudel, active now in the Parti Québécois, is the son of another FLQ player in the October Crisis.

There are so many Québécois children with a father to avenge! And they're not all boys. If we are to trust René Lévesque's complaisant biographer, Pierre Godin, Corinne Côté-Lévesque, the Premier's second wife, owes her nationalist fervour to her father's humiliation. He was demoted to being a humble labourer following a run-in with his superior, an anglophone. "This incident awakened in the young girl a new awareness that was not unrelated to her support for independence later in life." One could not be more clear.

We find the same conflict of love and duty in the life of Pierre Renaud, publicist and treasurer of the RIN in the time of Bourgault. Godin writes: "During the war, Léopold A. Renaud, a prosperous Montreal merchant, held the post of deputy-secretary to the Federal Commission on War Profits. The only francophone on the Board, he was barred from meetings of the Board of Directors . . . For him Canada was synonymous with discrimination." Scratch the surface of a militant nationalist's life, and more often than not you'll find a ridiculed, impotent father.

The father represents the nation in literature also. In *Maria Chapdelaine,* Louis Hémon conveniently disposes of François Paradis, the bad son who has sold off the land; this coureur de bois is a poor romantic who dies because he does not want to follow in the steps of his father. As for Lorenzo, the American, who sold his own land to go off and earn his keep in the United States, he is punished by Maria's rebuff, though he had tried to lure her with stories about movie houses, streetcars, and a fat paycheque. Maria will marry a second Samuel Chapdelaine, the farmer Eutrope Gagnon, stout fellow, who is as boring as all get out but who has the merit of being devoted to the land. Maria and Eutrope will marry in the spring, "when the men come back from the woods for the season of sowing."

The reader is asked to revere this race that does not know how to die, this land of Quebec where nothing changes and where nothing must change. A romantic dream, because in the real world what would have happened is this: Maria, unhappy to have lost her handsome François, falls back on Lorenzo, who's more interesting than Eutrope, after all. She follows him to Lowell, Massachusetts, where she gives birth to Jack Kerouac. But that's real life, less appealing to the ideologue than fiction, where you can keep tight rein on your destiny . . .

In Félix-Antoine Savard's novel *Menaud, maître-draveur,* which is the logical outgrowth of *Maria Chapdelaine,* the father Menaud loses his son Joson, who is drowned, and in his madness takes up Hémon's dictum and turns it into an incantation: "We are a race that doesn't know how to die!" The incantation becomes an injunction. "We do not know how to die": these are the words of a father who does not want to step aside, who resists change, who does not accept the laws of nature and who refuses to pass the torch, unless of course the son remains wholly compliant to his example, guaranteeing the father immortality and a triumph over life.

The entire nationalist discourse is that of a father who prolongs the minority status of his son, enslaving him to his dream of territorial integrity. The offspring imitates the father and never surpasses him—he is subservient to him, his lifelong lord. And the son, if he is unable or unwilling to assume the paternal legacy, is condemned for being weak. This is Félix Leclerc's song to his unemployed son, tenant in his own land, hewer of wood and drawer of water. You would think he would want to shake up this shiftless son by making him feel ashamed. In fact, all he wants is to harness him to his own dream before he dies, or to persuade him of his impotence. Stallion father, gelded son, would say the homespun psychologists.

The father's ascendance is a constant with nationalist sons, who succeed only on condition that they in their turn become dominators and castrators. Happily, from time to time a parricide turns up, but he doesn't survive for long. The collective discourse is tilted in favour of the patrimony, and it stifles all tentative gropings towards independence.

Take Bourgault and Lévesque. The first advocated independence in order to undermine British control; he was the rebellious son who dreamed of national emancipation. He was determined to do away with the father, whom he believed to be English. He was the parricide who wants to be head of the family. Because when you come down to it, that's what Quebec independence amounts to: a father-in-the-making. Along came René Lévesque, also a rebellious son, who had turned his back on Jean Lesage, founding father of modern Quebec, but was flawed in that he didn't demand enough, was too attached to Canada.

Bourgault became head of the RIN, but he was a headstrong youth, a son in fact. For him, Canada was a buck-naked Noah whose sons mock him in his drunken state. The RIN fervour cooled quickly. Quebec nationalism had been too long in the hands of the priests and the fathers for little upstarts to be allowed to fritter away its heritage. Not long afterwards

Lévesque wrested the paternal initiative from Bourgault, offering the electorate the respectability that comes from the experience of having been in power. In *Option Québec,* he launched into an incantation that justified his actions by invoking all of Quebec's fathers: Papineau, Parent, Groulx, and so on. Armed with such memories, this father was more presentable than his junior.

Suddenly Bourgault became a child again. The other father, to all appearances more competent, had absconded with his cherished political party. But what can you do, you have to reassure the ordinary Quebecker, who is so timid, and make a good impression on Wall Street, which is so nervous. And so René Lévesque, the great fantasist, gave Bourgault, the inadequate son, a cuff on the ear, and spent the rest of his life perverting the ideals of independence and trying to make his children, those good, supposedly gullible people, swallow the inane idea of sovereignty-association. Yes, he said, you can have your cake and eat it too, a Canadian standard of living and a country called Quebec.

It was a ruse worthy of an old deceiver, anyone could see that. As future negotiation with Ottawa would be out of the question, its failure guaranteed by the PQ, the Quebec government would have carte blanche to proclaim its independence unilaterally. The idea was to lead the Quebec people to independence without their noticing. A huge deception, yes, still and always, whereby a father lies to his children for their own good and tries to impose on them his dynastic fantasies.

In 1980 and 1995, Quebec's intellectual bourgeoisie willingly went along with this dupery. It knew better than anyone that sovereignty-association was a confidence trick and it agreed to pretend to believe in it. All to reassure us poor colonials, too simple to believe in ourselves and in our own greatness. Yes,

Madame, said Louise Beaudoin and Bernard Landry, of course you'll be able to keep your passport, and you, sir, you'll keep your pension. Nothing will change. And you, you two youngsters, whose jobs are contingent on federal contracts, of course you'll keep them; we'll even give you new ones, better paid!

Never had people been so lied to as at that time, and rare were those artists and intellectuals with the courage to stand up to such demagogy. One exception in 1980, Jacques Ferron, and one in 1995, René-Daniel Dubois. The few dissenters took refuge in timorous neutrality. In this, intellectuals on all sides failed in their duty as critics. Never, in Quebec, was the contempt of the intellectual class for the population so apparent.

What was most amusing was that certain nationalist intellectuals, just like the thousands of PQ militants who had become each more naïve than the next from reciting over and over father Lévesque's incantation, themselves lapsed into the kind of reasoning Jacqueline Pascal recommended to her brother, Blaise. Faith comes with prayer, she said, and what with repeating the act of prayer, well, faith comes to be. And so, reciting the magic formula, sovereignty-association, sovereignty-association, repeat after me, intellectuals and militants ended up as believers. I can excuse the militants, they were there to obey the founding father of the party, but I understand less well the intellectuals, who were well-informed people. Their complicity might be traced to the fact that in going along with the father's lie, in endorsing it and chanting it, they also shared in the prerogative of paternal dominance. Prevaricating along with Lévesque, the intellectuals found themselves in a position of power, just like the priests who had earlier held sway along with Duplessis.

Today still, Michel Seymour and his Intellectuals for Sovereignty speak of a Bouchardian partnership as though it were a viable option, natural and necessary. Imminent, as well.

They've concocted, as a bonus, the concept of "territorial nationalism," where love for the soil would supplant the ethnic glue. For my part, I'll believe in territorial nationalism the day a single Outremont intellectual will put his life on the line for Hull or Drummondville.

Let us never forget that these intellectuals form a class, one with perks and privileges: university tenure and generous emoluments for the right people. It's a pretty good bet that they would not bear the heaviest burden should the whole enterprise come a cropper. They could always take a sabbatical leave in one of their countries of reference, France or the States, and observe the fiasco from a distance, cozy and warm.

The population kept its cool during the two referendums, just as it had at the time of the colony or during the transfer of power. We never know all that well what it thinks. When one dangles before its eyes a partnership that's profitable and assured, it responds with a hesitant yes; when one talks in terms of a surgical procedure, it comes back with a firm no. It's as though this game afforded it a certain amusement, and it was keeping its options open pending a final decision. Healthy behaviour. It's like an enlightened consumer with a budget to balance, shopping around with eyes wide open.

And it's accustomed to these political oxymorons, whether it be the Quiet Revolution or sovereignty-association. Elsewhere in Canada there's a party that calls itself progressive and conservative, and another that claims to be reformist and conservative. I guess all these groupings that claim to advance and mark time simultaneously deserve to have across from them a party that wants both to take a powder and stay home. It's not hard to understand why these political bluffs aren't very effective. Just think how many times they've been trotted out.

The demagogy promoting an associative relationship is

irksome only to authentic separatists. They are rare, in fact, and seem to be the only ones prepared to acknowledge that finances in an independent Quebec would be chaotic and would impose new obligations with no new revenue to fulfil them. They know the situation would be difficult, but for some of them the penchant for martyrdom, so Catholic in spirit (as though nothing, after all, has changed), leads then to relish, even, the suffering to come. A guilt-ridden conscience, perhaps.

Independence holds the promise of a purifying sacrifice. Yes, we're going to get it in the neck, we're going to be miserable as all get out, but it will be worth it. We'll all help each other, and together we'll prevail! Pain will be superimposed on duty, and these two sufferings combined will redeem us. For that they are ready to sacrifice their individual freedoms and to muzzle the press, as counselled by Pierre Bourgault and the St. Jean Baptiste Society. This is to my mind colonized behaviour, in that they're following in the footsteps of those French Communist Party fellow-travellers who so bemused Albert Camus. It's bizarre, he said, this yearning for servitude. Here, in a Quebec that is so prosperous, with its North American standard of living, where we are heated in the winter and air-conditioned in summer, a willing subjection to shared wretchedness would lift the guilt off our cosseted shoulders, and grant absolution for all that material contentment. Give me a free Quebec so that I can expiate all this wealth! Unbelievable . . .

Let us here laud the courageous lucidity of Jacques Ferron, who did not shrink from saying in 1980 that the true separatists, in his opinion, made up no more than fifteen per cent of the Quebec population, and that only trickery and mendacious manipulation enabled the government to achieve a forty per cent yes vote in the referendum. Chalk one up for demagogy. It all goes to show that political deception has a future.

Fortunately, Quebec nationalism has in its midst some thinkers who talk straight. There is Laurent-Michel Vacher, for example, who denounced more effectively than anyone the golden calf of sovereignty-association, that fearful back-door separatism only good to dupe innocents. He pointed out in simple language that the approach was doomed. You do not forge independence by lying to free people whom you are claiming to liberate, and who will end up slaves to an illusion. Vacher spoke out, and many others no doubt thought as he did under their breath, but his words had no impact. The paternal discourse of Lévesque was too overwhelming for these daring dissidents.

Lévesque failed in 1980. Unable to rewrite history, he soon found solace in power, and to keep it, even relegated to the back burner the raison d'être of the PQ program. To do so he put his head on the block, as was his wont. "If you don't do as I say, papa will leave!" He lost some of his allies, but the party bent to the founding father. The dissidents went off to create a true separatist party, but it didn't get very far.

What came next was the final act of the epic struggle between Lévesque and Bourassa, the two Quebec fathers of their time. If I invoke these two men rather than Trudeau or Drapeau, who wielded power virtually uncontested in other domains, it's because they were so much alike, in both their methods and their ambitions.

~ Peers

BOURASSA AND LÉVESQUE. So different but so alike. Doubtless because they both wanted the same thing: their people's well-being before their own, like good fathers who sacrifice themselves for the sake of the little ones.

The match begins. In the left corner, the bohemian but patriotic journalist who talks so well when he isn't lying. "When you listen to him, you feel intelligent," said one commentator in the days of *Point de mire,* his television show on current affairs, and it was true. He was a genuinely imaginative man who wanted to see his people take their rightful place in the world, and who did much to further this end. That is undeniable.

His great flaw? A marked tendency for inventing tales where he had the leading role. Example: for a long time he nurtured the legend of the young war correspondent who witnessed the execution of Benito Mussolini, even though on that day he was thousands of kilometres distant. In his bitter retirement, ruminating on his failures and his backsliding, he posed as a martyr to federal trickery, although he was himself to blame for his misfortunes. Still the hero, but this time one who conjured a fictive victimization in order to evade responsibility.

Mind you, it was no doubt his longing for great accomplishments that led to his realizing at least a few of them. One could cite his reform of the electoral process, which was a master stroke.

In the right corner, the dutiful son of a good family, who, in the words of one observer I knew well, had the air of a diligent student who has skipped too many meals. He'd received a real education, this young man, and had everything it takes to make a perfect technocrat. With his degrees and his successful moneyed marriage, he could have lived a charmed life. But no, he loved power and only that. Namesake of another great man, Henri Bourassa, known best for his inconsistency and indecision, Robert set out to invest his name with real political weight. A noble ambition, and one that he realized.

A social democrat like his counterpart, and just as generous, he too made significant contributions to Quebec life. One need only mention legal aid and all the other incentives to social solidarity. His most remarkable feat? To have pulled off one of the most spectacular political comebacks in modern history, the equal of Nixon's or Mitterrand's. The most despised man in Quebec on November 15, 1976, the hot-dog lover mocked by Pierre Elliott Trudeau, not only did he regain power without the help of his earlier burdensome allies, but he was much mourned when he died. No mean accomplishment. His flaw: a passion for ambiguity, productive in electoral terms but resulting in the politician being better remembered than his policies.

There was a time long ago when Bourassa and Lévesque were comrades-in-arms. Daniel Johnson's Union Nationale party having defeated Jean Lesage's Liberals, Robert and René found themselves together on the opposition benches. The one saw his ascension to power postponed, the other badly missed his portfolio. They joined forces to propose a sovereigntist orientation for the Liberal Party. Bourassa went along with it for a while, then drew back when he realized that this detour would keep him out of power for too long. His calculations were correct. Lévesque went on alone, stumbled badly, and began an exile in the political wilderness that lasted nine years. Barely three years later, Bourassa was premier of Quebec.

Each continually raided the other's natural constituency. Lévesque needed grocers and people of substance to achieve independence for Quebec; Bourassa courted nationalists and the young to keep himself in power and obviate the need for independence. They went head to head three times, the younger winning easily twice, the elder prevailing the last time round. After his defeat in 1976, Bourassa in turn spent nine years in the wilderness before returning to power. It was a strange dance, where each masqueraded as the other. Lévesque was able to seduce property owners and business leaders who were tired of being tied down to the Liberal Party, while Bourassa succeeded in domesticating the nationalists. Lévesque won Labine's heart, Bourassa won that of Lesieur.

Bourassa's strategy was risky. He sometimes had to appear more zealous than his rival. That's why he worked so hard to draw the line between Quebec and Canada. And it's his fault that today there are two nationalist parties in Quebec rather than one.

Bourassa's second incarnation was more robust than his first. He had succeeded in freeing himself from his moneyed manipulators and had on his own reconquered the party that had held him in contempt just a few years earlier. Now his own progenitor, owing nothing to big business, having garnered even the anglophone and immigrant votes, he was master in his own house. Gone were the days when he submitted his Bill 22 to Montreal's financial community for their approval before presenting it to the National Assembly, a scandalous incident, and when his English-language ministers deserted him to protest his sign law, he kept his cool. The government man had become a statesman.

During his years of apprenticeship Bourassa had fashioned for himself an approach to the world that was wholeheartedly economic, although tempered by a certain sense of social justice. In the 1970 campaign, one of his slogans was "Federalism that pays." Premier a second time around, aping the nationalists, he advocated the "objectivation" of Canada, treating it strictly as a cash cow. That said, we would be wrong to hold it against him, or to say that he undermined our attachment to Canada. He inherited a fait accompli. What with Duplessis and his booty, Lesage and his demands, the elder Johnson and his separatist blackmail, Bourassa invented nothing new. It remains that the choice he made, however legitimate in its day, served to weaken for a long time to come the Canadian idea in Quebec.

To the point where in Quebec, Canada hardly exists any more. The alienation that was such a bone of contention for the earliest *indépendantistes* has become very real. A friend who grew up in the Lower St. Lawrence told me recently that in his region the only sign of the Canadian state was unemployment insurance. Once more the famous cheque from Ottawa, doled out with no quid pro quo, and tainted with negative associations. All the other visible, viable institutions were of Quebec origin. If one hoisted the Maple Leaf in the neighbourhood, either one was accused by the town notables of being provocative or one was subjected to ridicule. When the Canadian flag did make an appearance, it was assumed to be for the funeral of an old veteran, another poor sod crazy enough to have risked his life for a worthless country that isn't even a country, and that persecutes Quebeckers to boot.

Canada is now part of the past in many Quebec regions. Only some of the old people breathe its name without blushing, or call themselves Canadians without launching into agonies of soul-searching vis-à-vis their identities. The old are excused, their vocabularies have never evolved, poor people, you have to understand, they're all colonized—it's the old song.

Bourassa encouraged this disaffection. Not because he himself felt alienated. It was an electoral tactic, simple as that. Skilful politician that he was, he did what any good strategist dreams of doing: he lured away the natural constituency of his longtime rival, in this case René Lévesque. Unfortunately for him, and for Quebec's Canadians, he succeeded.

And then there was the Meech Lake Accord. Here again, Bourassa consciously made René Lévesque's humiliation his own. The latter, having poorly handled his referendum disaster in 1980, wanted to derail Pierre Trudeau's cherished constitutional reform. To do so he joined forces with seven provincial bigwigs, all jealous of their own interests, dyed-in-the-wool fearful conservatives hostile to change, who thought there might be something to be gained in making things difficult.

Pierre Trudeau was absolutely right to Canadianize once and for all the primary law of the land. It did away with an embarrassing incongruity and encouraged a natural evolution that was long overdue. He also held dear his Charter of Rights and Freedoms, a measure that would emancipate the individual once and for all from the dictatorship of the majority, and whose declaration was the main reason he entered politics. Nothing sinister in that, and it is astonishing today to hear indignant nationalists saying that not only did he repatriate the Constitution, but he also forced on us his Charter of Rights! It's an indignation that does not make many converts.

And so René Lévesque, to come back to him, decided to

scuttle the whole operation. The fox was in the hen-house, everything was on the brink of collapse, when the wily Pierre set a trap for his friend René, who went for it hook line and sinker. He deserted his provincial allies, who, doubtless relieved, threw themselves into the arms of the federal government. All but one, from Manitoba, a detail the nationalists never mention, as they want to credit the legend of a Quebec stabbed in the back by a band of cowards. Just as one conveniently passes over the fact that René Lévesque was the first to break ranks and betray his allies. Ah well . . .

This was the occasion for what nationalist scribblers called the Night of the Long Knives, an outrage supposedly perpetrated by Jean Chrétien. (In passing, we should note that "night of the long knives" is a phrase borrowed from the Nazi lexicon, designating the occasion when the ss liquidated the sa, consolidating Hitler's control over his party.) Jean Chrétien was at home that night, sleeping peacefully as usual. The expression has caught hold, however, belief having displaced the facts.

There are three little problems with the Night of the Long Knives. First, the self-styled martyrs in the Quebec press have forgotten Talleyrand's axiom, which asserts that exaggeration begets disbelief. If Jean Chrétien has never been lynched, it's because people must feel that there is some exaggeration in the choice of words. Second, this borrowing, with its foreign reference, reflects a colonized mentality typical of nationalists who love to display a European culture that only the lettered can properly appreciate. Finally, this term heightens the nationalists' ready-made persecution complex while exonerating René Lévesque, yesterday's conspirator transmuted into today's victim. But it's impossible today to refute this legend, or to employ a more judicious expression, because it's become an article of faith in Monsieur Lesieur's catechism. The fellow travellers in the nationalist press corps did a wonderful job.

Unhappy and blaming others for his own foolishness, Lévesque subsequently drifted from one embarrassment to the next, completing his mandate ingloriously. He gave Lucien Bouchard the task of reining in the unions, showing them he was but a fair-weather friend; he imposed on the party his "Renérendum," threatening to quit the leadership, and so on.

Retired, he published his *Memoirs*. Promoting the book in Ottawa, he spoke before a gathering of well-disposed book lovers, and at great length gave them chapter and verse on the treachery to which he had been subject, poor him who had never ever done anything bad to anybody. It got to the point where a ripple of disgust circulated through the audience. A lady who is most dear to me, charged with the responsibility of thanking him on behalf of the event's organizing committee, wished him well thus: "Monsieur Lévesque, good luck, and I hope your book sells as many copies as you've experienced betrayals . . ." It appears the lady was trying to say something nice. But Monsieur Lévesque did not much appreciate her parting words. Understandably.

Handed the torch of a humbled Quebec, Robert Bourassa found an unlikely ally in none other than Brian Mulroney. This last, seeking the support of Quebec nationalists and hoping to erase the memory of John A. Macdonald, Riel's executioner, decided to endorse the thesis of a federalist plot and to make amends to the Quebec government, victim of its own goodness of heart and Liberal duplicity. Thus compensated, Quebec would adopt the 1982 Constitution (as though it had ever been excluded!) "with honour and enthusiasm," words that were whispered in Mulroney's ear by Lucien Bouchard, who had been freed from the drudgery of his lucrative law practice to string together bombastic locutions for a princely fee.

Elected premier a year later, Bourassa received on a silver platter an unparalleled bargaining tool. A crafty politician, he put to good use Voltaire's insightful dictum from *Candide:* "Misfortunes give one rights." And so it went: "Pay me, and I sign. If you do not . . ." And we were back to the Bourassian blackmail of the 1970s: "Negotiate with me, because I'm your only chance . . . The others, you know . . ."

And we had the Meech Lake Accord. A stupid agreement, however worthy the signatories. Quebec obtained concomitant jurisdiction in the area of immigration, already a fait accompli thanks to the Cullen-Couture agreement, in force for twenty-five years and renewed quasi-automatically. That said, Bourassa was right to insist on it, since it was known to be a long-standing nationalist demand. Already, at the beginning of the twentieth century, Olivar Asselin had denounced, with reason, Ottawa's anglophile immigration policy and launched a movement in favour of French immigration, an initiative that had long remained a dead letter until Lévesque succeeded in imposing it despite his rivalry with Trudeau. When Quebec and Ottawa get together, over and above their divisions, they can do wonders.

There was the consecration of the presence of civil law judges on the Supreme Court, another practice already confirmed by necessity and tradition, there was the right to withdraw from programs with full financial compensation, fine, and there was the question of labour training, settled subsequently thanks to the Bouchard-Chrétien agreement, with disastrous consequences for the unemployed in Quebec, not that it matters to the Quebec government.

Finally, the distinct society, the grandest idiocy of this pseudo-compensatory operation. It would be from that time forward part of the country's fundamental law that Quebec constitutes a distinct society. First, as has been pointed out by the *National Post*'s Andrew Coyne, someone with whom I am

rarely in agreement, it was a mistake to constitutionalize a soci-
ological given. As he said, Canada is a predominantly white
society. Are we going to mention that in the Constitution?
Never would we do such a thing, it would be a thoroughly racist
and discriminatory declaration! And then, things change . . .

Quebec a distinct society? And then what? Who cares?
Newfoundland also has a distinct society, it's the most Irish
province in the country, but that doesn't give it any special
rights. If one had said that Quebec has a French character, fine,
but even there you have to be awfully insecure to constitutionalize something so obvious. It was said, if I remember correctly,
that one had to be very careful not to rob Quebec of its uniqueness within Canada, and so a distinct society, if you please!
Never mind that distinct societies in Canada are thick on the
ground, by definition and by their intrinsic nature: Mennonites,
Rastafarians, gays and lesbians, the Inuit, and one could go on.

The example I like to give is that of a Métis colony in the
West where the common language is Ukrainian. Imagine these
descendants of Indians and Slav colonists who speak a language
from off the steppes of Europe. Are we going to reserve a place
in the Constitution for this sublime instance of cultural cross-
pollination? No, it's not worth the trouble. Its distinctiveness is
obvious enough not to require any illusory constitutional protection.

Here it will be said that Robert Bourassa had no real choice.
He had to offer this tasteless morsel to his loyal lieutenant, the
failed father and apostle of special status, Claude Ryan. "Special
status," another exhibit to stow away on the shelf of political
tautologies, but Monsieur Ryan clung to this pathetic constitutional fig leaf. Bourassa wanted to appease a large faction of the
Quebec Liberal Party, and he imagined that at the same time he
could mollify the soft nationalists, thereby killing two birds

with one stone. A deft manoeuvre that would cost nobody anything. A good move also for Brian Mulroney, who thought Quebec would be ever beholden to his party.

It was a fiasco. Many Canadian Liberals, loyal to Pierre Elliott Trudeau's ideas, wanted no part of this crutch, and with reason. The PQ supporters had no interest in letting constitutional discord flag, and they voted against the agreement in the National Assembly. True to themselves, however, they insisted that it was because it didn't go far enough, though they later claimed Canada had rejected Quebec and persuaded many soft nationalists that that was the case. Bourassa and Mulroney had been outmanoeuvred.

Rebuffed, Robert Bourassa renewed the attack by asking for more, asserting even that Meech was only a minimum, a starting point, and that he had other demands up his sleeve. Brian Mulroney, who had thought he could make Quebec happy once and for all and pass into history as the Great Canadian Unifier, found himself inundated with demands for redress from one and all: First Nations Peoples, Québécois, Acadians, former Japanese internees, all the insulted and injured of the world held out their hands to him. Of course there were real wounds to heal, but Canada was now prey to a widespread neurosis, a hysteria of victimization. Lucien Bouchard seized the opportunity to pull his chestnuts out of the fire and give himself a historical role that would match his heroic ambitions.

Then came the Charlottetown referendum, which at least had the merit of creating a rare solidarity among Preston Manning, Lucien Bouchard, Pierre Elliott Trudeau, and Jacques Parizeau. Brian Mulroney had realized his fondest dream: to reconcile Canadian opposites. A tour de force from which his party has never recovered.

Since that time, nothing. Even if, implicitly, the Parti

Québécois has recognized the legitimacy of the 1982 Constitution, and, consistent with modernity and good sense, has modified the article concerning the confessional character of Quebec's school boards, it will never adopt this Constitution, which it abhors because it is not its own. Of course. Otherwise the PQ would be repudiating its founding father. Which is unthinkable. At least for now.

The Quebec Liberal Party cannot sign the accord either without demanding considerations that Canada would consider prejudicial to its integrity, in the words of de Gaulle. Bourassa's shrewdness had left Quebec paralyzed. Even if the QLP got Ottawa to give it the moon, the PQ would cry humiliation. Given that no compensation will ever do, and that Canada must always be refused, the Quebec government will never be able to declare itself wholly Canadian. Which is not so bad, when you think about it. It's fated to profit forever from the federation without having to recognize its legitimacy. It has nothing to lose and everything to gain at the same time.

We must reconcile ourselves to the fact that there will be no constitutional peace. But is it as serious as all that? In a way, yes, because in Quebec it will be a long time before we can talk about anything else. Don't expect the leader of the Quebec Liberal Party to one day square his shoulders, and say: If I'm elected, I'm going to Ottawa, I'm signing, it's all over, we're turning the page. A vain dream. Look at what Robert Bourassa's Liberal Party has become. It's a group scared silly of offending its soft-nationalist constituency, unable to voice its own option. On the scale of political courage, it doesn't rate very high.

As a consequence of playing two sets of cards, on the one hand a gainful openness to Canada, on the other the threat of independence, Bourassa created a Liberal Party that knows neither what it wants nor who it is. The QLP reached its lowest ebb with the Allaire Report, which called for nothing less than Lévesque's absurd sovereignty-association, the only difference being that Ottawa would be stuck with all the problems and all the bills. The PQ had succeeded in Finlandizing the Liberal Party of Quebec.

Bourassa himself, tired of it all, was quick to call a halt to this foolishness, and in so doing he at last showed his true hand. It had been a closely kept secret: Bourassa was a Canadian. He showed it during the Allaire episode and after the Charlottetown referendum as well, when certain journalists, Michel Vastel the first, went so far as to imagine that he would declare the unilateral independence of Quebec. Out of respect for his fellow citizens who had asked for nothing of the sort, Bourassa wisely abstained.

We can justifiably reproach Bourassa for having overused the time-honoured gambit of making demands. It's a degrading exercise that taints donor and recipient both. "Dear, don't go, I'll buy you a beautiful fur coat." "Thanks for the coat, but the others say it's not good enough and I've been short-changed. Now I want the car of the year. If I don't get it the others will want to separate, don't you see?"

He also played the fear card for all it was worth. It's what political scientist Léon Dion, Stéphane's father, called negotiating "with the knife at the throat." Another degrading game, except this one is dangerous. It's degrading because these are the tactics of a thug. It's dangerous because sooner or later the adversary stops being afraid, regains his courage, sends the negotiator packing with his knife and the hell with the consequences. "I won't play any more!" It's forgetting, also, that no one wants to negotiate with a knife at his throat, neither a Québécois from Rivière du Loup, nor an Ontarian from Peterborough. Meanwhile, who, in the midst of this vulgar squabble, thinks of the citizen's interests, or those of the consumer, or of the taxpayer who ends up paying the shot for these political manoeuvrings? No one, obviously.

"CANADA IS AT AN IMPASSE," declares *Le Devoir* with predictable regularity, to make things seem dramatic. Fine. In any federation worthy of the name there are always imbalances and frustrations of all sorts. The Sicilians will always resent Italy; the Bavarians, Germany; the Bretons, France, but still the grain and the flowers keep on growing. Who is bothered by our prefabricated crises? A few top bureaucrats in Quebec who can't enlarge their empires at the expense of the Canadian taxpayer, the 1532 readers of *Le Devoir*'s editorial page, a handful of right-thinking Torontonians with a lifelong case of guilt. The only happy ones? The fellow travelling journalists and the professional politicians who profit from the endless disagreements. All the others couldn't care less. And so we'll go on squabbling, looking over our shoulders, tripping each other up, imagining conspiracies, and carrying on with our unilateral declarations of indignation or humiliation, take your choice.

It should be said as well that adopting the 1982 Constitution wouldn't have guaranteed anything. Brian Mulroney and Robert Bourassa shared the immense but dubious talent of persuading their fellow citizens to the contrary. Total peace cannot be guaranteed. Monsieur Charest, elected premier of Quebec, could sign the document three times over, that would never stop the PQ from calling as many referendums as it wanted. Every constitutional solution is an illusion, but in the meantime, there's no denying it, we still have peace.

And so what should we do? Nothing. Let the adversaries grow old. And perhaps the day will come when we will have forgotten what we're arguing about. We will then, with great pomp, declare the disputes defunct, and all start talking about the latest pileup on Highway 20.

The duel between Bourassa and Lévesque had an unresolved ending, much in the spirit of the feigned assaults of the first and the sham retreats of the second. Bourassa had won the first two matches; Lévesque turned the tables in 1976. Bourassa wanted revenge, but his opponent left the field too soon. Lévesque died, Bourassa as well. Lévesque left behind him a paunchy PQ, Bourassa handed down a nationalist QLP. Their deaths blew the whistle on a tied game with both players unable to make a move. Each had lost and won at the same time.

～ The Parricide and the Good Son

THE YEARS THAT followed the first referendum were not so morose as was later claimed by the right-thinking bourgeoisie. The economy was in good shape, soaring real estate prices made a lot of people rich, writers wrote a lot and even well. Books like Yves Beauchemin's *The Alley Cat* and Arlette Cousture's *Les Filles de Caleb* filled the pockets of artisans more accustomed to pinching pennies than to racking up large sales. Cinema was going full blast, so we were treated to a number of films that embodied in no uncertain terms the resentments of the Quebec intellectual class. Including, of course, Pierre Falardeau's *Elvis Gratton,* a slap in the face to those materialists who had dared turn their backs on the Father-Nation.

There were two more interesting films, by Denys Arcand. The first, *Comfort and Indifference,* reeked of contempt for a Quebec population that was more interested in big cars than in national grandeur. Here too the intellectual was getting even with this recalcitrant nation, but in more refined fashion, without the vulgarity. Arcand fawns on the "people," those craftsmen and farmers who speak out and say what they think. They're the good guys, and they're in favour of independence (a coincidence, no doubt), while the bad guys are the gadget-happy property owners (probably another coincidence). It's a polarization dear to the heart of that venerable Quebec ideology which, from Monseigneur Laflèche to Pierre Vallières, has disparaged possessions and vaunted austerity. The same old wine in the same old wineskins.

Arcand went on to sharpen his attack with *The Decline of the American Empire,* a boot-licking title in that it was clearly aimed at the French market. It's a comic film that when you come down to it was just a cerebral version of Marcel Dubé's 1972 screenplay *Les Beaux Dimanches,* which portrayed a corrupt Canadian bourgeoisie besotted with sex and alcohol. The decline in question was made that much more comic by the fact that its theses were all wrong.

Thus (with a nudge in the ribs to the French, who must envy us, no?) the American Empire (of which we are a part), found guilty of having too much fun, was written off as doomed, and as is so often the case the dialogue conjures up that apocalypse once anticipated by the followers of Lionel Groulx. At last word the American empire was doing better than ever, the atomic disaster had not take place, and it's the Soviet empire that perished by its own hand, which is too bad for those Quebec intellectuals who so envied it its salubrious collectivism.

We should pardon Arcand for his error in judgement. Eager to please the French intelligentsia, he couldn't very well insult Communism, it would be taken badly in Paris. But he could in all tranquillity bash the Yankees. Arcand is apocalyptic, of course, because he is a nationalist, or at any rate he talks the correct nationalist talk. For example, he denounces the pleasure-seeking individualist who turns his back on collectivist austerity. His professors betray their vocation by committing themselves full-time to sex, they neglect the people while tucking into their food like pigs. In this quintessentially moral tale one character is punished with AIDS, while the others slip into conjugal mediocrity. They screw themselves to death, that'll teach them. You didn't want to build a country, idiots? Fine, you're going to go to the dogs and perish from pleasure.

In *The Black Sheep,* another film of that period, Jacques Godbout asked a group of young people what they wanted out of life. One declared that he was in favour of individual happiness. That was Joseph Facal, today the shrill minister and obedient son of Lucien Bouchard. He contradicted himself immediately: "What I don't want is in twenty years to be a character out of *The Decline of the American Empire.*" The contradiction should surprise nobody. In neo-Jansenist nationalism, only the collective has value, and individual happiness is suspect. It's a Tartuffian asceticism, obviously.

Patient still, the father was going to try one more time to impress his power on the nation. But who would the father be? Who would replace father-figure Lévesque, who had failed at his task?

His obedient son, Pierre-Marc Johnson, who did not go into politics to be leader of the Opposition, like his father, abandoned the field at the first shot. This man, twice a son, by birth and by adoption, was replaced by Parizeau, a true Monsieur, a Gaston d'Orléans who had made his mark and who lost no time dispensing with the paternal heritage. In other words, independence was put back on the front burner and sovereignty-association went the way of the dodo. In electing Parizeau, the PQ renounced Lévesque the father. Another *beau risque.*

Jacques Parizeau was someone to be reckoned with, another Québécois who had succeeded, like Pierre Trudeau, and who thought big in a way that was both dazzling and unsettling. Intelligent, cultivated, he was part of that generation that brought us the suave and learned Jean-Marc Léger, Pierre Vadebon-coeur, and so many others. An eloquent Finance Minister, he combined the interventionist energy of a Jean Talon with a taste for the good things in life more akin to François Bigot. A master of words and ideas, endowed with humour and elegance, he made the inner workings of power accessible, never lapsing into vulgarity. When you listened to him he made you feel more than intelligent—he made you feel brilliant.

As Leader of the Opposition he performed reasonably well, and profiting from the desire for political changeover common among the Québécois, who have always been a free people, the PQ regained power in 1994. And with Parizeau there would be a real referendum, with a real and clear question: "Do you accept that Quebec become a sovereign country?" Something like that. The people would be misled no more in the way Jacques Ferron deplored, and Quebec would enter history with its head held high.

But this was without taking into account Bouchard, who also wanted to be father. Seeing that the polls looked bad, he demanded a "winning" question. In other words, convoluted, like that of 1980, which could be made to mean anything at all. In short, a dishonest question. Once more one would try to hoodwink the Quebec people. Parizeau could see that his frankness would lead to defeat. The Québécois, so weak, so frail, wanted for the most part to stay in Canada, the country they founded and that was theirs. They therefore had to be lured with the prospect of a negotiation whose failure was predestined, and then presented with a fait accompli. They would thus gain independence oh so gently, and Parizeau's de Gaullian vanity would be satisfied, not to mention the vanity of the right-thinking bourgeoisie, neurotic to the bone: at last we will be a country like the others . . .

To avert disaster, Parizeau devised a trick as big as a barn door. He gave in where the quality of the question was concerned, on condition that Bouchard would agree to lead the negotiations with Canada that were sure to fail. He began to laud the talents of the man who had so deftly shafted the unions on behalf of René Lévesque. If the yes won, Quebec, which could never allow itself to see reason in Ottawa's terms, would declare itself independent, Parizeau would be the hallowed founder, and Bouchard would forever bear the stigma of the aborted negotiations. What a coup! Parizeau would realize his ambitions and in the process rid himself of both his precursor and his rival. He would win on all fronts. He would be father to the nation.

We know what ensued. The ruse failed miserably. Parizeau had to pack his bags and was immediately replaced by Lucien Bouchard, who donned the mantle of René Lévesque. The parricide was shunted aside, and the good loyal son, who had so often invoked Lévesque's ghost on the referendum hustings, assumed his legacy. The father was safe. The clan mothers, Louise Harel, Louise Beaudoin, and the rest, deferred politely to the new papa, and like Lévesque they would console themselves with power while waiting on history.

It should be said that Bouchard was then invincible. The terrible disease that had cost him his leg had also endowed him with a martyr's nimbus. His misfortune had gained him entrance not to history but to our collective memory, with its procession of torturers of Iroquois, deporters of Acadians, Orangist executioners of Riel.

More than Jacques Parizeau, with his air of an overnourished banker and his British tweeds emblematic of foreign success, Bouchard with his affliction embodied Quebec's age-old insecurities. He was a father who had known glorious suffering, like a figure out of the illustrated history books we'd once known, he was of modest origins like most of us, always quick to shower praise on his own father, Philippe Bouchard the truck driver, and he was married to a beautiful American. Another sign of success, but less suspect than Parizeau's. What more could the Parti Québécois want? René Lévesque lived again, reincarnated and improved, a reassuring continuance.

The difference was that Bouchard shared one flaw with Parizeau that Lévesque didn't have: the de Gaulle complex. A real papa, Charles de Gaulle, who called us his "children of Canada." Bouchard, whose admiration for de Gaulle knew no bounds, was said to unwind by listening to his speeches on cassette. He loved sprinkling here and there the General's words, whose source he was careful never to divulge. Pierre-Marc Johnson was thus "in reserve for the Republic," a phrase de Gaulle used in referring to Pompidou. Such examples abound in his vocabulary.

Words borrowed but not attributed. In this he resembles Jacques Parizeau, that grand bourgeois and citizen of Montreal going three generations back. Parizeau has passed on to us two of de Gaulle's locutions: "My dear and ancient country . . . ," an utterance de Gaulle used when he took in hand the Algerian affair. And this: "I've put the engine back on the rails . . . ," referring to the Culture Ministry that had been shaken by the dismissal of Marie Malavoy, guilty of electoral fraud. De Gaulle had invoked that same train when he left the government in 1946.

Messieurs Parizeau and Bouchard don't like each other very much. And not just because the latter outfoxed the former. The two plagiarists will dispute for a long time to come the title of father to the nation. But there is one important difference between the two, all to the advantage of the Parizeau. He speaks much better French, and never comes out with anglicisms painful to the ear. For instance, Monsieur Bouchard likes to say that he *s'est peinturé dans le coin* — has painted himself into a corner. There are days when you have to know English very well in order to understand the protector of Quebec French. There was also the time when this great "suppliant on horseback," to borrow a phrase coined by Gérard Filion, went on pilgrimage to the Élysée Palace seeking the assistance of the mother country, and declared in front of a battery of microphones: "President Chirac assured me of France's support, he told me so *en autant de mots*." That's very good English: in so many words. Monsieur Parizeau, that day, must have laughed himself silly.

Trifles, all that? Not at all. This weakness for plagiarism clearly reveals Bouchard the father's colonized mentality. In his mind Churchill's bowler hat rubs shoulders with the General's képi. It's not for nothing that his first child's name is Alexandre, a tribute to the conqueror, while the younger is called Simon, in memory of Bolivar — references he has himself admitted.

A strange man who hates his political vocation, which he performs very well, but who dreams of being a great political personage, the liberator of the French in America. Unlike René Lévesque, but like Jacques Parizeau, he only got involved in politics to enter into history. As for power, he's happy to have it while waiting to be consecrated in the history books, but he exercises it with little enthusiasm, subcontracting government business to Bernard Landry and the National Assembly to Guy Chevrette.

Since his ascension to power there's more and more talk of partnership, more even than with Lévesque. And Bouchard never misses an opportunity to remind his adversaries of the militant pasts of his predecessors, who like him had to defend the Quebec palisade against Ottawa: Jean Lesage, Daniel Johnson Sr., Robert Bourassa. He's a dutiful son as well, where France is concerned. He's not going to incite Corsica or Guadeloupe to secede, and never would he offend the spirit of the General. Under Bouchard, Quebec will be always the elder son of France. His great good fortune? He has opposing him a Liberal party that also would never lay hands on the paternal succession. Victim of his own complexes, Robert Bourassa dreamed of a Canada redesigned by Jean Monnet, a new European Community on Canadian soil. Always the paternal model, made in Europe . . . These days Monsieur Bouchard is waving the same flag Bourassa went seeking in Brussels, that of European Union.

One never dared tell Bourassa the father, either, that to transplant this formula, however appropriate it may be to a once fratricidal Europe, was utterly absurd and the sign of a bankrupt imagination. The 1867 B.N.A. Act preceded the advent of the Third Republic in France, the creation of Bismarck's Germany, and Garibaldi's Italy. Canada was Europe long before Europe, it pursued its own destiny and decolonized itself little by little, almost unwittingly. It's an unfinished task where our consciousness is concerned, but we've come a long way all the same. Yet, no. Monnet was to Bourassa what de Gaulle was to Bouchard and to Parizeau. No one in the QLP dared to challenge the father with the yen for Brussels, and the day when Daniel Johnson Jr. dared to admit that he was a Canadian before being Québécois, the putsch came swiftly. The Liberals liquidated the bad son, and went to Ottawa to seek out Jean Charest, just as they had repatriated Jean Lesage earlier on. Will Charest dare to break free from Bourassa's paternal fetters? Perhaps. He has just stated that from now on he'll move away from the kind of federalism built on making one demand after another. That's already something, but given how nationalist his party has become thanks to Bourassa's tactics, it's far from being a done deal. The Salic Law weighs heavy in the land of the fleur-de-lys.

So there will be a third referendum one day, that like Lévesque's will focus on sovereignty-association, only, if we are to believe Bernard Landry's bizarre promise, without the hyphen. More lies, presumably, that a father tells his spineless sons before pulling another fast one.

But suddenly an unexpected obstacle was raised that could force Quebec to grow up for good. Jean Chrétien, who has no complexes vis-à-vis anybody, be it Pearson or Trudeau, called to his side a university professor who quietly broke with his own father's views and chose his own way. Stéphane Dion is the author of a law that will bar Canada from embarking on any secessionist negotiation unless the question is clear, a measure that should please Laurent-Michel Vacher and Jacques Parizeau.

Right away, the good sons rose up in protest. From Gérard Bouchard to Michel Seymour, all grimly defended the Quebec government's sacred right to cheat. Every shred and tatter of borrowed vocabulary was trotted out for the occasion: aggression against the people; Canada, the prison of the Quebec nation; Stalinist shackles, etc. The St. Jean Baptiste Society threw itself at the feet of the *New York Times* and *Le Monde Diplomatique*. The militant Gilles Rhéaume even wanted to ask France to defend its endangered former colony. "Papa, come help . . ." It was almost touching in its absurdity. The fuss did not create much of a stir in Quebec or anywhere else, for the obvious reason that they were wielding a borrowed, archaic, senile and murky discourse, good only for eliciting smiles of sham commiseration.

But Parizeau the parricide was not going to let himself be outsmarted for long by the good son Lucien. This Montreal patrician with a doctorate from the London School of Economics, proprietor of a French vineyard and urban animal par excellence, has never had much esteem for the upwardly mobile pettifogger from Jonquière. He must have deeply regretted selling him his first PQ membership card, a partisan baptismal certificate fraught with symbolic irony. This little act of kindness, extended by a colonel in his best bib and tucker to a valiant corporal in rags, turned out not to be such a good investment.

Parizeau soon saw that this card would be used for little more than to weasel fat cheques out of the PQ government. He then looked on as Mulroney's new minion basked in the emoluments handed out by the shovelful to nationalism's apostates, who, it turns out, had not sold their souls, as it was claimed — they'd only leased them. But for the moment the corporal had garnered himself a marshal's baton in his new incarnation as a card-carrying Progressive Conservative. He moved up the ladder swiftly, became an ambassador, was elected member of Parliament, was appointed to Cabinet, then assumed the role of a martyr betrayed, founded his own party, and became a father himself. Finally this belated convert had the gall to steal Parizeau's party out from under him and to claim the mantle of a father who was supposed to have been dead and gone. That was adding insult to injury for Monsieur Parizeau, he who had stepped down for real on a true question of principle, who had endured exile in the wilderness, and had restored the PQ's soul.

And so the resentful parricide took on the role of retired statesman. He gave haughty advice to the good son but bad leader. He did not go so far as to wield a knife, that is not done between gentlemen, and besides, when confronting the enemy one must show a common front. But he irked the good son by gathering round him all the true believers in the party. To the point where Bouchard's number one companion in arms, Michel Venne, demanded that Monsieur Parizeau be silenced. It's only in nationalist circles that the right to dissidence is circumscribed in this way. Nobody protests, either, not even the person who has been targeted, free speech not weighing heavy in the balance next to paternal diktats.

Deaf to his critics, Monsieur Parizeau used his free time to lay siege to the party his rival had founded, a bit like having babies in another's nest, a neat revenge. With the Bloc Québécois as his tribune, he exhorted Bouchard to hold his referendum, held him to account and insisted he show his ideological credentials; he even called on him to put a clear question to the people, as he had wanted to do himself. But his rival knew this was a thinly disguised invitation to suicide, and so he played the daddy who pretends he can't hear when the kids are yelling their heads off. The game was a deeply irritating one for Lucien Bouchard, who had to make an enormous effort not to let slip his role of the good son anointed by the father, kindly to those who are restless and respectful of his elders. Hard, very hard.

Fortunately the party stuck by the father, tolerating at its head a man of the right even though it was on the left. The comrades-in-arms were staunch and kept a sharp lookout, and called to order this Parizeau who had become a rebellious son. The Harels, Beaudoins and Marois, those who overthrew the parricide to supplant him with the chosen son, remain loyal and do not conspire overmuch. They're waiting for him to fall on his face, at which point we will witness the most impressive combat ever waged among carnivores on the Quebec political stage.

The show goes on. Parizeau will perhaps succeed in pushing Bouchard into a referendum. If so, it will be dishonest once more. For the moment all is well, Monsieur Bouchard has his party under control. He has succeeded in purging the last Parizealots with knives between their teeth, and to govern he relies on the church mice of the party and ignores those who are tearing up their membership cards.

He still has a chance to get his name inscribed in the great history book, but it's not certain that he'll seize the opportunity. One thing is certain, he will not risk defeat, his vanity will not allow it. If the polls refuse him a third referendum, he'll take his leave in peace at the end of his mandate, for in his soul the man is more epicurean than kamikaze. He'll settle in Outremont, certainly not in Jonquière, will land himself a sinecure in a law firm, and will savour the handsome nest-egg he's put by. He might even go back into harness for the federal government; he'd make a wonderful Canadian representative at prestigious French funerals.

The hour will have come, then, for the clan mothers. They will fight to the last man for the high ground. It's a good bet, however, that the victor's reign will be as brief as Kim Campbell's. Whether it be Louise Harel or Pauline Marois, we may be sure that the psychodrama of the Quebec nation and its father will end like one of Michel Tremblay's plays: "Papa is gone, he botched things up, it wasn't his fault, maybe he'll be back one day, don't cry, mama is there. Mama will always be there. Go back to sleep . . ."

Jean Charest, newly elected, will lose no time lavishing honours on father Lucien, to keep him quiet, of course, and the latter will come to the sensible conclusion that a stretch of eponymous highway in the Laurentians is not a bad recompense for his efforts, certainly preferable to a statue crowned with the unsavoury discharge of pigeons. He will rub his hands together with glee at the thought that the parricide won't be getting a bust as father of the nation, either. All the while, the statue of the real de Gaulle will gather Quebec guano. Our colonial novel will have had a comic ending.

∼ The Cartoonesque

THE PATERNAL DISCOURSE of nationalist thinkers and politicians has just one goal: to infantilize the population in such a way as to bring it round to its own views and to control it. To this end it makes liberal use of the "cartoonesque," a word that to my mind captures well the style of our colonial novel.

Cartoonesque. You won't find the word in any dictionary, but rest assured, one day you will. It derives, of course, from cartoon: a crude vision of the world that trumpets ideologies in the simplest and most polarized terms. Think of Uncle Sam in his top hat or the Soviet bear whose teeth drip with blood. A few cartoonesque images of Quebec nationalism: the fat saleslady at Eaton's whom nobody has ever seen, and yesterday's "French pea soup" who cringed before his boss.

I say "cartoonesque" rather than "caricature" because the latter has the advantage, at times, of making us think. The cartoonesque, on the other hand, inhibits all reflection. I also like Flaubert's term, *l'idée reçue,* the "received idea"; unfortunately, it no longer means much to anybody. Which is too bad, because his *Dictionary of Received Ideas,* much admired by Kafka, is a marvel: "ENGLISHMEN: All are rich. GRAMMAR: Teach it to children, however young, as something clear and easy. HEBREW: Everything you can't understand." And so on.

In the same vein, the cartoonesque reflects with its broad crayon strokes a backward mentality oblivious to doubt and dismissive of all subtleties. Nationalism is the political expression of an adolescent cast of mind in the sense that it fears the unknown and thrives on absolutisms, and it incorporates an ideology and a language that make a perfect match for each other. It is no surprise that the great nationalist curates Yves Beauchemin, Josée Legault, Lucien Bouchard, and Pierre Falardeau are assiduous practitioners.

The cartoonesque, by definition, oversimplifies. Imagine, for example, a novel whose goal would be to urge its readers to vote yes in the next referendum. We begin with the story of a little girl from Rosemont who works very hard. By day she's an accountant's assistant in a clothing factory owned by Jews who are rich as Croesus, and at night she attends college and studies arts. At a party thrown by her employers in Westmount, where the champagne is flowing and oysters are in abundance, she meets a handsome, elegant young man, so beautiful that she thinks he may even be a bit gay.

She is captivated by his sparkling comments on Aragon and Picasso, dazzled by his refinement and intelligence. He offers to drive her home in his BMW convertible. Faking car trouble, he throws himself upon her and takes her virginity; then he opens the car door and tosses her out, shouting after her that she should wash between her legs the next time around. He takes off laughing, leaving her on the sidewalk, bathed in tears.

Her heart broken, ashamed, the young girl walks home in the rain. In the course of a sleepless night she resolves to avenge herself. At work she drives herself twice as hard and she doubles her courses at college, maintaining a feverish pace that helps take her mind off her pregnancy. Refusing to give birth in this accursed country where the injustices of the rich English prevail, she gives up the baby, conceived against her wishes, to a Swiss couple, both doctors. She flies off to Geneva between two courses to have the child, whom the Swiss, who are extremely wealthy, will raise in the lap of luxury and will instil with a love for the French language. As a friendly gesture, these good people offer to pay for the young woman's law studies at the University of Montreal.

She becomes a lawyer, defends the union members at her former workplace, and succeeds in ruining her one-time bosses, who are Jews, as I have said; they lose no time fleeing to Israel. She is elected member of the National Assembly for the PQ, is named minister, and is given the task of awakening in the Quebec people its latent desire for sovereignty.

Invited to a debate, she discovers that her adversary is none other than the rapist from twenty years earlier, the brute who has since become a rich real-estate tycoon and a Federal government minister. Guess what. She nails the wretch to the wall and passionately defends the honour of those Quebec workers who lived lives of humiliation for so long. There is jubilation in the land. She wins the referendum almost single-handedly. Her people are freed, the rapist goes bankrupt and ends his days indigent, impotent, and alcoholic, panhandling for quarters from his wheelchair on St. Denis Street.

The final scene of the novel takes place five years later. Our heroine is president of a free Quebec and is married to a former tenor with the Accueil Bonneau poor people's choir, now a professor at the University of Quebec. Her Swiss son, who has become an economist, comes to seek her out and asks her permission to emigrate with his wife and twin boys to this beautiful, new and free country. She says yes. The last word in the

83

book: yes. Isn't that beautiful? Say it's beautiful. You'd think it were Falardeau, or even Pierre Perrault.

I'm not exaggerating for a moment, and that's what is sad. On the eve of the last referendum, a biodegradable novel was published whose intent was just that—to make people vote yes. I forget the title, but it doesn't matter. Its author had paid no heed to what Proust had to say about the vulgarity of such texts: "A book with theories is like an object on which you've left the price." From one generation to the next, Quebec's writers have written scads of books to incite their fellow citizens to action. They've called for separation, for a break with the British Empire, for a return to the land, for the repatriation of Franco-Americans, for the colonization of Abitibi, for anti-Semitism, for the overthrow of Canadian power, for a yes in referendums, always with no result. And each time they have berated this people whose materialism has deafened them to their appeals.

It's an ancient misunderstanding between the poor wretches that we are and the literate bourgeoisie who control the universities, publishing, the press, and the Quebec State. Thus, the memory of the Conquest inspires no feeling of humiliation in these good people. The wise Toqueville saw this when he paid a visit to Lower Canada: "Up to the present, the people, having few needs and intellectual passions, and leading a very pleasant material life, has only dimly perceived its status as a conquered nation, and has provided weak support for the enlightened classes." I must myself be part of this labouring class, since never in my life have I given the least thought to the defeat on the Plains of Abraham, even though Victor-Lévy Beaulieu and Bernard Landry gripe about it all day long. Much good may it do them. The people still don't go along with it. They must be either stupid or colonized, or both at the same time. That's why one feels sorry for them or looks down on them, or both at the same time.

That's how the cartoonesque works: there would then be seven million cretins in Canada who aren't aware of the state of ignominy in which they live. The "enlightened class" would never entertain the possibility that it might itself be in error. No, never. Confident that it is in "serene possession of the truth," the Quebec intellectual class, from Groulx to Beauchemin, has always tried to force its own fantasies on the people it claims to serve, although, in truth, it dreams only of holding them in submission. The obtuseness of the people has one consolation: as they refuse to pay heed to their intellectual leaders, these last can seek solace in their feelings of superiority. The bourgeois thus becomes an aristocrat.

The cartoonesque is an art rich in "ideologettes," those shards of ideology that are so many false views of reality. Some of Félix Leclerc's songs, those reflecting his late-blooming nationalism, are cartoonesque: Québécois, unemployed, tenant in his own land, etc. In his world, polarized to the hilt, to be Québécois and to speak French is to be oppressed. The oppressor is a greedy foreigner, immigrants are impure and pollute our beautiful Quebec, Americans are vulgar materialists. This Leclerc knows no nuance.

Falardeau's films also embody the cartoonesque in its pure state. Thus Elvis Gratton, the big lout, is a federalist and votes no. He is there to make us hate Canada. In *The Party,* the convict is a really good guy who's had a lot of bad luck and a corrupt and oppressive society on his back; the prison guard is a crapulous, bourgeois, sadistic brute who sexually abuses young Haitian girls. Falardeau's not exactly a connoisseur of ambiguity ...

Another great artisan of the cartoonesque is Georges Dor. In his essays, the inarticulate Québécois is a vanquished figure whose ingrained submission to the conqueror has robbed him of all pride of language. He speaks badly because he is oppressed. Moving from one simplistic premise to the next, Dor asserts that the French speak well because France is a free country. In Haiti, the same thing. We, the Québécois, are the only people in the world who speak bad French, because our country was incorporated by force into Canada, a country that has nothing better to do than to assimilate us and turn us into robotic consumers, fodder for IBM and McDonald's. It's as simple as that.

Happily, the solution is as simple as the problem: Quebec has only to declare itself independent and it will be primed to do whatever it takes to improve our French. Presto! Everyone will speak really well. Not bad, eh?

It's pointless to go through all of Georges Dor's theses just to shoot them down one by one. If Monsieur Lesieur is a believer, Dor is a canon, and it's no use reasoning with him or the others. Besides, he's a likable fellow, and he's written us some very lovely songs. It's not up to me to teach him some basic truths. I'm not convinced, for example, that conquests always obliterate languages. Ukrainian, Byelorussian, Czech, Slovak, Polish, Hungarian, Armenian, etc., are there as living proof. Foreign occupations or Finlandizations of one kind or another do not necessarily produce spineless peoples, grovelling and submissive; there are even thriving cultures that have no tongues of their own, such as the Irish, whose genius from Swift to Joyce has enriched the English language. Yankee imperialism has not, at last word, done away completely with Brazil and Mexico. As for Haiti, well, only five per cent of its population speaks French, and it is this very bourgeoisie that stalks Falardeau's hate-drenched nightmares; the others speak Creole. That said, I don't for a moment doubt Georges Dor's sincerity. It's his vision of the world that is false, not him.

Georges Dor doesn't seem to realize how he's patronizing

those Québécois whose lot he wants to improve. In his world, the Québécois is a poor wretch so cowed by the colonizer (as though the Battle of the Plains of Abraham had taken place yesterday morning rather than several centuries ago) that he dares not express himself correctly. His own words have been taken out of his mouth. It's as though this pathetic loser had no life of his own, had no free will, and could not assert himself other than to play the fool. He will die the way he lived, witless, ignorant of his own social and cultural bankruptcy, between his six-pack and his poutine. When you think about it, Dor is looking down on the very men and women he wants to help. He is like a white missionary tending to Africans he considers so hopeless and simpleminded that they can't be civilized.

Monsieur Lesieur would not dispute a single one of Georges Dor's words. When he gets depressed he tells himself that the Québécois vote no because they are poor souls, lower class. And that makes him a Zolaesque aristocrat appalled by the working man who drinks rather than squirrelling away his pay. He knows independence is a must because he has read everything, understood everything, while the colonized masses with their Molsons and Chevies just don't have a clue.

One of my fondest memories in this regard is the final scene from Denys Arcand's *Comfort and Indifference,* a film which is rich in ironic nuances but which at times lapses into a cartoonism worthy of Falardeau. It's the moment when we drop in on a kind of car show for recreational vehicles, a great festival of kitsch for Quebec ninnies and materialists. The farmers and artisans who precede them, on the other hand, are simple and noble souls. They are perfect role models, whereas the guys with the carpeted vans are all Elvis Grattons. We don't know whether they voted no, but that's what we're led to believe; they're poor imbeciles who, up to their ears in an orgy of vulgar ostentation, are compensating for the collectivity's political failure. We dream no more, we create no more; instead, we consume goods produced by others. We might have expected a bit more subtlety, but instead the film lapses into a haughty contempt for this disloyal people that refuses to conform to the fantasies of its right-thinking elite.

I have the feeling that Arcand and Dor don't go out much, or if they do they don't spend much time with this lower class that they laud out loud but secretly can't stand. Adolescents that they are, in that they are themselves vassals to a borrowed and simplistic pattern of thought, they believe it's still possible to write *Uncle Tom's Cabin,* which did so much to help abolish slavery in the United States, *Oliver Twist,* which led to better treatment of children during the reign of Queen Victoria, *Germinal,* which dealt with the working conditions of miners, or *The Cancer Ward,* which exposed the predicament of Soviet dissidents. This is the naïveté of little boys who have never seen beyond their books and are astounded to find that their art is powerless to alter life.

They should have come with me to the funeral of my friend Paulo. Monsieur Lesieur should have been there too. Paulo was a garageman. A good fellow whose death saddened all who knew him. Carried off by a heart attack at the age of 48, a real waste. A Pierre Falardeau would have loved seeing his relatives and friends gathered together at the church. Aside from a few close relatives of the deceased, none of the men wore ties, they were all in working clothes; the women were better dressed. Enough to make Falardeau say: "Real Québécois, *hostie,* my people, *câlisse!*" But at the mandatory buffet that followed, Dor would have been distressed to hear them talk: "Hey, Larry! Remember the time poor Paulo forgot to *détailleter la bolte,* and *le fraime* came out at the same time as the *panne à huile* that was *jammée? Viarge,* but we laughed. But when you had to *bouster un char, chriss,* he was *le best, 'stie."* Dor the part-time linguist would call them poor unfortunates who don't know what they're doing. "My world," would boast Falardeau, who is master toady to a working class that never existed in Quebec.

If Dor were to get a bit closer to these poor Québécois, he would perhaps see something different than what he imagines. The friends of my friend Paulo are mothers and fathers, property owners or tenants, employers or employed. They are people who determine their own destinies, vote as they wish, yes or no, but either way make up their own minds — in short, they are free individuals who talk as they like or as they can, without asking anyone's permission and even less their forgiveness.

But the Dors of this world, including our friend Lesieur, have an unhealthy need to believe in the genetic inferiority of this poor Quebec worker who knows not where he's at. They are self-styled tragic souls who can see the apocalypse on the horizon, and this apprehension of what is bound to come elevates them from the bourgeoisie to the aristocracy. They have understood, and they have spoken, but the others, the colonized, the shallow, they have done nothing. And so Dor and his friends seek solace in the dandyism of the great unheeded.

The cartoonesque is not only juvenile, it is also dehumanizing in that it downgrades individuality in favour of the collective. Artists, thinkers, and politicians talk of the Québécois as though they were a single homogeneous group marching in step as in a Nazi film.

The cartoonesque also insults the intelligence, in that it distorts language for demagogic ends. It is worth noting that the cartoonesque is enamoured of foreign borrowings, a sure sign of a colonized imagination. Diaspora, genocide, apartheid (yes, you can find this word in the writings of Josée Legault, who does have the decency to bracket it with quotation marks) are all part of the militant nationalists' apocalyptic lexicon. The only word here that rings true is deportation. Yes, the deportation of the Acadians really took place, and we must salute the courage of this people, pioneer a second time in its own land. Elsewhere, there was neither dispersion nor genocide, whatever the demagogues may say, who know the truth and distort it knowingly. And when the politicians, taking their cue from these writers for whom exaggeration is a way of life, resort to cartoonesque rhetoric, they lapse into what de Gaulle called "blagology," from the French word *blague* or joke.

It's a blagology that has its flashes of magnanimity. During the 1995 referendum Bernard Landry, who had just chastized Yves Beauchemin for his remark about the still warm bodies, promised those "outside Quebec" that he would enact a Law of Return, like that in Israel. Thank you Monsieur Landry, you're too good. There's also Michel Vastel, a great nationalist fellow-traveller, who quite seriously called on Quebec to promote the repatriation of lost sheep from French Ontario and Acadia, a "quality immigration," as he termed it. That was most generous as well.

In their cartoonesque view of history, Bourgault and Falardeau put all the blame on the English. They make victims of the Québécois in order to obscure the shortcomings of those who led an ultramontanist Quebec after Confederation, a Quebec so subservient to the Church of Rome that it did away with its own Ministry of Education in 1875. "We didn't do anything, it's all the fault of the others." That's what devolves from the worst of cartoonesque thought: infantalization and the abdication of responsibility. For Bourgault and Falardeau, Quebec's history is an endless darkness that lifts only with their own arrival on the scene. Before us, nothing. Their nationalism is *sui generis:* they are their own progenitors, the new fathers of modern Quebec.

If they knew . . . If they knew that ultramontane Quebec has always been shot through with pervasive undercurrents, undercurrents that embodied free will and that were at odds with totalitarianism and one-track thinking. They represented a minority, but one that was very much alive. Take, for example, Honoré Beaugrand, who was a freemason, adventurer, novelist, and owner and founder of *La Patrie,* the dissenting Liberal newspaper of its time with a wide circulation in church-building Quebec. We know that as mayor of Montreal he worked with the English authorities against the Church to curb the typhus epidemic that was then raging. This freemason had doubtless heard talk in his lodge about the theories of a brilliant French chemist, Louis Pasteur.

In the twentieth century, over the protests of the church, the Liberals gave Quebec its École Polytechnique, the engineering school, as well as its business school, the École des Hautes Études Commerciales. They introduced compulsory schooling, a measure the Church fought tooth and nail, just as later it opposed old-age pensions coming from Ottawa. Duplessis responded the same way to grants for universities, pleading provincial autonomy. No, even if these times look from afar as though they were dominated by one camp alone, clerical-inspired conservatism, each had its own nuances and counter-currents. But demagogues abhor nuances. It is in their interest to do so, as they are enemy to the cartoonesque that makes for stirring speeches. And so we easily overlook the fact that the Duplessis era, with its Padlock Law and its persecution of the Jehovah's Witnesses, also saw the emergence of a group of young artists who joined together in the defence of knowledge and the imagination, and signed the *Refus global.*

Finally, the cartoonesque is what feeds most faithfully the apocalyptic demagogy behind Quebec nationalism since Lionel Groulx. In plain language, it affirms that if we do nothing, in other words, if Quebec does not become independent, the Québécois will assimilate and disappear off the surface of the earth like those *tourtes,* the birds consumed by the first settlers, of which all that remains is the word *tourtière*. Independence raises the spectre of the death of the Quebec people, so very fragile.

Recently Jean-François Lisée revived this demagogy of decline. "I'm afraid for Quebec," he said. At the beginning of the twentieth century, the nationalist seers were already forecasting imminent assimilation. At the start of the 1970s, folk singer Claude Gauthier said that we had only twenty-five years left to make love in French on Île d'Orléans. At the same time, a raft of articles was published dealing with the demographic decline of the Québécois and insisting that the only way to reverse the trend was to create a State that would send immigrants to French school and politely expel the English. Despite what Lucien Bouchard says, the Quebec people are not the only white race with a low birth rate. Monsieur Lesieur was shocked to discover an article in *Perspectives* claiming that by 2039 or so, not a single German would remain on earth! No more Germans, no more Québécois. The article left him depressed for several days.

Unfortunately for the nationalist zealots, their pessimistic gospel does not always take hold, and faith is more fickle than one might think. Monsieur Lesieur is a firm believer in the threat of disappearance but he doesn't think about it every day, sometimes months go by without its entering his mind. Happily, whenever his resolve starts to weaken, a timely article by Charles Castonguay on the imminent disappearance of the

Ontario French comes along in *Le Devoir,* to jolt him out of his lethargy. Or someone will comment that less and less French is spoken on the island of Montreal, and his faith is renewed. In short, Monsieur Lesieur's beliefs reflect a morbid view of the world, and only the prospect of an achievable independence can calm his eschatological anxieties.

In the meantime, the colonial novel looks to him like it will have a sad ending. He shouldn't worry. There are still some good laughs ahead, because you can always count on the cartoonesque to descend into self-parody all by itself. And so as they wait patiently for this Quebec apocalypse that never comes, people have closed their ears to its prophets, Bourgault, Legault, and the others. They present no danger because their road to power has been barred from the beginning. Bourgault gave it a good try, in vain, at a time when the electoral adventure required some boldness. Legault came up empty as well: the PQ riding association in Mercier, refusing to be a party to her driving ambition, sent her back to hearth and home. It's a good bet, however, that in twenty years these eternal adolescents will be mouthing the same arguments, still stunned not to be followed by the masses and to have only losers in their camp.

The fact is, the Bourgaults, Legaults, and Rhéaumes are becoming the Zouaves of Quebec nationalism. We all remember those quaint guardians of Quebec churches, whose name alone smacked of something old-fashioned and faintly ridiculous, and whose function was to lend ecclesiastical rites a certain pomp. They bravely showed their colours, shined their instruments, paraded flag in hand. Just like the Chartrands and Falardeaus who raise their standard to honour the Patriotes, under the kindly eye of a priest-like minister standing by with a little grant in hand. It all makes a little noise, it all feels a little good, but it doesn't frighten anybody. After the ceremony and the requisite sermons, a collection is taken. The onlookers smile, the young giggle, and we're left with a glass of beer and a bag of french fries. All's well that ends well, and same time next year. It's rather charming, when you come down to it. A bit like the now inoffensive Bérets blancs.

A word here about Zouave nationalism's official publication, *L'Action nationale,* founded by Lionel Groulx and home to the most gifted wordsmiths in Quebec. Some generous soul presented me with an unsolicited free subscription, proof enough that this right-thinking parish bulletin owes its survival to a thinly disguised charity. That said, I sometimes read it, and always with pleasure, as it's very well written. Like the French royalists, our intellectual aristocrats know their grammar, and their style is finely honed. It's a language infused with fleurs-de-lys, majestic drapery for a threadbare heritage. What is lacking, obviously, are new ideas.

And the revue's victimized tone is rather rebarbative. I've just picked up the most recent issue, that of June 6, 2000, and there I find a poem denouncing Canadian persecution. The author, Michel Garneau, expresses himself with barely suppressed anger but conserves his dignity. The incident, a true story, took place in Ottawa in 1960. Feeling a bit dry, Garneau went into the Yorktown Hotel and ordered a beer in French; the barman, a bad egg who did not speak his language, made him repeat himself in English. The nerve. But that was not the end of it. Garneau had just been served when the barman announced they were closing, and tried to take back his beer! Garneau defended himself with valour, of course, saying to him, in French if you please, that he would drink that beer to its last drop. And the poem ends:

> at which he snickered
> *we don't speak ffffrench here*

Chances are that Garneau would not harbour so painful a memory of a Berlin or Rome bar owner who didn't understand his French, any more than he would feel compassion for a Canadian from Toronto who said: "In Chicoutimi, when I ordered a beer, the waiter said: 'Hey, you English square-head, we speak French here, *'stie!'*" But wasn't that something? A poor little Québécois who had to mount a valiant defence of his glass of beer, how traumatic! And not that long ago, either: 1960 . . . No, next to that, the ten million Congolese assassinated by King Leopold II are nothing.

One thing is certain: with the arrival of Zouave nationalism, the end of the colonial novel looks to be long, drawn-out and folkloric.

~ Son Of

MY EXPERIENCE was different.

Jean-Marc Poliquin was a real father. The best of men. A just man. A cultivated gentleman who loved freethinking writers and who never forgot he was a butcher's son from Sainte Angèle de Laval, the second of a family of sixteen children. Grandfather Poliquin envisaged only two vocations for his ten sons: butcher or priest, meat or salvation. Jean-Marc and his elder brother, Renaud, were gifted; they were sent to the seminary. The elder was ordained and never dared leave the priesthood for fear of hurting his parents, who had sacrificed so much for him. A good son, then, a much-loved priest who ended his days at Jonquière where, as a Latin teacher, he had the young Lucien Bouchard for a pupil (our world is small, it's true, but sometimes beautiful as well . . .). The younger son went to see his parents and told them he was "leaving." "You've come to ask our forgiveness?" my grandparents asked. "No, I've come to inform you of my decision."

The next day the recalcitrant son took the train to Ottawa, a town where the small number of francophones meant more tolerance for the defrocked. He became a translator, then a journalist, married Annette Paris, who was Franco-Ontarian but didn't yet know it, and the couple had seven children, including me, the third, the child who liked to go off by himself and make up stories, and who always felt a bit hemmed in by such a large family.

My father admired the Jewish tradition that encourages a son to surpass his father. He had done so vis-à-vis his own father, rejecting the meat business and the business of souls in favour of journalistic notoriety. For us, the five sons of a well-known father, it was a daunting challenge. He used to say to us, with his conspiratorial wink: "I'll give you a leg up . . . ," and so he did. For my part, I was never conscious of his power, only his encouragement and his friendship.

And so I ventured fearlessly into his private domain: foreign languages and literature. No credit is due me, it was all that I liked. Now in the local neighbourhood, my father was regarded as a kind of superior being. He had learned Spanish, Italian, and German on his own, and had read Cervantes, Dante, and Goethe in the original. At university I applied myself to German, and I had two long stints in Germany. My father came to visit me once, in Kassel. He had been in Poland and had decided to come and see how I was getting along. I was delighted, as you might well imagine.

But I soon realized, in the course of a few conversations with friends, that all his German came from books and was of no use to him in everyday life. Goethe had not taught him how to casually order a beer. I was secretly heartbroken. So my father did not, as I had believed, know German well after all. It pained me that he could quote Schiller but could not say that it was a nice day. He saw what I saw, and that made it even worse.

He left the next day. I went with him to the station and had to buy his ticket because the ticket-seller had not read Kafka and had trouble understanding my father's laborious German. As we said goodbye on the platform, I looked him up and down for a moment, my eyes moist, and it was my turn to be silent.

"What's wrong, my boy?"

"Nothing. It's just that a little while ago I felt that I was looking out for you. And that made me feel strange, you're my father . . ."

"Don't worry about that, it's natural, that's the way life is. Remember what Balzac picked up from Chamfort and what you read in *The Country Doctor?* It's the story of a doctor who'd gone back to see his son, to whom he'd left his land. He was asked how he was received, and he replied: 'He treated me like I was his child . . .' Fair enough. And besides, your German is really very good. No accent, you'd think you'd been speaking it all your life! To tell you the truth I'm even a bit jealous, but proud to be so . . ."

I shook his hand and left the station immediately because I didn't want to cry in front of him. I'd ventured onto a territory where he was undisputed master, there'd been a test of strength and I'd emerged victorious, except that I owed my triumph to his early encouragement. An Oedipal murder without any pain, lucidly and joyously assumed on either side.

Many years later I published my first novel, an awkward beginning I have to admit, but my first novel all the same. My father was delighted and surprised, he who had never dared write except under a pseudonym for fear of ridicule. Still, he always admired the writing of others, with each new discovery claiming that he could never do as well, so why try? Now his son had tried.

My book was to come out on a Monday, and my father died the preceding Friday, without having dared to ask to see the manuscript. Out of respect, he'd told my mother. He'd been afraid of discouraging me with his comments, which would surely have been critical. He left just when we would have embarked on a definitive and fraternal test of strength in territory where up to then he had foreseen no challenges forthcoming. A gallant exit, as Sartre would rightly have said, one that it took me a long time to forgive. Not because I wanted to savour another victory, which would not have been a victory in any case, but because I didn't want to let him go. In other words, I loved him like a son. I loved him so much that I pardoned him his involuntary departure from the scene.

Yes, I still adore this father, while making my own distinction between what I owe him and what I acquired without his help. He helped me free myself from him, and I went the rest of the way. I also learned to see what I owed my mother. He had given me a taste for foreign lands and knowledge; she, the desire for roots and an imaginary world. I wanted to pass on to my sons what I had received from my parents. I allowed them to see my faults, as my father had let us see his with a good-humoured frankness that humanized him in our eyes. My sons are today growing straight and tall despite their tortuous interludes, each at his own speed, respectful yet also critical of me, and they mock me for my own shortcomings with princely forbearance. One day it will be my turn to step aside, and they will be the sole architects of their lives. I do not insist on achievement, it's their happiness that counts. We are a race that knows how to die, but that knows how to live most of all.

I feel the same way about the forerunners who brought me so much. Among others, Hergé, whose Tintin, the reporter, eased my francophone isolation in Ottawa, and whom I cannot thank enough for having rendered what was foreign, familiar. I later learned that he was a longtime anti-Semite. He had been a Rexist as well, and had even contributed to a publication with close ties to the Nazi occupier. A shameful episode that has in no way lessened my continuing affection for his picture books.

I make similar allowances for Sartre, who through his frankness opened the eyes of the little Poliquin in Ottawa who wanted to write. When I behold the doddering oldster, the pathetic Orgon plagued by Maoist Tartuffes such as Benny Lévy, I still remember the great writer who shrank from fathering children. And I respect Lionel Groulx, who was a true educator and along the way wrote some sublime pages. I'm not Jewish, and for all I care he can keep his subway station and his college, he didn't steal them after all. For all that, he's never been someone whose thinking I would ever want to emulate. My attitude towards him is akin to that of the excellent Olivar Asselin, who praised his fine writing while pouring scorn on his Barresian servility.

And now for Lucien Bouchard. I acknowledge his talent as a politician. I like his Saguenay accent and see him as a cultivated man who would have preferred to write works of the imagination but who found in politics a perfect outlet for his talents. He neither convinces nor intimidates me, certainly, but I know he is capable of generosity and is not a mean-spirited person. His one obvious flaw: his vanity, nourished by a vision derived from a France that no longer exists. In this respect he remains, as Marcel Aymé has said, the child of his readings, never sure if true glory is literary or political. In short, I do not dislike him, this gentleman whose sallies are often awkward or second-hand. He's only a man, but that's saying a lot.

Less gifted than Parizeau when it comes to his mastery of the French language, to learning, and to technocratic expertise, Bouchard outdistances him in one important way: he is a more likable and responsible father. Jacques Parizeau would have thought nothing of plunging the Québécois into the turmoil of independence, the Gaullist aristocrat in him being too avid for glory and too little concerned about its victims. Whereas Lucien Bouchard, the little guy who started out with nothing and who still remembers that it's with pennies that you make dollars, will always shrink from risking the hard-won well-being of his people. Forced to choose between the government of Quebec and the Québécois, he'll favour the person over the State. However in thrall he may be to the figure of the statesman in the books to which he's drawn, in the end, like René Lévesque, he'll listen to the little guy inside himself.

I also respect him for having largely renounced the role of make-believe martyr that he cultivated early in his career. He revelled then in all the humiliations he could call to mind, and his vocabulary was shot through with words like wound, affront, insult, destitution — without end. Worse, his own wound gave credence to his message. This low-grade demagogy worked well on the hustings and brought him to power.

Once he became premier, he perhaps came to understand to what extent these arguments had an invidious effect on his own citizens. In this post-Meech period when all hard-done-by Canadians were begging for some kind of compensation, he must have seen that he was fostering an insatiable neurosis. Yes, the imaginary victim is a life-long dependent, and Premier Bouchard didn't want to have seven million burdens on his hands, all absolved of responsibility by their memories of humiliation, and impossible to satisfy. When you're in opposition it's very effective to talk of martyrdom, but once you're in government you don't want the self-same laments thrown back in your own face, and by your own side! And so he began to speak of pride . . . And we saw how he treated the pesky Duplessis Orphans. He made short work of them. Yesterday's poor, bullied son had turned into a very strict father.

He must also have realized that he was fostering a doubtful legacy for Quebec culture. His most spectacular creation in this regard, you've guessed it, was Pierre Falardeau, an embarrassing comrade-in-arms for Quebec nationalism, whose mournful ideology Bouchard's arguments made respectable. This is one fathering of which he should not be too proud. It produced a classic case of proletarian nostalgia, clearly demonstrating that to assume the role of victim is to perform an act of self-exclusion: I dredge up 250 years of oppression to justify my powerlessness and, posing as one who has been wronged, I burden with guilt an audience from whom I may have something to gain. I become the eternal Son seeking a parent to bail him out. And finding him. And the Canadian State becomes a kind of stepfather, a vulgar provider with no legitimacy.

But be careful. It's not only Québécois who talk like victims! This is the lot of many minority communities, and if there are Québécois who are made uncomfortable by all this, they have only to visit us in Ontario and see the film *The Last of the Franco-Ontarians,* where self-pity and the discourse of decline reach comic depths. Or they can venture into certain Acadian circles where you would swear the deportation took place yesterday morning.

And Lucien Bouchard is far from being the only perpetrator. The groundwork was laid, he only had to appear. A whole swath of Quebec culture was, and remains, in a state of arrested infancy. Its prime exhibit: Réjean Ducharme, the brilliant adolescent author of *The Swallower Swallowed,* whose characters refuse to desert the magic island of their childhood and howl out their simplistic anti-Americanism. His plays on words were dazzling once, but in the long run became so incessant that his work lapsed into a kind of sad senility. Ducharme the wonder boy is now sixty years old, and he has aged badly. What is most unfortunate is that this eternal son has begat dozens of clones, and from one literary generation to the other, Quebec intellectuals go into raptures over writers of sparkling immaturity.

In this land whose literature dotes on child writers and greying adolescents, father Bouchard has it made. He's never criticized, certainly not within his own party where his shortcomings are passed over in silence like those of a father who drinks but who is so good to us. His comrades-in-arms in the press are complaisant, and pusillanimity is widespread. Spinelessness also. In fact, many are those who live off the federal government and remain dyed-in-the-wool *indépendantistes*. No harm in that. Lucien Bouchard himself, not long ago, was a perfect example of migratory and mercenary loyalty. Another instance of childlike behaviour sanctioned by victimist rationalizations: "I left home but I still have my income, and I have a right to it after all that's been done to me . . ." Or one plays at being a secret agent, another childish conceit: "Yes, I earn my keep on the federal side, but if you only knew what I really thought . . ."

One sometimes wonders if people will ever get their fill of such cravenness and whether its legacy will one day exhaust itself so we can move on to another life. "Of course," one murmurs, and here or there I hear intellectuals say they've had enough of this stultifying paternalism. But when they're invited to speak out, they still beg off. Understandably. The nationalist palisade is unforgiving of dissident children. It's dangerous to think the wrong things out loud in such a land.

In the meantime Quebec nationalism remains a topsy-turvy Virgilian fable where Aeneas bends under the weight of an Anchises who refuses to get off his back. Aeneas can struggle all he likes, but he can't move on. This is the pitiful ending to our colonial novel.

Is it comical or tragical? Or something else? Go figure . . .

AND LESIEUR AND Labine in all that? Let's put our cards on the table: these two gentlemen, so alike in many ways, diverge on one important point, which is their approach to the paternal discourse of Quebec nationalism. The first is all for it, the second will always hold back from it.

And so Monsieur Lesieur no longer likes Lucien Bouchard, but he still obeys his commandments. He too, like thousands of commited nationalists, considers the idea of "winning conditions" an insult to the people's intelligence. He finds it even more ludicrous when Bouchard says: "We'll have a referendum when we're sure of winning!" If independence can wait, that means it's not an urgent matter. And if there's no urgency, it might mean that it's not that essential. What is more, the very idea of a referendum is starting to make people smile, no? If the PQ leaders were so sure of what they're doing, they would have voted for secession a long time ago. Except that since they don't have confidence in their people, they make referendums, another Gaullist reference, with ambiguous questions designed to entice the people into believing that independence is what they want. Not too serious, all that.

But while awaiting the great day, those passionate believers in sovereignty-association play the Canadian game to the hilt in the morning, and the Quebec game after dark. It's like the Italian Communists in the little world of Don Camillo, all atheists in principle, the party line requires it, but good Catholics when you get down to brass tacks. Mayor Peppone is Bouchard incarnate when he says: "Comrades, I won't be at the meeting tomorrow night because, you know, it's my daughter's communion . . ." And the comrades nod their heads as though to say yes, of course, we understand . . .

When Monsieur Lesieur thinks of these thinly-veiled deceptions, he's not very happy. But it's not for him to dare contradict his leader, never. He grumbles, he murmurs, he gripes, but in the end he's mute in the presence of the Father, and will always accord him his vote. This is something the apostles of the no have to understand: the Lesieurs of Quebec yield before what is decreed by the ancestral spirits, and they will never shake off their voluntary servitude, that knee-jerk submission that will always carry more weight when there is a referendum than all the noisy, though empty, campaigns to drum up support.

By contrast, Monsieur Labine basks in a pervasive lightness. He is deaf to father Bouchard's harangues. He rather likes him, but he does not fear him in the least. Nor does the Canadian threat make him quake in his boots. Neither Jean Chrétien nor Pierre Trudeau have been paternal figures for him, and if these two men have one virtue, it's that they live far away. They don't intimidate him and he doesn't see them as interfering in his life or controlling it. Where Lucien Bouchard is concerned, and René Lévesque before him, the contrary is true. They force solidarity upon him, command him to think of the others, tell him he must do this or that, otherwise there will be a catastrophe. Sacrifices must be made, he will be guilty if or if not, either way it will be his fault . . . There's no end to it.

And so he shuts off the radio and goes for a stroll without caring to know if the colonial novel will end happily or not. That's what the militants of the yes side refuse to understand: that at the heart of the Quebec population there are millions of men and women impervious to the diktats of the paternal nation. Impervious because free.

The Québécois have always been free, silent and free perhaps, but free all the same, and they feign obedience only when it's in their interest. Thus, in the golden age of the French regime, they fled into the woods to illegally trade furs and contraband with New England. In the nineteenth century there was massive emigration to the American mills, notwithstanding the calls to return to the land. The worst years of Duplessis were also the formative years of flamboyant writers and artists such as Aquin, Ducharme, Blais, Charlebois. But the nationalist leaders see themselves always as commanders of these descendants of willing émigrés, playing out over and over again, from Duplessis to Bouchard, Montaigne's classic scenario: "Our kings . . . not having been able to do what they wanted, pretended to want what they could do." And the Québécois pretend to listen.

And to think that there are people in this world, still, who find life boring . . .

II

The Semi-Colonized

~ The Charming Hostess, At Last!

CHARLES-OLIVIER IS walking along St. Denis Street. His heart is heavy. In his overcoat pocket is my novel, unfinished. The idea that other people might be reading it depresses him. No, life is not a bowl of cherries, and he is distressed all the more by the frivolousness of his fellow citizens, who don't even have the gumption, as does he, to rage silently at Second Cup and McDonald's for their English-language neon provocations.

Speaking of fellow citizens, here are two coming down St. Denis, arm in arm, amorous as they will ever be in their lifetimes. Yes, it's the little cashier and the young salesman, and they're most certainly not giving any thought to the extinction of their race. Tonight they're going to whip up a little lovers' meal, and they couldn't care less that it will be well beyond their budget.

They pass Monsieur Lesieur without seeing him. It's evident, by their gaiety, that they're already sharing happy memories, and he can't help contrasting their carefree obliviousness with his own misery. For an instant, he even thinks of reproaching them. But he quickly changes his mind. They might speak badly of him at the bookstore, where he is known.

And so he decides, as he does every week, to treat himself to a good meal in that restaurant where he is a respected regular and where stars of stage and screen and Montreal theatre people go to rub shoulders. There, at least, he'll be able to dine in the company of people who can afford to vote yes. That will console him.

Decidedly, this is not his day. He has barely crossed the threshold when he spots right in front of him at the first table two people that he had refused to link in his mind: Frank Labine himself in the company of the charming hostess from the bridge club. And that's not all. They've seen him, too, and Frank has already risen and is inviting him, in his resounding voice, to join them. There's no way out, the whole restaurant is already looking up, and what will the waiters say if they see him beating a retreat? He mustn't risk losing the respect of his loyal servants. So he'd do best to accept the invitation and to make his exit as quickly as he can on some pretext or other.

Frank has pulled up a chair and ordered a third place setting. "I can't stay long," says Lesieur, who refuses to remove his coat. Labine and the lady insist. "Well, all right, I'll have a beer just to keep you company for a couple of minutes, there's someone waiting for me." Labine: "You know our charming hostess, Irène Campeau." Lesieur almost comes out with an enthusiastic yes, but he stops himself in time. "We've been introduced, I do remember. Good evening, Madam . . ."

Irène Campeau and not Ariane Daviault? His heart sinks for the third time tonight. All of a sudden he likes her less than before. With a name like that, no wonder she's a friend of Frank Labine. He must get out of here, and fast.

But Irène is still seductive. "We were talking about Italy," she says, with her loveliest smile. "I've never been there. Have you?" When you hear her voice, you want to say yes, no matter what. And Frank is so kind. He's ordered veal kidneys, a specialty of the house, for the new table companion—it's his favourite dish, in fact—and has discreetly indicated that he'll be picking up the bill. Irène has chosen only appetizers, but the most expensive. Lesieur vows to call Frank François from now on, that will make him more presentable, and will constitute one small victory over Canadian vulgarity.

The Beaujolais Nouveau has arrived at the table. Lesieur finally agrees to take off his overcoat, but as he does so my book, which has been burning a hole in his pocket, drops onto the floor. Helpful as always, Labine picks it up and exclaims: "My, my, our friend is doing some dangerous reading . . . If you're a nationalist, even if you're moderate and open-minded, I wouldn't let your friends catch you with this book. Hide it immediately. Irène, this is the book I was talking about, I was going to give it to you, I'd even written something inside it, but it got lost . . ."

Monsieur Lesieur is suddenly hot, very hot. He'd not been able to decipher the words Labine had scrawled on the flyleaf, but now he knows. Fortunately Frank has not opened the book, but if he had . . . Lesieur remains silent for some moments, lets the heat abate. Labine has already moved on: "Let's try this excellent wine, it goes well with the kidneys, does it not, Irène?"

His first victory, and unanticipated. Irène is no longer smiling, she is even a bit cool. "It's too bad you lost that book, you could have read it yourself. I have to say that politics, ideologies, all these quarrels are of no interest to me. I prefer flowers and computers."

"What? You never vote?" Lesieur asks, thinking the day may not be lost after all. "In my view . . ."

Irène cuts him off. "That's not what I mean. Everyone has a right to his opinions, and mine are part of my private life. Look, during the sixteen years that I was married there were two referendums, and neither my husband nor myself knew if the other voted yes or no. There are enough stupid conflicts in married life without throwing in politics as well. When I vote, I'm alone with my conscience. It's not for nothing that we vote inside a polling booth."

And so Lesieur plays his apolitical card: "Well, I didn't vote in the 1980 referendum . . ."

Labine interrupts: "Neither did I, I was on my honeymoon in Italy!" Now, that! Lesieur clearly remembers that he had married a certain Cheryl from Sudbury, it was in the book! His eyes grow wide. Was it all a lie?

Seeing that he is being gawked at, Labine explains that his first wife died in 1978. He remarried a friend of theirs, a widow herself, originally from Calabria, and they spent their honeymoon in her native land. So what is he doing with Irène, Lesieur wonders, suddenly, like a lot of unhappy people, becoming moralistic. He must be looking for a mistress. Perhaps Irène thinks less well of him now. He has to score another point as soon as he can. "You must not have seen Florence, then?"

"No," replies Labine, sadly. "And we never went back to Italy. Giovanna died also, three years later. From the same illness as my first wife." He is silent.

And now Irène is holding his hands in hers, it isn't fair! She's gone all tender, he's free, I've lost my advantage again, damn! "A widower twice over, and so young . . ." she says, her voice truly consoling. Labine withdraws his hands with a smile that's almost too noble. "Be careful, my lovely friend, I'm a jinx." "But no, silly!" she replies laughing, too merry for Lesieur, who, suddenly melancholy, contemplates the jar of pickles in front of him, wondering if to take one would make him seem uncouth.

Irène rises. "Ah, there's the man I was waiting for. Excuse me, I have to leave you. Frank, you've been charming! I'll expect both of you Friday at three. Gentlemen . . ." A man twice as elegant as Labine appears at her side. Smiling, he holds out his hand to the two still at the table. And he greets them in English.

"Bernie Nussbaum. How do you do? Forgive me for absconding with this rare beauty. Enjoy your dinner, gentlemen!" And he ushers Irène to a table near the back of the restaurant.

Labine, the poor ninny, smiles back at the man. And he just keeps on eating, as though nothing has happened. Lesieur is disgusted. She's gone off with a Jew! And that's not all, because his friend adds, with his mouth almost full: "You know Bernie Nussbaum? Best dentist in Montreal." That's all he needed. Filthy rich, too. If there were only Labine there was a bit of hope, a chance he could outmanoeuvre this insurance agent who jinxes women and hasn't even seen Florence. But the Jewish dentist, with his millions and his tailored suit, forget it. Life is cruel! Lesieur thinks of Gabriel Arcand's drunken misery in the Plouffe Family film: "Is there a place anywhere in the world for an Ovide Plouffe?" The pickles cheer him up a little.

Still smiling, Labine has ordered a *vino novello* this time. He knows Bernie Nussbaum well. A few years ago he sold him a big life annuity. An intelligent man, who speculates in real estate for the fun of it. He buys lofts in the Plateau Mont Royal, renovates them luxuriously, and resells them to the beautiful people. Irène Campeau is one of his associates, she helps him with the decoration, it takes her mind off the pharmacy and it's a lucrative hobby for her as well. Bernie is also the most flamboyant homosexual of Marie-Anne Street. Labine knows all that, but having carefully registered everything Irène said about respecting others' private lives, he prefers to keep his counsel.

That will perhaps stand him in good stead later on. She is so charming . . . That said, Labine hasn't the faintest idea that the friend before him has a yen for Irène as well.

Over dessert, Lesieur makes a noble vow. Since Labine is no longer a serious rival, he will offer him his friendship. After all, even if a man's a Canadian, if he treats someone he hardly knows to an expensive meal, he can't be all bad. But the first chance he gets he will jettison this poisonous book inscribed to a thankless woman who gives herself to foreigners. That way he will punish both Labine and her for their bad judgement. And he won't have to read another word. Both men are in excellent humour by the end of the meal.

They leave together, and when Labine suggests walking with him to the subway, Lesieur accepts. They've exchanged a number of confidences already, and have arranged to dine together after the next afternoon of bridge. Serene, Lesieur tells himself that Labine basically is a good man, even if he doesn't always know what he is doing. He might even be able to convert him to the yes side. As for Irène, who knows, perhaps one day he'll take her to bed. The wine has truly lightened his heart.

As they pass the bookstore where it all began, Lesieur has a sudden impulse. "François, I want to thank you for the wonderful meal, and if you'll allow me, I'd like to offer you the book you lost. It's not very good, it's badly written, but I'm sure you'll appreciate its point of view. Come on in. I don't usually approve of this sort of writing, but it's my pleasure."

Labine demurs. "Listen, I don't have that much time to read. It was going to be a present, and as you saw, it would not have been well received . . ." Lesieur insists, especially since he feels guilty for having in some sense stolen the book. And he doesn't want to feel beholden to this man who's so good that he seems somehow superior. That he cannot swallow.

Lesieur wins out. They go in, but unfortunately the book is already unavailable; the fourth printing won't arrive until next week, but if you would like to leave your name, your telephone number . . . They browse a bit just for form's sake, and then leave. Another disappointment for Monsieur Lesieur. Not only is this cursed book selling well, but he has lost his chance to draw even with Labine in his own eyes.

They walk in the evening air, unusually mellow for the time of year. Labine talks about being a widower, something that weighs on him; he longs to be part of a couple again. Not a word, however, on the subject of Irène. In the street leading to the subway, the two men chat a little longer. "Yes, we'll have dinner together after bridge, and it'll be on me," adds Lesieur.

"A good and honourable man," thinks Labine, happy with his new acquaintance. "A good man," thinks Lesieur. "A bit thick, perhaps, even if he dresses well. A poor colonized soul. I mustn't forget to get rid of that awful book with its compromising dedication."

They pass a wastebasket, Labine has his back turned, a quick movement and the deed is done.

⁓ It's All Albert's Fault

Monsieur Lesieur did the right thing. If he had read any further, he would have ripped my book to shreds. Because it's not Frank Labine who is colonized, it's him, Charles-Olivier Lesieur. That's right.

Lesieur, colonized? Impossible, he's a nationalist. That word is his clan's favourite insult, to be thrown in the face of whoever doesn't agree with them. Poor Labine, *he's* colonized, or Stéphane Dion, and all the others who vote no. (That would make for millions of colonized individuals in Quebec, quite a crowd.)

I answer to that, as calmly as I am able, by saying that there is no one so colonized as a nationalist. Pierre Falardeau, Josée Legault, Georges Dor, Jean Larose, Michel Venne, Jacques Parizeau, Lucien Bouchard, all are colonized. Or more exactly, semi-colonized.

There are days when I tell myself it's all Albert's fault.

Albert Memmi, a great writer, was the author of, among other books, *The Colonizer and the Colonized,* a remarkable work in which he risked a first sociopsychological explanation for the phenomenon of colonization. There is no colonized individual, he wrote, who does not dream, at least one hour a day, of being a colonizer. Colonization is an alienation that leads to the denial and even the hatred of oneself. He who is truly colonized takes himself for another. The education and socialization of the Senegalese or Tunisians at the hands of the French colonizer in the 1930s led them to think of themselves as French. At school they were taught that their ancestors were Gauls with blond moustaches and horned helmets; their history and cultural identity were negated so that they might share in the glory of Napoleon and Louis XIV. The truly colonized prided himself on speaking the best Parisian French, dreamed of passing competitive French exams, hummed the airs of Charles Trenet, admired Jean Gabin, and in general aspired to a French metropolitan success that would whiten his skin. The French were the great colonizers, from Guyana to Indochina. France was and remains an empire whose approval is coveted by the old colonial bourgeoisies, that of Quebec included.

The phenomenon is not only French. There are also colonized Moluccans who dream of opening a restaurant in Amsterdam; Indians or Pakistanis who wreak their vengeance on the colonizer by mastering his language and carrying off the best literary prizes; the colonized of Portuguese Africa, Spanish-speaking America, and the French West Indies. Everywhere in the European empires of yore we have seen people who only yesterday were deprived of the right to vote assume the voice of their masters to make it the instrument of their personal and collective liberation: Salman Rushdie, Édouard Glissant, Cesaria Evora, Nelson Mandela, and so on.

Memmi's book was a huge success in Quebec. People fought over it, that no one would dispute. Gaston Miron and the early separatists swore by it; students photocopied passages that they handed out free at the doors of university classrooms. Everyone was so convinced that the portrait was a perfect fit for the Quebec situation that it became, in nationalist circles, a primary source. In fact, it still is.

There followed an authentic cultural revolution that nationalist thought has never quite outgrown. With Memmi's theses as a guide, Quebec's history was reinterpreted, and the new historical school of the 1950s that had already, under Groulx's influence, dropped Providence as a historic force, now transformed Quebec into an occupied territory and the Québécois into a colonized people in need of liberation. The Quebec cinema turned away from harmless documentaries about Western wheat to produce anticlerical and antifederal fictions where the leading men sported the stubbled cheeks of terrorists. Quebec got modernity and entered the Third World at the same time.

It was the same in literature, where Hubert Aquin was to write *Prochain épisode* with Memmi's ink, while his brother François, a member of the now "National" Assembly, delivered a speech on breaking with federalism, several pages of which were inspired by Memmi's book. Michel Tremblay, with his dazzling *Les Belles-Soeurs,* introduced the brilliantly transgressive *joual,* and Claude Jasmin published the excellent *Pleure pas, Germaine.* Robert Charlebois, with his powerful songs, some written by Réjean Ducharme, consigned to oblivion a whole industry of imported or translated ditties, while Michel Garneau gave us a stunning translation of *Macbeth* into Quebec French. French Canada vanished, the Quebec genius was born. Nothing would ever be the same. It was the golden age, and no doubt about it!

The Memmian ideology transformed the political scene.

From one day to the next nationalism tossed the cassock onto the ash heap and garbed itself in the leopard-skin gear of Latin-American guerrillas. One put away Groulx and swore only by Marx, Mao, and Guevara. The FLQ was born and the PQ came shortly after. The October Crisis crystallized Albert Memmi's influence: there were the *Poems and Songs of the Resistance,* there was the cartoonesque Léandre Bergeron with his little Marxist history of Quebec, and a whole lyric generation battened onto Memmi's thought, often without bothering to read him. There was no need in any case. His ideas were everywhere.

Take the case of Hubert Aquin, whom we've already mentioned. The first words of *Prochain épisode:* "Cuba is going down in flames in the middle of Lake Leman while I descend into the heart of things." It is a key passage in the history of the Quebec novel, where the writer links Quebec with Third World freedom-fighting and gives vent to his obsession with bourgeois life and its crippling apathy. All through the novel the Byron of the Greek resistance crosses paths with Chénier the Patriote, and the author denounces those Balzacian influences that cripple his imagination. At the end his vaguely combative disgust is transformed into a compensatory declaration of love: "Here I am, defeated as only a people can be, more futile than all my brothers . . . I lie down on the page of Abraham and I stretch out belly-down to perish in the blood of words . . . I burn to be done with it all and to put a full stop to my indefinite past."

No, no one in Quebec or elsewhere in Canada has so keenly felt, under his skin and in his work, the psychosis of this troubling decolonization. Aquin's drama expressed the intellectual's painful awareness of his impotence vis-à-vis a situation he abhors. In that, like Tardivel and so many others, Aquin is reminiscent of Henri-Louis de Boishébert who, as commander at Michillimakinac in 1702, wrote to Callière: "It is a great privilege, Monsieur, and an honour for me to be entrusted with your commands, but it is also a great pity to have no other resource than paper and ink to execute them."

Still very present in Quebec, Albert Memmi has made much ink flow and blackened reams of paper. His thought continues to influence nationalist party programs, literature, cinema. Jean Larose invokes his name to air the contempt he feels for himself and his kind, and Pierre Falardeau, who never stops talking about how he is colonized and conquered, considers him essential reading.

If I were Albert, I'd be exceedingly proud of myself. Of all the foreign thinkers of the twentieth century, his influence on Quebec nationalism has been the most enduring, and he will have been for our time what Louis Veuillot, Charles Maurras, and Maurice Barrès were for earlier generations. My compliments . . .

THE PROBLEM IS, there was a problem. Maybe even two. The first is that Quebec was not Memmi's Tunisia. Miron, the Aquin brothers, and the FLQ all made the mistake of applying a foreign model to the Quebec situation. The second is that their decolonization was accompanied by a recolonization by those same forces that were supposed to be avenues to freedom. And so the Quebec of these thinkers was a unique arena in which decolonization and recolonization, in parallel, generated a confusion that was fertile, dramatic, and farcical. In that order.

Fertile, because there truly was a liberation. In the 1960s the church was ousted from the schools and the hospitals, and the State gave itself the means for important developments such as Hydro-Québec and its own investment bank. The Québécois discovered pleasure, the body, the word, and the world. Our own culture and literary language asserted itself; and gone were the days when you needed a French accent to get ahead. So far, so good.

Dramatic, because the Memmian theses could only be applied in part, and often not at all. The Québécois were neither Arabs nor the Blacks of Frantz Fanon, they were closer to being Pieds-Noirs themselves. Colonizers more than colonized. We have even, in our time, been cruel colonizers who didn't hesitate to massacre the Fox and the Natchez in the eighteenth century. Our forerunners were willing collaborationists, they advocated annexation by the United States, and they gave Duplessis the nationalist carte-blanche to sell off our natural resources for a song. The Third World view of our situation adopted by Quebec intellectuals cleansed this guilty conscience in the purifying fire of martyrdom; it's no surprise that they threw themselves into Albert Memmi's arms with so much enthusiasm. But this error would lead to painful misunderstandings.

Farcical, because these same misunderstandings would also give rise to scenes that were downright comic. I've already mentioned the nationalists' distortions of the truth, reflected in Pierre Vallières' *White Niggers of America,* to cite just one instance. But the very idea of independence was itself distorted, turned into sovereignty-association, an absurd, pusillanimous, and demagogic concept: Social Credit with a university degree. The examples are legion.

However, it's hard to blame Miron and Pierre Vallières for straying into Albert Memmi's Maghreb and mistaking Montreal's Main for the casbah. In those days, appearances were on their side. The incomes of Quebec's anglophone households were on average seventy per cent higher than those of the francophones. The odious practices of the capitalist Price in the Saguenay were still fresh in people's memories. In order to succeed, one had to leave the French language behind. Until Lesage, the Quebec Finance Minister was more often than not English-speaking; capital was English only, engineering also, just like the federal civil service. Had I been twenty years old in 1960, I too would have swallowed Memmi whole.

In the 1960s, which were not always all that beautiful, let's be frank, a Gaston Miron had good reason to denounce Montreal's bilingualism. Looking for work, he was always asked if he spoke English. He said no. He was then threatened with the withdrawal of his unemployment insurance. He protested, properly insisting on his right to work in French. In those days no one required an equivalent bilingualism from his anglophone fellow citizens. They, even though in the minority, didn't have to take French classes, but Miron, as part of the majority, was forced to learn the minority language. An absurd and unjust situation, truly alienating in Memmi's sense, and urgently in need of change.

But the real problem derived from the fact that the Quebec situation was not one of classic colonialism. Whatever wrongs they may have committed, the Anglo-American colonizers bore no relation to the bloodthirsty Belgian King of the Congo, Leopold II, who caused the deaths of ten million men and women. And whatever legend or the histories may say, it was not the conquering English who were to blame for Quebec's backward education system, but the triumphant ultramontanism that had given the Church a free hand in that domain.

No, we didn't want to think about home truths, with all their complexities. We forgot, as though on purpose, that French Canadians had colonized Northern Ontario and the West, and that a hundred years after the Battle of the Plains of Abraham. We preferred the abstract and arbitrary imposition of the foreign model, and in taking these borrowed ideas for present realities, the Quebec intellectual elite quite simply recolonized itself. It's so comic in some respects that it's embarrassing.

Thus, by invoking Memmi the intellectuals washed their hands of their past sins. They discovered affinities with the Indians their ancestors had driven off, and they even applied to themselves a vocabulary of oppression much more suited to those Native peoples, which is quite a turning of the tables, when you think about it. Worse, by blaming the English colonizer for all their troubles, they absolved of any responsibility all those Quebec authorities that had been accomplices to or even the cause of an unacceptable state of affairs. Whining away in a vein of victimish self-exaltation, the intellectuals set out to spread the Memmian gospel and free a free people from its chains. Here's where the farce begins.

Still, the Memmi "made in Quebec" would take its toll of real victims. There was the night watchman assassinated by an FLQ bomb, and the Quebec cabinet minister Pierre Laporte, valiantly throttled during the October Crisis by the members of the Chénier cell. Fortunately, the comic episodes were much more numerous.

In the 1970s I often felt sympathy, pity even, for the young converts to Albanian or Chinese Communism who were handing out tracts at factory gates or in the subway. In the cold, in the humid heat, or under the rain they harangued the passers-by, ardently mouthing their sermons, forever prophesying an imminent apocalypse for capitalism, before retreating to their chill and smoky garrets where they would chew over second-hand slogans imported from Albania, Vietnam, Nicaragua, countries none of them had ever seen. They were not easy to live with, that I remember. They were always right, the others were always corrupt; they were intolerant, long-winded, tiresome. But they had convictions, there was some compensation in that;

there were even those who religiously shared things out, levying a tithe on their salaries for their comrades. They were a pain in the you-know-what but they were sincere.

These young people didn't know it, but they were perhaps the last truly colonized Québécois. Mao had replaced Maurras, the Vatican had shifted to Peking. All have recanted today, and there are no more Marxist-Leninists around than members of the FLQ. They came to the sad conclusion, ultimately, that their books had lied to them and that the individual, in Quebec, is always stronger than the group. Thus, as Jean-Marc Léger said ruefully, there are workers in Quebec but there is no working class. These militants are now paunchy grandfathers and grandmothers with white hair. To quote the time-honoured surrealist Raymond Queneau, all that remains of their fantasies of being colonized is "the feeling of having had a youth." Which is at least something.

No one had told these poor young people, nor anyone else for that matter, that the decolonization of Quebec under the aegis of Albert Memmi had already given way to an enduring recolonization. Not without its plusses, but not without its drawbacks, either.

THE FACT REMAINS that those years of opening up to the world did some good. A lot, in fact.

I knew that period too, and it left me with some good memories. At home, as in many other families, our discovery of the planet began at the dinner table. Ask any Canadian who is more than forty: "How old were you when a bottle of wine was first uncorked at supper? Or when you first ate Roquefort? Or yogurt?"

I was fourteen years old, and my father had called the

family together when he walked in the door. "Children, today you're going to taste a food that the French call *yaourt,* and the English, yogurt. You can say either one. It's like curdled milk, it tastes good and it's healthy, but you have to get used to it. Here, taste this . . ." We tasted. We found it a bit bitter, and so as not to hurt him—he seemed so happy—we told him he was right, you had to get used to it. At Christmas the same year, at the home of my Uncle Robert, who was a lawyer and a sophisticated man of letters, we ate for the first time French cheeses with a hard loaf that was still called French bread (yuk, we hated it!).

At the same time thousands of families were setting aside the traditional meat and potatoes to try the now commonplace lasagna. Rice was already around but less current than today, as was the spaghetti that we did not yet call pasta. We began to turn away from beer in order to drink those wines that before you found only in fancy restaurants. Good things to eat were suddenly within everyone's grasp. The exotic as well, what with pizzas, followed by souvlakis, shawarmas, tabouli, and that sushi that ties Falardeau's stomach in knots. Listen to him, on intellectuals: ". . . those sushi sucklers, those baklava slurpers . . . they're the same mincing types who every Christmas turn up their noses at our mothers' tourtière and pigs-feet stew." You have to read it to believe it.

This widespread loss of innocence coincided with the great cosmopolitan festival of Expo 67. Canada was born to the world, while Quebec asserted itself with a promotion of the French language that was timid at first and then went all out. Along with the wine and the cheese, Brel, Ferré and Reggiani were now making regular appearances. Our best and brightest took off for France on jam-packed planes, where their Frenchness would be renewed; some came back alienated for life with a brand-new accent and accused us for the rest of their days of speaking badly. In our venerable universities we quietly distanced ourselves from the wholesome Catholic writers, Saint-Exupéry, Claudel, and Bernanos, and discovered Boris Vian. Quebec became more secular and more French at the same time.

In Quebec the governments were the great architects of this French revival, which was long overdue. In the previous century, Curé Labelle signed his letters with his title, which was seven words long and contained two anglicisms, a pretty good average: "*député-ministre* du *Département* de la Colonisation." In the television series *Les Belles Histoires des pays d'En Haut,* Labelle became *sous-ministre,* which was real French. In the 1960s, you could still find *shérifs* in all the small towns, as well as a *solliciteur général* in Quebec. But suddenly there was no more *Commission du service civil* or *Commission des liqueurs,* and that was just as well. Advances were made on all fronts, and slowly but surely, Quebec became French.

Still, some things were overlooked. Even today the august Laval University retains its *École des gradués,* from the English "graduate school," rather than the *Faculté des études supérieures et de la recherche* that you find everywhere else, even in Ottawa. (That one I like . . .)

This French revival in Quebec would enable the language to move into areas from which it had long been barred. One now mastered business, engineering, and the automobile in French. The same explosion carried Pierre Elliott Trudeau to power in Ottawa and led to the creation of the Parti Québécois. It was a blessed time when you had the impression that something new was happening every day.

There were the birth control pill and *made in Québec* dirty movies, but also Jacques Godbout's novel *Salut Galarneau!,* Réjean Ducharme's *The Swallower Swallowed,* and Marie-

Claire Blais's *A Season in the Life of Emmanuel*. There were *Le Grand Cirque ordinaire,* Raoul Duguay, *le Jazz libre du Québec, l'Osstidcho*. Blais won a major literary prize in France, the Prix Médicis, and Charlebois created a sensation at Paris's Olympia Theatre. What a great time we had! We were as good as anyone now, we were ourselves at last, and soon Daniel Lavoie would come out of Manitoba and an Acadian writer, Antonine Maillet, would get the Prix Goncourt.

The French revival, begun in those years, was Quebec nationalism's finest moment. A happy time when the nationalist and social forces melded perfectly; each was an apt complement to the other. For example, it was the working-class ridings of Montreal that sent the first PQ members of the National Assembly to Quebec City. In those days, young people from the Saguenay and the Gaspé were still flowing into Montreal only to find, to their displeasure, that their largest city spoke mostly English. On arrival the majority became once more a minority. It was a classic Memmian situation, which would soon change with Bill 101, and so much the better.

When I think back on those years, one thing is obvious: nationalism was and will perhaps always be necessary. If that movement was so widespread and attracted so many followers, and if it led to the election of four PQ governments, that's because it also answered to a need for social justice. Had it not, it would have languished just like the Marxist-Leninism of those petit bourgeois of that same time who were briefly transformed into proletarians. When this convergence came to an end, the movement retreated into a spiteful and fantasist nostalgia.

What I like about this nationalism that fought for social and linguistic justice is that it prevailed. I dare not say, however, that its work is entirely done. The PQ, spurred on by Miron's passion for justice, made the French fact predominant in public spaces and in the workplace. It is now routine and even preferable to work in French in Quebec, and in imposing this new order through its laws, the Quebec government simply kept pace with the natural evolution of the French language, which would not have taken place even in France without the active support of the State. No, there are times when the mobilization of collective resources is essential, and when the collectivity acts in the interests of justice and not of a State corporation like Hydro-Québec, its views take hold effortlessly, and they endure.

Here, the chasm between English-speaking Canada and French Quebec proves at times to be unbridgeable. Rare were the Canadians of that time who understood that the French State could legislate in linguistic matters. For many anglophone citizens, language belongs to the private domain, and state intervention was seen as an unspeakable violation of privacy on the part of the government. A mistaken assessment that I can understand, but that in no way lessens my high regard for this just and victorious struggle.

When I discuss these questions with my English-speaking friends, I defend Miron and Laurin without hesitation. Justice and the morphology of the French language proved them right, it's as simple as that. I also remind them that the nationalist ideology never, even in its worst moments, claimed that one should not learn English. On the contrary. Most of the best nationalists have never turned their backs on this international language, and in asserting the right to use their own mother tongue, also an international language, they have acted properly. At least now the rest of Canada understands that this fight was undertaken in the name of justice and no longer takes offence at our accomplishments and our vigilance. Except, of course, for that right wing with its roots in the West, which always requires one or two generations more to get the drift. Its capacity for understanding does accelerate, however, once it aspires to power and actually achieves it.

Good years, militant and victorious, but French Quebec was about to halt its drive towards decolonization, or to slow its momentum, at least, with a descent into recolonization.

~ Bienville, Black, and Bouchard

IN RETROSPECT, the movement towards decolonization was destined to fail. Quebec has always been a colony, and both its intellectual and its governing elite have seen to it that it would remain one. And there's nothing to be ashamed of in that, given that Quebec is no different in this respect than what it still mistakenly calls English Canada.

LET'S FIRST MAKE it clear that with us, an individual who is perfectly colonized is a colonizer who has achieved success. One need only cite the number of cases in point from the French regime, liberally replicated on the English side once Canada had passed over to the British. And that's just for starters.

Take, for example, Bienville, one of the many sons of Charles Le Moyne. The father, a former underling to the Jesuits in Huronia, started with nothing, made his fortune in the fur trade, and crowned his success by establishing a barony in Longueuil and ennobling all his sons. His success was typical of the Canadian experience in that he succeeded during his lifetime in doing what it would have taken four generations to accomplish in France.

All his sons became rich in both money and double-barrelled names: Le Moyne de Longueuil, d'Iberville, de Sainte-Hélène, de Maricourt, de Sérigny, de Chateauguay, and little Bienville. D'Iberville, before going off to perish from ague in Havana, received the ultimate consecration. He married a French noblewoman, who gave him two beautiful children and an estate in France. As for the young François Le Moyne de Bienville, he became on his own merits Governor of Louisiana, made a somewhat dubious fortune, and was living at his death in a superb mansion in Paris. This son of pioneer New France died rich and respected in the mother country, where he had not been born. A perfect paradigm.

There were many others like him. At the time of the surrender in 1760, some thousands of petty noblemen, merchants, and churchmen sold all their belongings and left for or returned to France, depending on the case. One of their number, Marin de la Malgue, an interpreter for the king and an officer, set foot in France for the first time, re-engaged, and went off to die in Madagascar.

Another example is that of Juchereau de Saint-Denis, whose family, one of the oldest in New France, had served the colony especially well. After the surrender of Montreal, Juchereau also set sail for this unknown France, had a successful career in the military, participated in the bloody repression of a rebellious Corsica, and had an end perfectly fitting for one with his service record: the sans-culottes, ten years later, paraded his head at the end of a pike. Which just goes to show that loyalty to France was not all that rewarding. He would have been better off following the engineer Chaussegros de Léry's example. *He* returned to the colony under the English regime and died in his bed.

Many historians have wrongfully condemned those Frenchmen whose flight to the mother country left the colony, in effect, with no head. We shouldn't hold it against them. They were convinced they had no more future in a land destined to become English, their only loyalty was to their own fortunes, and they hoped for greater advancement. Their emigration then was individualist, but since our continent has favoured this stance ever since its European beginnings, we can hardly condemn them for that. Unless, of course, one is a nationalist, for according to this ideology all individual expression is suspect. No doubt staunch nationalists must find some consolation in the destinies of Marin de la Malgue and Juchereau de Saint-Denis, as their self-interested disaffection was so severely punished.

If even so we deplore the conduct of these inconstant ancestors, we only have to look at those we still call, with a certain time-lag, the English to see that there was nothing exceptional in their behaviour. There is the exemplary case of Donald Smith, who enriched himself in the nineteenth century thanks to the fur trade and the railroad, and died a baronet in the land of his birth just like those other great forefathers Maisonneuve and Frontenac, who themselves were only passing through. And there was R. B. Bennett, lawyer and member of Parliament from Calgary, prime minister of Canada from 1930 to 1935, who, once he retired, lost no time emigrating to England, where he had himself ennobled and nibbled away at his nest-egg while waiting to die. In our own day, a certain magnate of the Canadian press, whose dream is to follow in the footsteps of Ontario's Lord Thomson of Fleet, is jumping through hoops to make it into the peerage and become Sir Conrad or Lord Black. Yes, Louis Hémon was right when he said nothing changes in the land of Canada.

At the same time, the powerful United States has had a field day on our side of the border stocking up on Great Americans. There was the young Torontonian with the boring name Gladys Smith who would become Hollywood's Mary Pickford, followed later by Michael J. Fox and Jim Carrey from Vancouver, Gordon Lightfoot and Geneviève Bujold, Shania Twain from Timmins, and Céline Dion from Charlemagne, Quebec. We could also include Alexander Graham Bell, with his profitable telephone, the economist John Kenneth Galbraith, or Nobel Prize-winning Saul Bellow. To succeed in the States, whether one speaks French or English, is a goal as eagerly sought after as a London peerage or literary consecration in Paris.

But back to the French. Nostalgia for the mother country has always been, with us, a sure sign of greatness. Octave Crémazie was writ larger in our imagination thanks to his Paris sojourn. Even today the *Petit Robert* biographical dictionary acknowledges only one of his literary achievements: the diary he kept during the siege of Paris by the Prussians. The poet Paul Morin, during the 1920s, was well regarded thanks to his long exile in France. Robert de Roquebrune, Jean Éthier-Blais, Anne Hébert, Jean-Paul Riopelle, Alfred Pellan, so many have come back from Europe ennobled by their mandatory stay in Saint Germain des Prés.

To sum up. Our intellectual bourgeoisie had always been colonized. From the anonymous author of the *Diary of the Siege of Quebec* who allowed as how he missed the King of France, to Jean Larose with his slack-jawed admiration for that France that he deems so cultivated, Paris remains a fundamental reference point and magnet. How many books have been written and published in deference to aesthetic criteria prevalent in the mother country? In this respect the Quebec intellectual, aside from the fascinating period when *joual* came to the fore, has never for long been absent from New France.

That said, we are wrong to speak of colonization by France.

However much that country may harbour hegemonic tendencies in cultural matters, what we are really talking about is self-colonization. It is not so much Paris forcing itself on us as it is we who throw ourselves at Paris's feet.

The most blatant example of self-colonization today is Lucien Bouchard himself, who will hold forth at length on the subject of the blessed day when he shook the hand of God the Father, Charles de Gaulle. Michel Vastel, his hagiographer, gives an emotional account of how the young Lucien was almost disfigured in his haste to approach the General. He must have been happy, father de Gaulle, to receive this homage worthy of the Sun King, healer of scrofula.

Lucien Bouchard has repeated it over and over again: he's never been as happy as when he was Canada's ambassador in Paris. He didn't miss us at all, and we can understand. Paris! Ah, Paris! The Paris of his dear Saint-Simon and his dear Proust! The Saguenay lawyer was accredited at Mitterand's Élysée Palace, was admitted to Rocard's Matignon, was received in the fanciest salons the City of Light had to offer. He had realized Bienville's dream, and all it cost him was a few speeches, a real bargain. The self-colonized boy had made it.

Self-colonized, and not only vis-à-vis France. On a recent trip to the United States Bouchard told his hosts that nowhere in the world was America so much admired as in Quebec. (He's from the Saguenay, Lucien; overstatement is second nature to him.) If that's not prostrating yourself before Washington, I don't know what is. In that he's a worthy successor to his spiritual father, René Lévesque, Americanophile in his bones. As Jean-François Lisée showed so well in *Under the Eye of the Eagle,* Lévesque always took great pains to assure the Americans that Quebec would never be another Cuba, our allegiance to Pepsi was much too profound for that.

Lucien Bouchard outdoes his mentor in bending his knee to both France and the United States. There was Hanoi, for instance, a few years ago. A week earlier he had been in China to sell maple syrup, and he had made it clear to his hosts that he would not, in his meetings with Chinese leaders, broach the subject of human rights. Quebec, he said, fully respects Chinese sovereignty. The Chinese leaders must have been impressed by the fact that Lucien Bouchard from Jonquière had come to tell them in person that they could continue executing their dissidents in peace, and that they had nothing to fear from the Quebec Provincial Police.

The following week Lucien was in Hanoi at the Francophonie summit, far from the discomfiting Chinese, who would have booted him out the door had he ventured to preach to them. In peaceful Vietnam our travelling salesman suddenly decided to express concern for dissidents on other shores. It would look good on his record, it could embarrass Jean Chrétien, it might even please the Americans, who knows? He was immediately taken to task by Jacques Chirac, who was there to sell arms, wine, and atomic reactors. Human rights? Forget it! It was the Élysée equivalent of Duplessis's "Shut up, you!" Bouchard quickly went to ground. You have to give him credit, he obeys.

That very day I couldn't help thinking, with some emotion, about the Memmian PQ of yore. It was, for example, going to do away with private schools. Once in power it quickly changed its tune, given that that's where most of its ministers were sending their kids. The good bourgeois were jealous of their privileges, a failing that in their dear French Republic, one of their favourite touchstones, would have merited them the scaffold. Lucien Bouchard himself preached by example, sending his son to a "good school" in Outremont, private of course, causing

135

Vastel his hagiographer to write that this wonderful pater-familias placed the interests of his children above those of the State. (He was joking, surely.) We should however take note of the fact that Pauline Marois, former Minister of Education, was an admirable exception to the rule. She had the rare courage to show confidence in the schools she administered. This is so unusual that it deserves special mention.

The PQ, so beautifully egalitarian in theory, had also planned to implement a foreign policy worthy of its allegiance to emancipation movements around the world: no more NATO, no more NORAD, it would be a non-aligned nation that frater-nized with Latin-American countries and even thumbed its nose at Washington by courting Cuba. Priorities would include the recognition of the PLO and the defence of Soviet dissidents. Quebec would set the example of a humane foreign policy. It would be a country that did things differently, with consumer co-ops, savings and credit unions, self-managed factories, unions on an equal footing with big money. The dreams of May '68 would bear fruit in French America.

What happened to those dreams? Not much. Some soft-pedalling here and there, and then the foot on the brake, as the Third World hot-rod came to a bourgeois halt. *Prochain épisode*'s opening augured right: Cuba went down in flames into Lake Leman . . . The college profs gave way to the pharmacists, and the militants turned into church mice. Under Lucien Bouchard the PQ had become a party that is even more a party than the others. What will that Quebec resemble, that only yesterday one dreamed of liberating? Especially if it secures that sovereignty-association now piously dubbed a "partnership" in the new free-market ideology masquerading as social democracy?

A part-time sovereign state that will have inserted a ring in its own nose, what with ceding its currency, the primary instrument of sovereignty, to an outside power, Washington or Ottawa. A client state also of Paris, white and American rather than black and African, that will tie itself in knots to please the decision-makers at the Élysée and the Wall Street financiers. It's long ago and far away, the RIN that dared to dream of change.

Lucien Bouchard can't take all the blame for this downward slide. It's inscribed in the genetic code of nationalist ideology, colonized from the very beginning.

～ Already Yesterday

IT IS A SUBLIME irony that Quebec nationalism has evolved in such a way that it was born on the right, grew up on the left, and has aged again to starboard.

It is its genetic destiny, as I have said, in that the colony's very baptism was reactionary. As the few attempts at Protestant colonization in America had more luck in Brazil than Canada, the Catholic State took over from Huguenot private enterprise to create not a new Jerusalem that might want to secede but a new France. Richelieu immediately banned the settling of Protestants on our shores. He wanted to reproduce France, not build a new country.

The devout soon got very involved in colonization. It was, for instance, the Compagnie du Saint-Sacrement that sponsored the founding of Montreal. The Compagnie was founded in 1627 by a young noble, the Duc de Ventadour, lieutenant-general of the king in Languedoc and viceroy of Canada. In today's terms one might say it was France's right wing that opened up Canada to colonization. And the traces remain.

The Jesuits arrived soon after, followed by the ultramontane Laval, as well as the religious communities of the Counter-

Reformation. Loyola's Society was not long in chalking up its first martyrs. Its college in Normandy, Henri IV de la Flèche, had for its boarders' chaplain Father Massé, who had been one of the first Jesuit missionaries in Canada. Among the good Father's students were Paul Le Jeune, the first author of the *Jesuit Relations,* and Charles Lallemant, uncle of the martyr. Another of the college's alumni was René Descartes, apostle of philosophic doubt, an ironic coincidence and not the last.

Champlain had barely set up his little fort at Quebec when he installed there the mystics Marie de l'Incarnation and Catherine de Saint-Augustin, the first a beneficiary of the Duchesse d'Aiguillon's largesse, niece of the Cardinal, and muse of that devout faction that later interned Ninon de Lenclos for being too much of a free-liver. Maisonneuve's Ville-Marie was also a Catholic citadel, as decreed by the Société de Notre-Dame de Montréal, whose founders were all members of the Compagnie du Saint-Sacrement, yes, the same that persecuted Molière, who got his own back by inventing the character of Tartuffe. A wonderfully nasty trick, that Monseigneur de Laval repaid in kind later in Quebec, when he threatened to excommunicate Frontenac and his friends for wanting to stage *Tartuffe.* The same episcopal authorities had not said boo when Corneille's *The Cid* had been presented. Of course, it's the story of a son who avenges his father . . .

Langres, where in the next century Diderot would be born, he of the heretical *Encyclopédie,* sent us a saintly nurse and ardent Catholic, Jeanne Mance, another nice coincidence worthy of that linking Descartes and Laflèche. The hazardous seventeenth century gave us writers, Ragueneau and Marie de l'Incarnation at the head of the list, who condemned materialism and exalted sacrifice, more in the tradition of Pascal, who hated his ego, than of the free-spirited Madame de Sévigné.

Fortunately, as a complement to the admittedly passionate *Relations,* there are the accounts of those nation-builders Champlain and Boucherville, and the too-rare instance of a story-telling adventurer, Radisson. For the most part those who thought and wrote in New France were closer to the Restoration than the Revolution.

The eighteenth century would bring to our shores La Hontan and Bougainville, free spirits quickly cast out by a lettered class that took its morality very seriously. For a long time they pilloried the entire pack of sulphurous scholars that included Voltaire. They, for their part, wanted nothing to do with Canada. In fact, the French left never liked these few acres of snow, which they associated with the sugar colonies where the black man was enslaved. They never warmed to these compensatory adventures that bled France and made no apparent contribution to the well-being of mankind.

The American ideas of freedom and equality did at one point penetrate Canada. Benjamin Franklin and his invasion force briefly occupied Montreal. This escapade would give us Fleury Mesplet and his *Gazette.* But the French Revolution, decried by our clergy, shipped us for the most part emigrants like Abbé Calonne, who forgot nothing and learned nothing. Our intellectual elite, though titillated at times by the advanced ideas of the age, was for the most part four-square for the reactionaries, just as it had earlier stood behind a fiercely apostolic Counter-Reformation.

There was a small detour to the left in the first decades of the nineteenth century with Papineau and Garneau. That gave rise to, among others, the daring but terribly outnumbered Patriotes: six parishes out of thirty-six. In the budding Outaouais region, the famous Jos Montferrand spoke out in favour of the colonial government, ushering in a live-and-let-live approach that is still very popular in that area. In Quebec, in the Gaspé, in the Beauce, not a Patriote in sight. Not many, at least. A last word on Papineau: the great man, who so adored his people, fought tooth and nail to preserve the seigniorial regime with all its privileges, justice be damned. In that he anticipated those PQ ministers who leaped to the defence of private schools.

In 1837–38, those advocating independence were rare. There was Robert Nelson and his cohorts, but their impact was small, whatever modern champions of the nationalist ideology may say. Taking their cue from a few notables at the time of the American invasion in 1775, the Rouges who succeeded the Patriotes were more inclined to advocate annexation to the American Republic, a nice foreshadowing of Lévesque's and Bouchard's Americanophilia. More recently, the disillusioned separatist Pierre Bourgault has said that he'd prefer joining the United States to sticking with the Canadian federation. If Quebec can't be a better France, at least it can become American, there would be something to gain in that.

One thing is certain: the colonized cast of mind endures. We seek not the originality but rather the authority of foreign models. The idea circulating in New York, Paris, or Rome quickly becomes our truth. What Papineau and his comrades sought from Montesquieu and Jefferson, the ultramontanists, from Bourget to Monseigneur Laflèche, would find with Louis Veuillot. Always we turn to a European tradition, and the ideology of the right has dominated Quebec for three centuries. For one Arthur Buies, who dared join Garibaldi's army, there are four intellectuals who will fight with the papal Zouaves or for Mexico's Emperor Maximilian against Juarez. The Index on one side, the Institut canadien on the other—the left exists, fights the good fight, but the right always comes out on top.

At the end of the nineteenth century, Tardivel returned to

Quebec. He dreamed of founding a French-language theocracy, a State that would counter American materialist values. His son-in-law, Omer Héroux, led a similar campaign in *Le Devoir*. Still nothing indigenously Québécois, here it's Rome talking instead of Paris.

And then there is the sterling example of Lionel Groulx at the beginning of the twentieth century. But be careful! The canon was not totally colonized by the French. No one in the country wrote better French than this man, but he soon learned to keep his distance from the Church's elder daughter and French ideology. His dream was French Canadian, and in this he was more a child of the colonizing Counter-Reformation than of the Restoration. He too was more committed to Rome than to Paris.

The young Groulx had read the Revanche authors, Barrès and Maurras. It was a time when France, afflicted by the loss of its Germanic provinces Alsace and Lorraine, saw in Canada a small branch of its people that had not, oh joy, been contaminated by the *Encyclopédie,* the Revolution, and the lay Republic. Here was this beautiful people that Louis Hémon had exhumed: "We came here three hundred years ago . . . if it's true that we have learned little since, assuredly we have forgotten nothing . . ." You would think you were rereading the famous comment of Bainville concerning the émigrés returned from London in 1815. And so the enduring link was re-established between the nationalist right of Quebec and that of France.

Groulx, however, if he was enamoured enough of Maurras' *Action française* to want to found his own, did not swallow everything whole. No, he was selective, and he even distanced himself from Maurras when the latter was condemned by the Pope. Once more, the Vatican overruled the Académie. But Groulx remained loyal to Maurras' quasi-pagan celebration of the French race.

Lionel Groulx could have written *Colette Baudoche,* Barrès's novel. It's the story of a young Alsatian girl who has remained loyal to France, and whose family is forced to shelter a German schoolmaster who has arrived to "germanize" the population. Slowly, a rapport develops between the Teutonic sausage-eater and beer-drinker and Colette, who is no Joan of Arc out of Lorraine but whose faith matches that of Maria Chapdelaine. The German teacher is not a bad man. He sets out to learn about this France that has so recently been his enemy, and he responds to its charm. He even sets aside his beer in favour of the local wine, the French Alsatian *vin gris,* and claims (you have to read it to believe it) that changing his drinking habits has "endowed him with wit." And so Germanic rudeness is tamed by French civilization, which is, as everyone knows, more refined than all others, the German in particular. Back from vacation, the young schoolmaster asks for Colette's hand in marriage, but she turns him down cold. French honour is saved. The end.

We don't know to quite what degree Groulx lapped up jingoistic rubbish of that ilk. One thing is sure, his writing reeks of Barrèsian ideology. Thus, in *The Call of the Race,* discussing the fight for French schools in Ontario, he exclaims, "Ontario must become our Alsace-Lorraine!" Who, what, how? It's clear where Father Groulx got that.

The poor canon was raving. There was no imaginable connection between the little Baudoche girl's Alsace and Lantagnac's Ontario. On the one hand, you had a province whose population expressed itself largely in a Germanic dialect, not even in French, and on the other, a region where the French had been colonizers just like the American Loyalists. They had nothing in common, other than that the French had suffered a defeat in both cases. Hiking up his cassock, Groulx leaped elegantly over the discrepancies and hung on to the one remote similarity. That's what it's like to be colonized. Your imagination is so impoverished and neurotic that you superimpose foreign concepts on your own situation, and define your identity in terms pertinent only to your borrowed model. Groulx was a wannabe Barrès just as Aquin, later, fancied himself Memmi.

But Groulx was in good company. In the Ottawa of his novel the architects were replicating Tudor, Victorian, Edwardian styles. The reigning Anglomania was echoed by Groulx's pseudo-Barrès. Colonized here, colonized there, the two bad plagiarisms deserved each other.

Susan Mann Trofimenkoff makes the convincing case in her book *L'Action française* that Groulx, all the same, was far from being servile right down the line. For example, he quickly turned his back on Maurras to obey the papal injunction. The canon was looking for a Canadian solution to a Canadian problem, and that is a point in his favour. It must also be said that he was suspicious of this Combist France with its hostility to good priests. In that respect he was a worthy follower of Bishop Laval, who was hostile to Frontenac, and of de Pontbriand, the ultramontane preacher who heaped scorn on the French court. Groulx had spent time in France, and had not appreciated the gibes that his clerical collar, so venerated here, had attracted there. And he saw the Communist horror making inroads in the mother country. No, much better to take refuge in Catholic Latinity, inclined perhaps to well-meaning authoritarianism but so well-disposed to his true mother, the Church.

In his predilection for Fascism and anti-Semitism, two imported products, of course, Groulx was followed, and is still followed, by a large part of the intellectual bourgeoisie. Many, like him, praised Salazar, Franco, Mussolini, etc. Today André Laurendeau and Henri Bourassa are being let off the hook for their follies on the grounds that they were but products of their time. With such pusillanimous reasoning, one will soon be exonerating Adolf Hitler. It is claimed as well that they didn't know, couldn't have known . . .

And then all these good people threw themselves into the arms of Marshal Pétain, who must have been amazed. Long live the defeat of the French army, now a rural and Christian France will be reborn! Its people will be saved from the Communist temptation by Mussolini-style corporatism. France will be free as last from Jewish and Masonic tyranny. A second Restoration was nigh. Groulx and the others were delighted. What others? André Laurendeau, whose belated recantation must nevertheless be counted in his favour, Camille Laurin, Jacques Lazure, later, and Doris Lussier, who signed virulent texts attacking General de Gaulle, that "felon." Not very pretty, Quebec's nationalist right in the years when France was offering more collaboration than resistance.

The years between the wars favoured the coming together of the French and Quebec movements on the right. One need only recall the French Fascist Drieu la Rochelle and his novel *Gilles,* whose exemplary character Carentan lauds this good Canada that has been spared all revolutionary horrors: "a French people that did not experience 1789, nor the eighteenth century, nor even in fact the seventeenth, nor the Renaissance and the Reformation, they are French through and through, unadulterated."

We remember also the anti-Semite Céline who, with his typically troubling drollness, dreamed for a time of fleeing his decadent France for the land of priests. In 1936, speaking of Canada, which he had visited and where he had been well received in right-wing circles, Céline prophesied: "Only a single country will resist for one more century, that where the priests rule, the most tedious of all lands . . . but I'll go there, I'll serve at mass. I'll teach the catechism, there's no other choice if you want to save your . . . and that I'm determined to do." Robert Rumilly, the former Royalist, had already trumped him by eight years.

To my Quebec nationalist friends who are made uneasy by such kinships, I recommend reading Proust's *Time Regained,* in which, describing the clients of Baron de Charlus' pederastic bordello, he notes the esteem in which were held Canadian aviators: "Some of them specifically requested Canadians, perhaps charmed by their accent, so subtle that it was hard to know if it came out of old France or England . . ." (Just a little pleasantry on my part, of course.)

BUT IF YOU REALLY want to have a good laugh, then cast your mind back to the General's great caper on our shores. Yet another episode in the ongoing tragicomedy of the fathers, Sophocles rewritten by Aristophanes. A good time will be had by all, and there's more to come.

General de Gaulle arrived at Expo 67, opened wide his arms, and pronounced the words we now know so well. Over and over he called us his "children of Canada." Very sweet, that. Pierre Bourgault would claim thirty years later that he was decolonized in a flash. Guy Bouthillier would say much the same. They both got it wrong. The General's declaration would have just the opposite effect. Quebec nationalism would recolonize itself with unprecedented zeal. And that just as Tremblay was completing *Les Belles-Soeurs,* and Charlebois was singing *Lindbergh.*

Much has been written about the General's motives. He's been accused of senility, which is unfair. The General never succumbed to the Marshal's disease. All sorts of explanations have been proposed, from geopolitical manoeuvrings to block American hegemony, to premature ejaculation. Did he really want to take back Canada from England, a country he looked down upon for having become a colony of its own colony, the United States? I doubt it. He was too lucid not to have known that this sort of thing was no longer done, and not to understand that Canada had not been a British possession for a very long time.

De Gaulle a decolonizer? Don't jump to conclusions. He had perhaps broken with France's colonial past, but he hadn't entirely given up on the Empire, as can be seen from his discussions with Peyrefitte on the subject of Polynesia. He certainly wanted to decolonize the untenable parts of the French Empire, the Maghreb and black Africa, and to liberate the territories of other countries, but he didn't want to give up Martinique, Guyana, and what he called the "pastilles" of the French Empire.

A third hypothesis: the strategist in him dreamed of re-establishing in America a French bridgehead that would enable him to harass the giant down below. That doesn't make sense either. No doubt he would have loved to vex the successors to Roosevelt, of whom he had such unpleasant memories, but France, a traditional ally of America since La Fayette, had no interest in pushing that game too far. And the General knew the history and geography of Canada too well not to foresee how risky such an enterprise would be. He always had to take action, of course, it was in his nature, but he did so intelligently. With no arms to match his ambitions, he repeated his exploit of June 1940 in London, when his only asset was a microphone. No, he never retracted anything later, and the governments that succeeded him have continued to work towards close ties with Quebec, with greater or lesser conviction depending on whether they were of the right or the left.

One thing is sure, he did make an error in judgement in evaluating the situation. He who referred, with reason, to the Russians rather than to the Soviets, had forgotten, like Marcel Rioux at the same time, that we were no longer French; he also thought English Canadians were British. Jean Drapeau had to remind him that French Canadians were free people, the work had already been done thank you very much, and we were the sole masters of our fate. The free citizens that we were didn't have to be liberated, even by a noted liberator in search of a cause. There were, then, some things the General didn't understand? And him so intelligent?

Let's say that he understood them in his own way, in the light of his own interests. The General's cry, in my opinion, was a response to imperatives dictated by internal political affairs. We were in 1967, five years after the Evian accords that gave Algeria back to the Algerians. There were then on French soil over a million former colonists, impoverished overnight, many of whom were, understandably, embittered. One day they had native labour at their beck and call, and the next they were ordinary citizens of a land that was, in many cases, totally foreign to them. A bit like our own émigrés of 1760. There was profound disappointment too among those nostalgic for the Empire, dispossessed forevermore of their coolies and negroes.

Transport all this into the context of the General on Montreal's City Hall balcony, crying out to all those below who'd heard nothing from France for two centuries. But imagine the microphone is turned not towards Montreal, but in the direction of Paris: "Dear Frenchmen of France, to those of you who reproach me for having sold out the Empire, I offer you this American France regained. A land rich in possessions and possibilities, whiter and more French than that miserable Maghreb, a land where you will find real cities, clean ones, and real universities, and where you can roll around in great big American cars fuelled by gas that's a lot cheaper than what you get at home. A land of dreams that has cost us nothing and that will cost us nothing. A bargain for our France that craves greatness but still can't afford it! Here then is this new frontier worthy of our past, where your innate yearnings will find a legitimate outlet! You will perhaps not be masters of this land in the making, but at least you will have a home away from home worthy of your aspirations. France can only be enlarged. I'm thinking above all of you, you colonists so unhappily dispossessed by native peoples not your equals. Here you will be at home, you will be better off and will in the end pardon France for the painful decisions she had to make in a changed world. I invite you to come in great number to populate this Quebec which can offer a bright future to all enterprising Frenchmen who have initiative but lack prospects. For you I have come to liberate this land, but don't thank me, I know you rarely appreciate my great undertakings. Never mind, here is my beautiful gift to make up for your lost Algeria. Admit that it's better than nothing. Long live a free Quebec! *'Vive le Québec libre!'*" A surrogate reconquest, then, and not too exacting, either. A microphone did the trick very nicely, just like the last time.

That wasn't all. He was farsighted, de Gaulle. He knew this remote French Canada better than anyone. He remembered that its intellectual bourgeoisie had twice been loath to come to the aid of a France invaded by the Germans. With his cry, he pardoned them just as he had pardoned a collaborationist France.

In 1914 Henri Bourassa had let it be known, and rightly, that French Canadians didn't have to don the uniform of an empire that had treated its loyal minorities poorly. Bourassa was only partly right, however, and fortunately for Quebec's pride there were others as nationalist as he, but more clear-sighted. Olivar Asselin, for instance, who recognized that a greater drama in Europe was posing a threat to democracy and justice. Reasoning as he did, Bourassa was proclaiming the independence of a French Canada that had known for a long time that it was different from its mother country; for his part, Asselin was also acting as a free individual, and one who was all the more liberated in that he felt he could in good conscience help out the land of his forefathers. Two sides of the same coin, of equal value, a rare paradox in our history, with inner conflicts worthy of a great creative imagination. The problem for de Gaulle was that the Bourassas outnumbered the Asselins.

In 1940 the right-wing clergy refused once again to fight for this France, once denounced by Monseigneur de Pontbriand for its impiety, its loose morals, and its penchant for the freedoms of the *Encyclopédie*. It went so far as to choose the glorious, submissive Marshal over the France of the Resistance. Twice, then, the nationalist right rejected conscription in the name of a purity of heart that set it apart from a forgetful France. The General knew that better than anyone, he who had been kept up to date on Quebec opinion by the representative of Free France in Canada, Élisabeth de Miribel. He also knew that both times it was the young, adventurous heretics who had signed up voluntarily to save the honour lost by Bourassa and Groulx. Including the young Quebec lawyer Georges Vanier, who left a leg in France, and the ordinary soldier Jacques Dextraze, a volunteer in 1939 who would one day command the entire Canadian army. Them and millions of damned Englishmen from Canada.

De Gaulle knew all that. Which explains the uneasiness experienced by nationalists such as Lucien Bouchard, who have a hard time evoking the glorious past of the Canadian forces in the service of a humiliated France without risking accusations that their spiritual, ideological, and intellectual forerunners tried to prevent our young men from going off to be killed at Ypres and in Normandy. It's indeed an embarrassing moment: the intractable isolationist extolling the courage he didn't have and that belonged only to a wrong-thinker who was right.

But with his cry, the General forgave. He forgave the actor Doris Lussier, an *indépendantiste* of the first hour, who had once said horrible things about him, and he forgave the young Lazure and Laurin, who were to leap to the assistance of the fleeing d'Ermonville, assassin of French Resistance fighters. The Quebec right had been Vichyist, while the Canadian Quebec had participated in the liberation of France. De Gaulle knew about betrayal, and he knew from experience that forgiveness is more of a unifier than even the most well-founded resentment. In short, he delivered a master stroke worthy of the great politician he was. He opened up a new frontier for a France that was imperialist still, but idle, staking a claim in America that might somehow pay off, who knows, and he rallied to his side an elite that asked for nothing better, since it had so much to atone for. In according it such a magnanimous absolution, de Gaulle retrieved the sceptre of Louis XIV and an immortal France while eliciting a pardon for its own long-standing inattention. Not bad at all.

Except for one thing. Was this not a cruel rebuff to those Canadian combatants, the young Ontario farmers, the Native people, the French Canadians who had sacrificed their lives to save France? I think here of Laurier Fortier from Timmins, who signed up with his three brothers to liberate France. They were all lucky enough to make it back, but thousands of their comrades were left behind. Did de Gaulle think of them at all, those who had sacrificed so much for France? It would appear that he did not. And that I can understand. He, who always said that the building of empires had nothing to do with being on the side of the angels, had been loyal only to himself.

In effect, this was what he had to say to Laurier Fortier: "You paid with your life to save my land, which thanks you and considers that its debt has been paid. If I have offended you in any way, know that I forgive myself, my interests required that I defend a cause that is more dear to me than your esteem. Sorry . . ." A cruel irony, the General turned his back on his saviours and opened his arms to those who once held him in contempt.

The Montreal thunderbolt would not have enormous consequences. Yes, one fussed, and one amused oneself as well. Canada sent the great man back to a France that needed him more than we needed her. Quebec got more involved with France, and that gave the French-language revival, already underway, a shot in the arm. And the intellectual bourgeoisie bowed down before the liberating father-figure.

Taking its cue from the city of Montreal, which had purchased its subway cars in France, the Quebec government became Jacobin in the extreme. This gave rise to a centralizing movement that held the municipalities in contempt, and to a massive bureaucratization that cost the taxpayer dearly. This recolonization, essential and beneficial in certain respects, would produce the most perfect tribute imaginable to colonial apery: not the statue of the General that took its place along with the bust of Louis XIV on Place Royale, but the Olympic Stadium, the work of the Frenchman Taillibert that was cobbled together with baling wire. And so today, in the centre of Montreal, we have a rickety masterpiece that leaks everywhere when it's not outright crumbling, a costly parabola that is an enduring laughing stock. It is the perfect emblem for France's recolonization of Quebec.

As I've said, the business of the balcony had few after-effects. Of course, France is still very present in the minds of our thinking and governing bourgeoisie. One dreams of being published in Paris, of living there wealthy and respected. We even concocted a little festival of Quebec cinema, in Blois, which is as everyone knows a great metropolis much favoured by film enthusiasts from around the world. The festival, by the way, died its own natural death. What else? We've been honoured with the odd historical plaque, but not much besides.

Pompidou was not so stupid as to renounce the General's Quebec legacy. He still had to humour the same clientele of nostalgic idlers, but he was quick to cut his costs. Wily as he was, he didn't invest more than he had to in this nascent adventure that he saw as a folly, and that was more suited to the world of dreams than of political reality.

With Giscard, the same thing. Yes, one had to give René Lévesque a little medal, even an audience, that was part of the game, but the game stopped there. He preferred the Canadian West, its ranches and its oil, to this New France, whose only merit was to avidly consume his wine, his cheese, his books, and his perfume.

Compared to their sympathies for the Sandinistas or the Kurds, Mitterand and the left never gave a thought to the General's ambitions. Nothing. Ever since Voltaire, the left has been indifferent to us. And if they showed any interest at all, it was for a Canada that was plural, dynamic, federated, and tolerant. Like modern Europe. The result: from Mitterand to Jospin, the General's neocolonial dream had no takers. There was one fleeting exception: Rocard, who suddenly discovered he had affinities with the Quebec sovereigntists. But this was a flirtation with no future, at best a one-night stand.

One thing is certain: thanks to de Gaulle, the French right and nationalist Quebec renewed their marriage vows. Who was the primary artisan of Gaullist politics in Canada? A certain Phillipe Rossillon, who, as Michel Winock has noted, was a former partisan of French Algeria. The same man, later dropped by Georges Pompidou, who considered him capable of the worst excesses, ended his days as protector of the French language, a role that suited him well and that was right in line, if I may say, with his lifelong vocation. Who are today the French politicians who most actively encourage Quebec to accede to that independence that will bring it forever into the orbit of the Élysée? Jean-Marie Le Pen and Pierre Messmer, an unashamed racist and a historical Gaullist, the latter more pardonable for his loyalty than the former for his convictions.

When all is said and done, the French left cares little for Quebec because, like everyone else, it has other things on its mind. When it pays heed to our disputes, it listens as much to René-Daniel Dubois as to Pierre Falardeau. It lends an ear also to John Saul, Atom Egoyan, and Margaret Atwood, as did Lionel Jospin on his last visit to Canada. On which occasion Jospin mouthed the usual homily to the effect that Quebec is a beautiful branch on the French tree, blah blah blah, and one must cultivate one's uniqueness wherever one is, etc. Bland pronouncements. But during all the Mitterand years, the left never supported the secessionist idea, not on your life. It prefers Canada, a space more congenial to its European point of view. It has reason to be wary, especially when it sees Le Pen making common cause with the PQ. It too was looking on, the night of the lost referendum, when Parizeau denounced the ethnic vote. Ever since, there has been no doubt: an independent Quebec is for the French left a reactionary aspiration, just as were the origins of New France. Some things never change.

What remains of the Gaullist adventure? A statue that the General himself would never have wanted. But admiring as he is of this guiding father, the semi-colonized Lucien Bouchard, who bloodied his face to shake the General's hand, did yield to the temptation, perhaps in order to bury Quebec nationalism's Vichyist past. And Quebec's left in all that, which, more than the right, has pushed for secession for forty years? Well, its thinkers look a bit silly when they throw themselves at Lionel Jospin's feet, he who is more apt to listen to John Saul than Gérard Bouchard. They can't figure out why they don't garner more support from people who court Castro while cozying up to Guyana. They are bitter, feel misunderstood, but they say nothing, because inside the palisade it's not good form to voice your doubts or second thoughts.

AND ON IT GOES. On and on. We make ourselves small before the paternal Élysée, like Gilles Vigneault, who wanted France to "love us and help us," or Jean Royer, who wrote recently that the day after the referendum defeat of May 20, 1980, "France was disappointed in us." Imperial France perhaps, but I suspect that the French in France didn't give a hoot, and they are right.

Even today, the culturally colonized coo with joy when they hear the French say, as at the Paris book fair in 1999, that Émile Nelligan is the "Quebec Rimbaud." As though Nelligan couldn't just be Nelligan. (There is in fact in the Nelligan cult, with all its silly parallels, a Parisian pretense that would bring a smile to the face of Albert Memmi himself.) But of course, these same culturally colonized individuals will never say, for example, that Rimbaud is the "French Nelligan." Ah, no. The French wouldn't understand . . .

The language of the French right has even worked its way into the thought of the Quebec left. Here's a little test. Take this sentence: "North of the north, books are written and tell of the

Latin blood that flows in our dreams, from our beginnings to the days to come." Who wrote that? Lionel Groulx, you'll say. No, it's the poet Claude Beausoleil, who is still steeped in the ideology of blood dear to the Groulx and the Roquebrunes of the 1920s. No, nothing changes. (Sigh . . .)

Let's now move on to another imported product that was once all the rage among our nationalist elite, on the right especially. A poison that will dishonour them forever. Anti-Semitism.

~ The Fault of the Jews

ANTI-SEMITISM. It is here that the colonization of minds among our newspaper-reading bourgeoisie manifests itself most clearly.

Careful. This is a taboo subject. It's not nationally correct in Quebec to speak about it, other than to say that the Québécois are no more anti-Semitic than anyone else, and this plague was limited to a few isolated pronouncements by misinformed and well-intentioned individuals who have been quoted out of context by malicious people who only want to sully our image abroad. Among their number, the nasty Mordecai Richler, whose Jewishness, in this connection, one assiduously neglects to mention.

I use the words "nationally correct" advisedly—it's a Quebec phenomenon. Indeed, many are the contributors to *La Presse,* to *Le Devoir,* or to Radio-Canada who deny the existence of political correctness in Quebec, or who deplore its effects. Endowed as they are with a superiority complex inherited from Abbé Groulx, they will insist that this is an Anglo-Saxon phenomenon to which their independence of mind renders them impervious, and that it afflicts only narrow-minded academics from New England or Toronto. (The intonation at the end of that sentence should be ever so slightly contemptuous . . .) We have no truck here with any of that, after all we're more evolved and less up-tight. Here we're not afraid to say that even though a blind person may have been elevated to the rank of the visually impaired, he still can't work as a taxi driver. We say that, and we laugh. We're above it all, are we not . . .

No, we're not. Political correctness exists in Quebec, too. And it's not such a bad thing either. It represents a sociolinguistic evolution whereby those marginalized in the past demand the right to participate wholly in all spheres of public life and to describe in their own terms their own reality. Thus the Eskimos have become Inuit and masters of Nunavut. It's a simple matter of respect and dignity. If the old now want to be called elders and the blind, visually challenged, so be it. I don't see it as a threat to my freedom of speech. And in any case, Quebec has kept pace with the international movement by replacing its *infirmes* (crippled) with *handicapés* (the disabled). And so much the better.

So let's not say that we are more intelligent than others. It's true that we do not resort to the linguistic contortions that are cause for ridicule in Toronto as well as New York, such as "temporarily able-bodied female" to describe a woman, or "physically challenged male" for the handicapped. If we are immune to these abuses we shouldn't be patting ourselves on the back — it's the limits of the French language that protect us, not our intellectual superiority.

We have gone along with the movement in everything. And why should anyone complain? There are some jokes, for instance, that are no longer acceptable. Jacques Godbout, in *Salut Galarneau!,* wrote "happy as a homosexual in prison." He would never write such a phrase today because it is now respectable to be gay, and we are more in touch with what goes on behind bars. So there is political correctness in Quebec, like everywhere else, and it's not a problem. If you please . . .

On the other hand, the linguistic absurdities absent from Quebec have been more than adequately compensated for by the idiocy of national correctness, a rectitude that is every bit as inhibiting for thought and speech. Thus, one must never say "Canadian," except to snigger or malign. "French Canadian" is even more taboo. It is good form also, in certain academic circles, to ramble on about "territorial nationalism." After all, ethnic nationalism, that sounds a bit Serbian, and it calls to mind some embarrassing associations we'd prefer to forget.

National correctness rules out any reminders of Quebec nationalism's anti-Semitic past. Other than, of course, to down-play it or excuse it.

In my native Sandy Hill we had a neighbour, an upright gentleman, staunch Catholic, who sported a pencil-thin mous-tache out of the 1930s. He was handsome in the style of Clark Gable, though not so elegant. He had almost completed his bachelor's degree, and his vocation was intellectual: he was a journalist at the newspaper *Le Droit,* where he toiled for starva-tion wages. He had two sons, friends of my brothers. This good patriot hated the English and all their works, especially the Beatles, corrupters of our youth. All his ideas were ultramon-tane; he detested unions and everything foreign. In short, a man who would have been dear to the heart of Abbé Groulx.

One summer evening my brother was invited by this man's eldest son to have a Coke out on the balcony. The father joined them for a chat. And in the course of the conversation he declared that no Jew could be superior to a French Canadian. "Not even Einstein?" asked my brother. No, not even Einstein. Besides, we don't even know if the theory of relativity is true, and so . . . One can only imagine what he thought of Marx, Freud, or Mahler. My brother couldn't believe his ears. Being a well-brought-up boy he didn't say anything, preferring to let the conversation flag and expire on its own. He left without telling him off once, no small feat for a member of my family.

This is the milieu I knew. And remember, this fellow was educated and a journalist, therefore well-informed. And the bad news is, he was far from being an anomaly. From Gratien Gelinas to Raymond Villeneuve, our most outspoken anti-Semites have always come out of that educated class that was perfectly positioned to combat prejudice. But that's the opposite of what transpired and transpires still. It is the notaries who are anti-Semitic and not the workers, and many more lettered than illiterate individuals share the prejudice.

Note here the observation of Michel Winock, who discerns among French nationalists a cult of the collective that applies equally well to their Quebec counterparts. The solidarity (which, by the way, is an illusion) that they attribute to the Jews, reflects a jealousy that mutates into self-hatred, for not being able to muster it themselves, they consider themselves wanting and diminished by their failure. From there, self-hatred becomes hatred of the Other. It's as clear as spring water.

Now let's have a little laugh. At the height of the Galganov affair, involving a gentleman who was defending his right to use the English language in his store, the Bloc Québécois wrote to the Canadian Jewish Congress to ask it if it supported the person in question. It seems incredible, but no, it was an official letter with a signature, stamp, postmark, everything in order. The Bloc was merely reasoning like a classic anti-Semite who endows the Jews with a solidarity he envies: he's a Jew, Galganov, and so the others must be on his side. This time, so as to embarrass them, we'll ask them publicly whether they're going along with Galganov. (Tee-hee hee . . .)

It was a disaster. The Bloc looked more ridiculous than ever. The Canadian Jewish Congress must have replied: "Would you be so kind as to inform us as to what this is all about? Galganov's battle, sorry, is not our business. We have given no directives to this gentleman, and believe it or not, there are Jews who go ahead and do things on their own, without our consent. You have the wrong address . . ." The English-language press had a field day, and understandably so, with the poor Bloc. An editorial writer even made the point that the Bloc never wrote the Vatican to ask it if it supported the court challenges of federalist Guy Bertrand, who was born Catholic. No, the Catholics, it would appear, can exercise free will, but the Jews are all hand in glove.

Which is to show considerable ignorance of Jewish diversity, whether in Canada or in Israel. Thus, Mordecai Richler himself has not shrunk from launching a few well-aimed barbs at the Knesset for the brutality with which Jewish soldiers put down the Intifada. But to say that doesn't help, because there will always be someone to reply: "Yes, but I know them, and I'm telling you that they stick together, those people. Mind you, they're good at it. It's just that . . ."

The Bloc quickly dropped the matter. Curiously, the French-language press took no note of its initiative. Perhaps they all stick together, these Quebec nationalists, members of Parliament, and journalists. If that is so, we should feel happy for them, as it must mean that their old dream of solidarity has at last come true.

That is how nationalist anti-Semites in Quebec think. And at times they append collusion with the English to their fantasy of solidarity. The author and editor Michel Brûlé has written in *PQ-de-sac* that the Jews and the English are indeed guilty of collusion, the proof being that the former have their own movement called the B'nai Brith. And in the word "Brith," there are the letters "brit," no? Brit as in "British." Is that not proof positive? Now we've got them! It's very simple, you just had to think of it . . .

Poor boy. This is an anti-Semitic stupidity of the first order, to be inscribed instantly in the already massive collection of howlers one may attribute to Quebec nationalism. The B'nai Brith is an association dedicated to the encouragement and education of Jewish youth. *B'nai* in Hebrew is the genitive plural of *Ben,* which means "son," and *Brith* signifies "alliance." B'nai Brith, the Sons of the Alliance. Like the Bloc, Michel Brûlé was out to lunch.

If there is a reproach that may be made to Mordecai Richler, since his name has come up, it is that his book gives the impression that there is a kinship between French Quebec and the anti-Semitism that led to the Jews being rounded up in France. Hardly. The nationalists are not all called Groulx or Falardeau, and they're not all in cahoots like the Jews . . . Mordecai could have reminded us, and it would have been most appreciated, that the Assembly of Lower Canada in the time of Papineau gave Jews the right to vote twenty-seven years before the British Empire, or that Aaron Hart, the Seigneur de Bécancour, received his title before the Barons Rothschild.

That said, Richler was perfectly correct in denouncing the link, however distant or close, that has always existed between Quebec nationalism and a hatred of Jews. And I understand the anger he feels towards the memory of Groulx. It's true that in France there is no Lycée Édouard-Drumont or Lucien-Rebatet Bridge, but there are times when Richler lays it on a bit thick. Groulx never called for a pogrom, we can agree on that. And as I've said, Groulx the historian, whatever his faults, was after all the progenitor of what would become the University of Montreal, and is due his subway station, his college, and a few hills in his name. Anti-Semitism was not the cause of his life, and in the end, after the discovery of the death camps, he renounced it. It was late in the day, but still . . .

Finally, Richler could also have said, and this is what is most important, that our anti-Semitism was the work of the intellectual bourgeoisie, and was not adopted by the people on whom it has always looked down. A point in favour of the Québécois, who did not make an offering to their learned elite of any pogroms, à la Poland or Germany. It would have been kind to have made that clear.

The recent debate on anti-Semitism has only highlighted once again the colonized cast of mind of our intellectual bourgeoisie. Thus, the thinking bourgeois is a grand neurotic, easily humiliated, and above all anxious about what people think of him in other countries. Note the nonsense bruited about concerning the prime minister, Jean Chrétien — that we are ashamed of the way he looks, that he expresses himself badly, etc. Personally, I've never thought about what might be said abroad regarding the prime minister, especially since I've already seen a certain Joe Clark in that post. Sorry, but opinions abroad have no effect on the way I vote or the way I live. Among the thinking bourgeois, things are different.

I have no reason to believe that Lise Bissonette or Jean Larose are in any way anti-Semitic. But it can be shown, the evidence is there, that where Richler is concerned their behaviour and that of many other nationalists betrays a colonized cast of mind. In *Le Devoir* Lise Bissonette, with her customary zeal, defended the tarnished honour of her newspaper and assailed her denigrator in no uncertain terms, going so far as to suggest, rather crudely, in fact, that his argument was the product of an alcohol-clouded brain. (That must have enchanted the pamphleteer in question, who likes nothing better than to be seen in a Hemingwayesque pose, whiskey in hand, cigar between his teeth. A colonized look in itself, if truth be told . . .) That said, there was good reason to contest the vagueness of Richler's sources, but what the editorialist reproached him for most bitterly was having discredited Quebec nationalism in foreign eyes by calling attention to its former follies.

In simple terms, what she wanted to say was that the nasty Mordecai had no business talking about our affairs in the *New Yorker,* to those good Americans whom we so admire and want at all costs to reassure. (After all, there are so many Jews in New York, you never know . . .) Bad boy, don't do that any more!

The same story from Jean Larose, who, in *La Souveraineté rampante,* sees someone colonized behind each tree. "Richler wanted to shame us and hurt us." We have to reassure these grand neurotics by informing them of the following: The Americans, the French, the Germans, they don't think anything about Quebec, nothing at all, and they themselves have too many sins on their conscience to condemn us for anything. Here, the colonized intellectual is a great unfortunate, convinced of his vulnerability and his inferiority. As for the so-called ordinary Quebeckers, they don't care, and they're right. Richler hasn't stopped them from going off to warm their skins in New England in summer or in Florida in the winter. They have other preoccupations, and they're not so colonized as to ask what everyone thinks of them. What is more, I would wager one of my sons that they've never met a single American who has asked them: "So, is it true, in Quebec the nationalists were anti-Semitic before the war?"

Let's just say I'd be surprised.

~ Françoise and Charlus

BUT IT IS IN THE realm of language, clearly, that the colonization of people's minds is most ardently felt.

I'VE ALREADY MENTIONED the fierce desire of our bourgeois intellectuals to succeed in France, where they establish themselves once they have made their reputation here. So it was with the three daughters of George-Étienne Cartier, who, upon the death of their father, went off to Cannes, where they quietly lived off what the good man had left them, and died, all three, as spinsters. François Hertel, poor man, who thought himself too renowned in our company, followed suit, as did Félix Leclerc, until the nationalists decided to honour him as a father and tout him as our national singing laureate. He reciprocated with a string of appallingly jingoistic ditties. He pronounced on the pure and the impure, a Quebec sold off to the Americans, the apocalyptic suffering of an Île d'Orléans forced to speak the English of the conqueror. Memmi, always Memmi, whose ideas had turned the head of this poor man, once a great singer and a great writer. A shame . . .

An even better example: the cult of speaking and writing well. We can gloss over those instances of self-flagellation where Quebec literati castigate their fellow citizens for not knowing how to express themselves, not reading Barthes, or preferring Schwarzenegger to Philippe Noiret. That's where ordinary folks assert their freedom and the bourgeois savants express their ongoing servility.

In French civilization, as Claude Duneton has shown better than I ever could, the correlation between social status and command of the language is taken for granted. The right people speak well. And if you use all the good verbs and adopt a French accent, then you've got it made. In Jean Larose's terms, you're decolonized. No kidding. But the poor people who speak so badly and don't know how to use the conditional tense, well, they're colonized. You love the people, you stroke them and disdain them at the same time, and you think to help them by mocking them. Always this superiority complex vis-à-vis those we consider inferior, which becomes an inferiority complex as soon as someone turns up who's even more refined.

My grandfather, Elphège Poliquin, a butcher in Sainte Angèle de Laval, P.Q., was not the least bit colonized. He had completed only a few years of primary school, but that still gave him more education than the president of the school board, a congenial illiterate who held his prayer book upside down in church. Grandpa spoke like everyone in the district, that is, like a farmer, and it didn't matter. His favourite expletive was *"Hèle de hèle!"* and he was blissfully unaware of its English derivation. His *char* had a *moffleux* and he put on the *brèques* to stop, like everyone else. Yet he loved language, and he gallicized all his borrowings from English, again like everybody else. And when someone spoke well, he liked that. He said: *"C'est le fonne,* listening to a man who doesn't have to make an effort to speak well, I like that, it's very beautiful . . ."*

He was sincere when he said that, but I can assure you he wasn't intimidated,. Example: he had a friend, a Frenchman whom I will call Monsieur Roland, who was a travelling salesman. My grandfather often invited him to eat and to sleep over, and the fellow loved the cooking and the colourful conversation of my grandmother Gertrude. He was a good man who had come to seek his fortune in America and had no more thought of France. He had been nothing much in his native land, and emigration had boosted his social standing beyond his expectations. His diction was taken for learning, and he was credited with refinements that he didn't possess at all. A common phenomenon. If an opera was broadcast on the radio in his presence, someone was sure to say: "You must know what they're singing, eh? The French, they're cultured, no?" He realized at a certain point that he should always say yes, so as not to disappoint the questioner.

My grandparents loved to hear him talk, they listened to him for literally hours. As he was generous with his opinions, they asked him to hold forth on the great issues of the day, international ones especially, because, as he came from France, he must have travelled and seen things that in Sainte Angèle you could find only in books and newspapers. "Monsieur Roland, do you think there will be a war with China?" asked my grandmother with concern. "No, Madame Poliquin, don't worry. The Chinese soldiers only eat rice, they can hardly stand on their feet, the poor souls. A little atomic bomb, like in Japan in '45, and that'll be the end of it. No, it's Germany you have to watch out for, the old foe, a warlike people who are jealous of French greatness!" "Ah, but he knows how to talk," everyone said in unison.

One day my grandfather made a resolution, and, in his authoritative way, addressed him: "Monsieur Roland, I like the way you speak. And I'd like to sound educated, like you. So as of now, every time I make a mistake, you're going to correct me. I think that would help . . ." Monsieur Roland, who had only barely passed his school-leaving exams but was now being elevated to the status of an expert in grammar, replied between two mouthfuls of tourtière: "If I can be of service, of course . . ."

The next day, after the first bowl of tea in the morning, my grandfather said to his guest, "Monsieur Roland, excuse me, I have to put some wood in the *fournaise*." His tutor jumped at the opportunity to accede to his host's wishes. "Monsieur Poliquin, a small observation, if you'll permit me. We don't say *fournaise*. In good French, we say *chaudière*. It's easy, no? First lesson of the day. I hope that pleases you . . ."

Grandpa didn't see it that way. He fixed him with a reproachful gaze and replied: "Come on now, are you crazy? A *chaudière* is a bucket for carrying water, it's not a *fournaise* for heating a three-storey house. If I had to heat with a *chaudière, hèle de hèle,* we'd be freezing our asses in here!"

"But no, Monsieur Poliquin, I assure you that in France . . ."

"No, no, no, a *chaudière* to heat a house, maybe it's good in France, but here we're in Canada and we're going to heat with a *fournaise!* Besides, *fournaise,* I've said that all my life. I can't have been wrong all that time!"

Grandfather was an imposing figure, grandmother's delicious crêpes were there waiting in the buttered pan, and so Monsieur Roland didn't pursue the matter. "But I would never say that, Monsieur Poliquin! So much for the *fournaise!* Madame Poliquin, your crêpes smell so good . . . I have tears in my eyes!"

In short, there was no more talk of a chaudière in that house. Not for heating, in any case. And grandfather's French lessons fell by the wayside as well.

How would a bourgeois intellectual have reacted in the

same situation? Like a colonized soul who prostrates himself before foreign authority. "*Chaudière?* Ah, you're supposed to say *chaudière?* Excuse us, we didn't know. We always say *fournaise* in Canada. You understand, we're so far from France, and we can't all know how to speak well like you. It's not our fault. And then, the English influence doesn't help. And besides, we have no real culture, it's not like in Europe. Well, if you'll excuse me, I have to go fire up the *chaudière.*" There, it's not hard at all.

The neurotic, the colonized, you don't find them among those good people whom Dor scorns and Falardeau strokes. You find them among the Dors, the Bouchards, and their ilk. These people have read widely, have studied, and imagine that all the Paris waiters have read Proust. They are the ones ashamed of Céline Dion and Jean Chrétien, the first because she has so much money she doesn't know what to do with it and the second because he makes mistakes in French that we forgive Lucien Bouchard.

The French Canadian people are descendants of colonizers, not the colonized. They are a silent people among whom nostalgia for the mother country, a sign of status for the right-minded, means nothing, and for good reason. Take the case of Guillemette Hébert, daughter of Louis, an apothecary and first colonizer of Quebec City, and of Marie Rollet, much appreciated in the young colony for the quality of the beer she brewed. Guillemette was very young when she arrived in Quebec. Her family had no problem surviving the first English occupation of Canada, from 1629 to 1633. They came to an understanding with the new masters, the Kirke brothers, and didn't go back to France like Champlain and the Jesuits because they didn't have the means. The Héberts were at home despite themselves, and here their conduct anticipates that of the sixty thousand inhabitants of 1760.

Grown up, Guillemette married Guillaume Couillard, and their union was a fruitful one. As Allan Greer tells us in his *The People of New France,* when Guillemette Hébert died in 1684, she left behind her no fewer than 143 children, grandchildren, and great-grandchildren. As of 1738, her descendants numbered 689. One per cent of the population, in other words, a fecundity worthy of my grandparents, Elphège and Gertrude.

What I'm getting at here is that no descendant of Guillemette Hébert could have asked her: "Grandmother, what was it like in France?" You can imagine her reply: "I don't know, my boy; I don't know, my girl. It was such a long time ago . . ." All that remained to her of France were the memories of her parents and her husband. Her recollections were above all informed by her Canadian experience, and what came her way via the many arriving ships. She had known the building of the palisade, its consolidation, its anxieties and its self-confidence, its joys and its sorrows. She became Canadian as a matter of course and, so it would seem, was none the worse for it. All her descendants had the same experience, and more. If some returned to the old country they had never seen, it's because they became successful, like Bienville or Anne Hébert. For the descendants of Guillemette it made no difference, French regime or English regime. Canada was the land they had founded, and it still is.

Elphège Poliquin felt inferior to no one. Not superior either. He was himself. A descendant, like many others, of those courageous settlers who had preserved their heritage almost without meaning to. He was not anti-Semitic like the notary on the corner who read *Le Devoir,* and he did a brisk business with the Jews of Three Rivers. He himself didn't speak a word of English, but he was delighted to see his grandchildren speak it with ease. A free and independent man who admired neither the Queen nor France, nor the United States, and harboured no neurotic imaginings concerning Paris waiters who read Proust whereas he did not.

Man that he was, he resembled Françoise in *Remembrance of Things Past* as much as Jean Larose does the Baron of Charlus. I adore this Françoise who, according to little Marcel become big, "demanded only one right as a citizen, that of not pronouncing like the rest of us," and giving words whatever gender she deemed fit. Like her, Elphège made the sort of mistakes in spelling, vocabulary, and gender that elicit cries of rage from the semi-colonized Georges Dor.

Elphège and Gertrude never knew the pangs of statelessness that afflict the Quebec bourgeoisie today. We all remember Denise Bombardier's appearance with Bernard Pivot on French television, when she lit into the sodomitic pedophile Gabriel Matzneff. It went something like: "Know, sir, that I come from a continent where there are laws that punish such behaviour . . ." Never mind the moral status of her pronouncement, because that's not what's at issue here. She said "continent." She did not dare say "Quebec," because it's not a country. Nor did she say Canada; her ideological peers wouldn't have liked that. She preferred "continent," because it smacked of America. Now the French adore America, everyone knows that. Cowboys, Chicago gangsters, Rockefeller, Louis Armstrong, Jerry Lewis, and Marilyn Monroe, it's *chouette!* France, to Charles de Gaulle's distress, was Americanized a long time ago, and that has given us Dick Rivers, Eddy Mitchell, and Johnny Hallyday, who was so skilful at imitating American styles with his versions of Presley and Hendrix and yet so good when he was just French Johnny. Even Sartre dreamed of Buffalo Bill when he was a kid, he tells us so in *The Words,* and who has not heard Yves Montand singing the praises of Gene Kelly?

I don't hold Denise Bombardier's "continent" against her. She was only reflecting the colonized cast of mind of a generation that used to rail against Yankee imperialism and, from one day to the next, rediscovered America. This intellectual generation is acutely aware that, except for a few far-right politicians or old-time Gaullists, France is not the least bit interested in Quebec; it prefers the West, the Rockies, Ontario industry, and the Inuit. It's still on its knees to Faulkner and Michael Jackson. And so our bourgeois intelligentsia has reinvented itself as American.

If you don't believe me, you have only to look at how American is the literary vocabulary in Quebec. In music and in publishing we tie ourselves in knots to show France that Quebec is in fact America. The much-touted reclamation of Jack Kerouac is typical of this new brand of self-colonization, whose thrust is more sycophantic than self-affirming. Yes, he's a status seeker, this colonized Québécois trying his best to please a mother country that's already self-colonized. America, America . . .

The political rhetoric was not long in following suit, with the Free Trade movement leading the way. Lucien Bouchard, in Atlanta, thinks he's being shrewd when he says the Québécois are gaga over Coca-Cola. He's talking for his caste, but I'm not sure he's speaking in the name of all his people.

RECENTLY THERE WAS an amusing instance of colonized language being dealt to us from on high. Newfoundland asked the Canadian Parliament to modify the constitution in order to inscribe there its true designation, Newfoundland and Labrador. This banal request is, in juridical terms, requisite—it's a formality. It's been two hundred years since Newfoundland and Lower Labrador were amalgamated, and it's logical that that be reflected in the country's defining law.

Immediately we were treated to what the journalist Paul Wells amusingly refers to as a unilateral declaration of indignation on the part of Lucien Bouchard. In other words, one of those howls of victimization he executes so well. It was all, apparently, a provocation. Provocation? As though Quebec were Chile, and suddenly cut off from the Andes. Again the foreign reference. The only thing lacking was for Lucien Bouchard to use this border incident as a pretext for massing his troops at the gates of Labrador.

The excitement lasted several days. We were even reminded that the recovery of Labrador was part of the Parti Québécois's original program. The provincial map in Premier Lévesque's office had displayed a Quebec that included Labrador, just as Duplessis had wanted it. Then a few geographers with impeccable nationalist credentials made some embarrassing declarations on the air and in the newspapers. Having studied the question in depth in the 1970s, they had concluded that Newfoundland really did own Labrador, that there had been no cheating or theft, and that the current state of affairs had been dictated by geography and history, not politics.

A bit more fuss was made for form's sake. Bernard Landry threatened to go to court, but then the memory of Hydro-Québec's lucrative contract for the exploitation of the Lower Churchill Falls eventually muted Lucien Bouchard's Balkanish impulses. Money speaks louder than national humiliation, and Monsieur Bouchard quickly reined in his counterfeit indignation.

Three days later, we were on to something else. This time it was Stéphane Dion's Clarity Bill, another "act of aggression against the Quebec nation." Always the foreign turn of phrase. Once colonized . . .

BUT THERE WAS A time, now forgotten, when one dreamed of doing other things, and of cutting Quebec's ties with the mother country for good. It didn't last. "Cuba went down in flames . . ."

The high point of the *joual* "rebellion" was in my opinion the appearance of *It's Your Turn, Laura Cadieux,* by Michel Tremblay. It was a novel written in pure spoken Québécois, without a false note, and yet French. And one could say that if there was a true Memmian liberation that did some good, it was in our literary language. At last, after years of the ersatz French dialogue written by Marcel Dubé and Françoise Loranger, we truly saw ourselves on stage, on television, and in our books.

The revolution was short-lived. The writers of *joual* began to dream of making a splash in France, and cleaned up their act forthwith. In order, of course, to sell over there. They didn't give up on their working-class, Montreal-based subject matter, but they were soon foraging in the dictionaries they'd been deriding so recently. Thus Michel Tremblay adopted a semi-colonized style, beginning a sentence with a few conventionally respectable words, then throwing in a bit of lingo from the old neighbourhood, and finishing off with an ultra-bookish bit of vocabulary. I call that squinting: a wink of one eye to Saint Germain des Prés, a wink of the other to St. Denis Street, so as to be accepted on both shores, obviously. And there you have the style that would characterize all Quebec literature through the 1970s, 1980s, and 1990s. That's not all. Tremblay was called a genius. His abnegation, his return to the fold, was celebrated. It brings to mind what Cocteau said about Frédéric Dard: the brilliant left-handed writer was now writing with his right. Outremont pardoned the delinquent of yore.

Tremblay was not the only one to recover his French virginity. After *L'Hiver de force,* Réjean Ducharme also started to write like a "bourgeois gentleman." Robert Charlebois acquired a slight accent, while losing his voice. And so on. But the champion here, the best Tremblay imitator, is without question Victor-Lévy Beaulieu. He is a writer whose essays and editorials are worthy of note, who in his beginnings was a bad imitator of Céline, and who found a lucrative niche as the reincarnation of Claude-Henri Grignon. With wood-stove TV serials and all.

Here, we're in a perfect semi-colonized world. With Beaulieu, the written and spoken language is hopelessly confused. "I saw the chief of police. The latter is angry with me." It's laughable, of course, because no one talks that way. Except the semi-colonized, naturally. And so you have farmers who speak like notaries, bums who swap passages from de Chateaubriand, a madam who quotes Mallarmé, and so on. But what counts for the author is not believability, or even the picturesque. What counts is to show that he himself has read. Only, his grafts from the great books don't take, in the countrysides or the lanes that he describes. They're just tacked on. This is a colonized imagination in full flight.

All is not lost, however. Yes, there has been a recent, massive return to "fine writing" in our literature, and there is no end of neo-colonized authors flaunting their newly-acquired vocabularies, with narrators who can't get over having discovered the dictionary. But there are also talented writers who employ an appropriate French, make no concessions to France, and write with a Québécois accent that you can hear clearly as you read. I won't name them, because they would never forgive me. In the long run, the liberating effect of the *joual* revolution will have endured.

WHERE DOES THAT leave me? Well, it leaves me with the thought that my own language, my natural idiom, is a Creole of the North, the language spoken every day in the schoolyards and garages of our land. And it's very helpful to know it, especially at the garage. "Monsieur Poliquin," says Gerry the mechanic, *"chauffer* with your wheels all *désenlignées* like that, it's a real *hasard!"* I understand exactly what he's saying, and I myself speak Northern Creole with an ease that can make me look like a character right out of a Michel Tremblay play. And I'm not ashamed of it, any more than I'm ashamed of my grandfather Elphège.

I also speak French, less well but all the same. For me it's a learned language, not the way English is, of course, but still learned. All my life, in my reading, I've come up against words that meant nothing to me. As a child I was distressed to learn that the angelica so coveted by the Sophie of the *Malheurs de Sophie* didn't exist where we lived. I had to wait fifteen years to taste it, and to find out at last what the word really meant.

And it's not over. I'm still learning this language that always eludes me a little. On my forty-second birthday a friend gave me a little lesson in the pronunciation of a very simple word. I'm not surprised to see *Le Devoir* mixing up words, and I'm more understanding of Lucien Bouchard than I appear.

I will navigate all my life between my Northern Creole and French, without being embarrassed by it. Diglossia is a perfectly natural condition, after all.

SOME WILL SAY that I am too hard on the poor nationalists, that I treat them like caricatures. Let me assure those bleeding hearts that the other side is just as hard on us. And it's about time it learned that so-called English Canada, over the same period, lived through its own decolonization movement, with its own parallel recolonization. And the tug-of-war is still going on. Let's take a little tour over there. It will boost our morale, if nothing else.

~ The Other Side of the
   Looking-Glass

I TAKE THE FLOOR at a nationalist gathering.

"I'm going to talk to you about a village we all know well. About two hundred souls where, thirty years ago, there were two thousand. A church, a post office, two stores, a drug store where they sell more sardines than medicine, a bar that is well-stocked on the first of the month especially, when the welfare cheques are due.

"There are no more than ten or so farmers left in the district, and their sons are regular clients of the bar's table dancers. Everyone lives poorly; the only agriculture now is subsistence agriculture, like in the old days. As for the neighbours, they're vacationing city-dwellers who come to roll around in poultry dung in the summer or do cross-country skiing in the winter, and these would-be pioneers have had the gall to plant pines and fir trees where once there were beautiful furrows. The hippie return to the land has gone bourgeois.

"Once there was an industry here, prosperous enough to give people work in the summer so they could get unemployment insurance in the winter, but it had to close its doors after gobbling up several federal grants. The road leading to the village is in disrepair; travellers prefer the highway that passes twenty kilometres to the south. There are a few lakes in the area where there are water-skiing competitions in the summer and snowmobile races in the winter, exasperating the city-dwellers who are dismayed that the expensive summer homes they've had built are at all times of the year besieged by noise. Their owners, the McKeowns, the Millers, the Cohens, and the Matwichuks, protest to the town council, but never get any action.

"The farmers are not very friendly, the old priest will tell you that himself. His church is almost empty, and is used mainly for burials. The only civil servant in town is a social worker with a big heart but too much to do. He asked for a transfer three years ago but is still waiting. The poor fellow can no longer bear to see this once well-off village wither away from boredom and despair. Exactly half the population is on social assistance or one form or another of government charity. One out of three families is single-parent. In every family, an alcoholic; in a third of them, one or more cases of incest. The mayor himself, a retired postman and notorious drunk, was accused last year of having assaulted his grandson. Out of shame, he didn't run again in the elections but he was elected all the same, by acclamation, because no one wanted the non-paying job.

"If you really want to get depressed, you can go there for the national holiday. You'll see boys with slicked-down hair, in white T-shirts and jeans, a pack of cigarettes between sleeve and biceps. They're the same ones who sleep on the worn couches that you put out on the veranda in summer. While they munch greasy fries and drink beer from the bottle, they talk of the cars they've already had or that they're going to buy for cash when they win the lottery. To kill time they paw the rear-ends of the girls or chat up the girls of their friends, then get into fights that will be patched up later after a good binge. The girls, as you may have guessed, have false teeth just like their boyfriends, and hair like Farrah Fawcett. Heavily made up and decorated like Christmas trees, they look cheap. Their one edge over the boys is that they talk of getting the hell away from here, and they often do leave so as to escape the guys who beat them.

"Everyone chews gum . . ."

"Enough, for God's sake!" you cry. "Stop insulting our exploited, colonized, humiliated people! Damn you! It's just like a sushi-eating intellectual who turns up his nose at our mothers' pigs-feet stew to spew out abominations like that!"

Relax, ladies and gentlemen. Your knee-jerk indignation has given you a bum steer. Who said I was talking about a Quebec village? The town in question, which I will call East Gull, is fifteen kilometres from Kingston, in Ontario. It was originally a Loyalist settlement, populated mostly by Irish families in the nineteenth century. No French Canadian has ever lived there. Until the 1960s, agriculture flourished, and then things changed. The old priest is a recently arrived Pole, and the rumour is that he won't stay long. Nor did the last one, a Vietnamese.

Yes, there are damaged towns in Ontario with their share of unemployed, property owners too old to leave, and broken families, and whose sole revenue comes from fussy holidayers. Yes, there are millions of Canadians who are poor and speak English, often badly, and who can't expect much from their representatives. In New Brunswick, Newfoundland, Manitoba, everywhere.

Poor English? Impossible! No, they all drive Mercedes and live in big West Island mansions, everyone knows that. In their factories they make the poor colonized employees work their fingers to the bone for starvation wages, while the boss's sons take advantage of their daughters when they're not slaving as maids. The foreman, a monster who speaks part English, part French, is called Trudeau or Chrétien. Yes, there are still English, and they're in league with the Jews, and they're all against us. Boo-hoo-hoo! And there you go. You have in hand Pierre Falardeau's next script (and the last and the one before that, too) or tomorrow's column by Pierre Bourgault in the *Journal de Montréal.*

If Bouchard, Falardeau, or Larose denigrate so-called English Canada, it's because this fiction feeds their self-colonized fantasies. You have to despise your imagined enemy to really feel that he exists; the trumped-up hatred of the Other is what keeps one going. And you have to know as little about him as possible for fear of discovering that reality is not what it used to be. Otherwise the whole neo-colonized structure is liable to collapse. Above all you must refuse to read that country's writers, because that's how the self-styled oppressed show contempt for their imagined persecutors.

And it works! We do not read Laurence or Davies, we turn up our noses at Glenn Gould and Atom Egoyan, we pretend the country doesn't exist. There are of course a few ecumenical spirits who break the mould, but they are in the minority. Most frequently, all collaboration is actively discouraged, nor do you venture into the Other's territory for fear of coming back changed. And if you do so, you'd better, when you return, show clearly which side you're on, like Robert Lepage who, back from Ottawa, sided publicly with those who vote yes. The weight of numbers will have its due. Robert, you're a good boy at heart, that is, someone who defers to the collectivity.

I WAS BORN ON the other side of the looking-glass.

I went to high school in Ottawa during the 1960s. In English class we read Shakespeare, Coleridge, Byron, Twain.

Almost never a Canadian writer. Here and there, perhaps, a poem by Bliss Carman, today legitimately forgotten, or a novel by Hugh MacLennan, now of only historical interest. Our literary references were all foreign, as was the case for music and painting. The same for film, except for a few National Film Board documentaries that bored us stiff. You would have thought that anglophone Canada had nothing to say for itself, that it was a culture whose proper names didn't belong to us.

In this proudly colonized environment, my elders went dancing at the Empire Hotel, dined at the Queen Elizabeth, took King Edward Street to join the Queensway. Canada was a British colony and proud of it, with its borrowed flag and no constitution of its own. A white country, very white, where the Chinese were restricted to their laundries and their restaurants, where anti-Semitism and English clubs were into their last days, where segregation of Blacks in Nova Scotia schools had just been abolished, and where Native Canadians, the only authentically colonized people in Canada in the Memmian sense of the word, had only had the vote since 1960 and languished quietly in reserves where alcoholism ran rampant. The Italians paved the Ottawa streets while waiting to open their restaurants, and we accused them unjustly of being dirty and dishonest. The only cultural institutions with a bit of life in them were radio and television, where to succeed you needed a British or mid-Atlantic accent.

I remember a certain lady, daughter of a prominent Westmount family, who, the evening of her wedding, had found draped over her marriage bed a huge Union Jack. She also told me that when she informed her guests that she and her husband would be spending their honeymoon in England, people said, "So you're going back? Isn't that lovely!" Not going to the mother country, going back. You can appreciate, I hope, that

that particular Canada does not make me nostalgic in the least—and in that I am not alone.

Then the earth moved, but as always in Canada, no one noticed. Here, these things only register later on. The one obvious sign of this secret revolution was the adoption by the Pearson government of the new national flag, and that after a bitter struggle. The flag debate in the House of Commons, the most acrimonious in our parliamentary history, lasted eighteen months, and the Conservatives didn't hesitate to call the proposed replacement for the Union Jack a "rag." Never have so many insults been bandied about in Parliament. And when the flag was eventually raised, the leader of Her Majesty's Loyal Opposition, John Diefenbaker, averted his eyes. Looking back now, it's either a laughing matter or one impossible to comprehend. It was yesterday, and thank God for that.

English-Canadian universities were pathetically colonized, to their core. When they weren't aping Oxford, they were imitating Harvard, and badly. In one Western university, in the Sociology Department, seventeen professors out of twenty had American degrees; the three remaining were British. One suspects that all their methods and references had more to do with Chicago than Winnipeg.

In a Department of French Studies with which I was familiar, the professors were French, New Zealanders, Canadians, Scots, and Americans. Not a single Québécois. No Quebec books, either, that goes without saying. It was a time when Jean Éthier-Blais himself, at Carleton and then McGill, denied the existence of a French literature in Canada. To students who wanted to discuss Marie-Claire Blais, one replied, But why? We already have Balzac, Georges Sand, and so on. Our writers were not even on the program at the University of Montreal, Laval University, or anywhere else. Yes, times were hard.

I don't know who woke up first, but suddenly a whole generation found its voice. Our cinema saw the light of day, and a young man from Ottawa called Matt Cohen published a first novel in Toronto edited by a poet who was going to make a name for herself, Margaret Atwood. They were both about the same age as Réjean Ducharme and Marie-Claire Blais.

Before Cohen and Atwood, and a whole group that was going to enhance the reputation of English-speaking Canadian literature, we hardly knew anyone other than W. O. Mitchell, a kind of grandfather of letters analogous to Gratien Gélinas in Quebec. He had given us a first novel set in the prairies, called *Who Has Seen the Wind,* and would be a mentor to the first great writers out of the West, Wiebe and Kroetsch. Then everything happened at the same time. There were Margaret Laurence and Robertson Davies, a bit older than these young Turks but no less dazzling, then Govier, Ondaatje, Marian Engel, Dennis Lee, a surprisingly long list.

In December 1999 I was at Matt Cohen's funeral, and I can assure you that it was touching to see around his coffin all those who had contributed to the literary decolonization of Canada. Now they are prosperous, celebrated in Hollywood, like Ondaatje, or the subjects of Sorbonne theses, like Atwood. Who can today deny the existence of this literature? No one, not even Canadians themselves, which is saying a lot.

Today, whatever may be said by Lucien Bouchard, who as someone who never left the Saguenay before he was forty-five is not particularly well-informed, Canada exists, and it has a lively culture to prove it. In song, cinema, television, radio, it is brimming with confidence. Obviously, for a nationalist of the stripe of Lesieur or Bouchard, the country remains primitive, or at best a pale American copy where one eats and dresses badly. But this sort of nationalist doesn't get out much and when he does open his eyes, despite himself, he carefully avoids looking west of the Outaouais or east of the Gaspé peninsula for fear of being refuted by what others have clearly seen.

That said, this decolonization of English-speaking Canada did not come easily, and you would have to be pretty naïve to consider it complete. The same Canadians who took so many years to accept their own flag for a long time resisted their own evolution. Many only resigned themselves reluctantly to the 1982 Constitution, because they thought it was just fine where it was, in London. What do you expect? Former colonies are fertile ground for conservatism. Just look at our place names, which evolve with the speed of an iceberg.

In Quebec, for example, we jealously hold on to the Chemin du Roy, the Place Royale with its bust of Louis XIV, d'Aiguillon and d'Auteuil Streets, the Auberges du Gouverneur, all symbols of a (neglectful) monarchy. The province has even endowed its flag with the monarchy's colours, a white fleur-de-lys on a blue background, a remarkable display of loyalty considering it was in no way reciprocated. It's like a cuckolded knight who insists on defending the honour of his lady.

It doesn't surprise me either to find loyalist or monarchist nomenclatures in Ontario or Nova Scotia: Kingston, Queen's Quay, Regency Park, Victoria, etc. On this point, however, Canadians are no more colonized than anyone else. The Americans have conserved many colonial vestiges in New England. For example, Massachusetts and some other States are still called "Commonwealths," harking back to the Puritan Cromwell. They have retained the names of French colonizers in the Midwest and Louisiana: the names of cities such as Des Moines, Roseau, and Baton Rouge; the names of cars such as Marquette, LaSalle, and Cadillac, all luxury models; and the names of men—the Governor of Montana is Marc Racicot, Ronald

Reagan was born on Hennepin Street in Dixon, Senator Landrieux and Senator Breaux are from Louisiana. Not to mention the extensive Spanish heritage in New Mexico and California. Such is the North American continent. It continues to honour its pioneers, but doesn't know anything about them. In this, Ontario and Quebec are within the norm.

This toponymic cryogeny extends to other ethnic groups determined to glorify what they have left behind. Kitchener, once Berlin, still rowdily celebrates its Oktoberfest, the Portuguese avidly follow the football played in their mother country, the Irish fiercely defend their culture even though they express it in the English language, the Chinese celebrate the dragon, Jamaicans and Haitians recreate their costumes and dances on our shores as though they'd just arrived here yesterday. All this appealing behaviour is very Canadian.

Bad news for the nationalists, however: English Canada does not exist. Or at least, hardly anything remains. It's either dead or very old. Jacques Ferron, in 1946, was able to describe the English in these terms: "The English are inoffensive people. As long as they have beefsteak to eat from the Atlantic to the Pacific, they're happy. When they talk to you, if you cannot answer them in their own language, they're astonished because you're giving them something to eat that is not beefsteak. They don't get angry. No sooner do they show their disapproval than they smile, just as they hasten to adulterate everything they eat with a hot sauce." If he were to return from the dead, Ferron would be very disappointed, because the English are not what they were. But I daresay he would not complain. Except that he too was fond of his stereotypes, just as some Scots are of their pompommed tartan berets.

Just a few years ago, however, a few die-hards were challenging the adoption of the metric system, for them the ultimate outrage perpetrated by the devil Pierre Trudeau in his campaign to Frenchify everything. In 1984 there was still a service station in the Ottawa area that sold gas by the gallon to defy the authorities. Such last stands make us smile today, when even Ontario awarded itself a black lieutenant-governor not long ago, while that of British Columbia was Chinese. When Kingston celebrated its Loyalist bicentenary in 1984, a mayor with a Greek name welcomed the Queen of England.

The statistics speak volumes. In 1947, eighty per cent of Toronto's population came from the British Isles. Today only half its inhabitants are white. There are no more than 739,000 Anglicans in Canada; they lost 277,000 adherents and closed 523 churches between 1985 and 1997. According to sociologist Reg Bibby, of the University of Alberta, there will only be 100,000 practising Anglicans left in 2015. These Anglicans are the same English mocked by Ferron, and still feared by behind-the-times nationalists.

I have a young friend who makes for a good example. She is Cindy Runzer from Red Deer in Alberta, and her French is far better than that of PQ minister Guy Chevrette (which isn't saying much, I agree, but all the same . . .). Her maternal grandfather was English, her maternal grandmother, Finnish. On her father's side, a Romanian and an Austrian. Four major ethnic groups come together, then, in my friend Cindy, which perhaps explains why she's so pretty. To a nationalist who's still back with Ferron, however, she's still English. As in "damned English." Cindy calls herself Canadian, which makes sense, as she can't swear allegiance to any one ethnic group. Abbé Groulx, in his time, wouldn't have been pleased.

And that's not the end of it. The day is not far off when, given the high Native Canadian birth rate, the mother tongue of the Saskatchewan premier will be Cree. British Columbia's premier is already from the Punjab. The mayor of Winnipeg, today an avowed and proud homosexual, tomorrow will be Ojibway, and that of Vancouver will have a Japanese name. In this light, to continue talking in terms of English Canada reeks of stupidity, bad faith, and ignorance.

Besides, it feels good living in this new Canada. You eat better, for one thing, and have many more things to eat. In my native Sandy Hill there was, not long ago, a greasy spoon on Wilbrod Street where you could get hamburgers and passable club sandwiches—what is called, doubtless as a joke, "Canadian cuisine." It became a Chinese restaurant, then was bought by a Peruvian who served Argentine and Tex-Mex dishes. Now it's a Somalian restaurant. Everywhere you see the same evolution, the same diversity, more hospitable than troubling.

No, Canada is no longer very English. That's just what's dreaded by the militants of APEC—the Alliance for the Preservation of English in Canada—an outfit that has been the butt of Mordecai Richler's sarcasm, just like the Office de la langue française. There are some interesting people in that crowd. One of its prominent members has even written a book that exposes the plot being hatched by the Québécois to infiltrate Canada and make it totally French. Thus, during the war, camps were set up in northern Quebec where fertile French Canadians were ordered to procreate on demand and inundate Canada with little Jean-Baptistes. Rare are those citizens who do not roll around on the ground laughing when they hear such paranoid ravings.

Theirs is the apocalyptic vision of a dying culture. You have only to attend an APEC meeting to see the age of the members. The room is filled with heads white or bald, many sets of false teeth—nothing very dangerous. Of course these rancorous elders love to repeat how bilingualism spelled the death of the Armed Forces and the Mounted Police, how someone they knew lost his job in the civil service because he didn't speak

French, and so on. But the revulsion of these senescent loyalists isn't reserved only for francophones. They feel the same way about taxi drivers who wear turbans or TV newscasters with Middle-Eastern features.

So is that gang dangerous? It's in the interests of the nationalists to believe they are, and to make us think so, but there's nothing to it. Until the 1980s you could still get elected in New Brunswick by presenting openly anti-French resolutions in the legislature. Twenty years later that's unthinkable. Of course, there will always be loyalist outbreaks, but rarely will they amount to much. There is still the Canadian Alliance, you will tell me, and with reason, because its Reformist predecessor demanded the abolition of the Official Languages Act. But its opposition to State bilingualism barely had any impact except in Alberta, and its members ever since have been turning cartwheels trying to wipe from our memory those evil tendencies. They've realized that tolerance pays better dividends at the ballot box than hatred does. When generosity becomes more advantageous than intolerance, it has a future.

If there is still a Ferronesque English Canada today, you'll find it largely in the comic novels of Robertson Davies, with their tea-drinking damsels and sherry-sipping clergymen. Davies painted a brilliant portrait of this colonial society that was on its last legs but didn't know it. It was an act of parricidal burial whose ironic tone, though without a sense of regret, recalls the disappearance of that small class of Jewish immigrants lost to bourgeois living, the class described by the no less talented Mordecai Richler.

BUT DON'T TALK to Lucien Bouchard or Pierre Falardeau about any of that. You'd be wasting your words. Their demagogy can't survive without victimization by good old English Canada.

Let's take another look at Jacques Godbout's *The Black Sheep*. A revealing scene: Jacques Parizeau enters the offices of the *Toronto Star* to meet the editorial team. He is very much himself—that is, robust, kingly, serenely confident, and totally at ease in this bastion tailor-made for great financial movers and shakers. Suddenly the manager of the *Star,* John Honderich, says: "Monsieur Parizeau, I can't get over it . . . You say this is the first time you've ever set foot in Toronto?" Imperturbable, the Quebecker replies yes.

Remember, Monsieur Parizeau was well over sixty years old at that point. This Oxford-educated scholar, who was for a long time Finance Minister in Quebec, had never seen Toronto. He prides himself, mind you, on his knowledge of the City of London and Wall Street. But Toronto? No thank you. The same man has many times told the story of his journey from Montreal to Banff in 1967. He got on the train a federalist and got off a separatist. Along the way he saw the Loyalist red brick farmhouses of Southern Ontario, the Ukrainian isbas of Manitoba, the teepees of Saskatchewan, and the ranches of Alberta. He then concluded that such diversity was ungovernable, and above all foreign to Quebec. So, burn all bridges, and let everyone go his own way. Free at last of such pointless interdependences, Quebec would light out for a brighter future.

One thing about Jacques Parizeau: he must have incredible eyesight to have seen so much from so far away. Chances are, however, that he didn't often get off that train, and that he didn't fraternize more than he had to with his fellow citizens. Nothing scornful in this attitude, just the ingrained haughtiness of a grand bourgeois who knows he belongs to a superior civilization. A superior caste as well.

So far so good, he's free to assume whatever stance he likes.

One thing is sure, no one will accuse him of being open-minded or curious about his fellow man. If he's decided to slam the door in his neighbour's face, that's up to him. The problem is that Jacques Parizeau has frequently taken it upon himself to interpret English Canada to the Québécois. An inexcusable presumption, since he doesn't know anything about it. A Quebec student who has spent one summer washing dishes in Banff knows more than he does.

Parizeau hasn't read Alice Munro, who could have taught him that her Loyalist Huronia, with its hard past and precarious existence, has more in common with Victor-Lévy Beaulieu's Lower St. Lawrence than with Yorkshire. Digging a little deeper, he would have found that the perspectives and interests of auto workers in Oshawa and Sainte-Thérèse are very similar. But no, he wraps himself in his aristocratic iciness and majestically turns his back. And his Canadian remains an Englishman in a bowler hat whose ancestors were ardent conquerors. His cartoonesque vision, with its Ferronian embroidery, is still intact.

The other problem is that he is not alone with his biases. A few years ago a Montreal columnist admitted on Toronto television that she knew nothing about English Canadian literature. She'd read a bit of Atwood, but clearly not much, as she confused that Margaret with the great Margaret Laurence, who wrote so many masterpieces. No, the name meant nothing to her. She was proud of her indifference, and for the first time in my life I saw an intelligent and cultivated woman vaunting her ignorance. And there are many like her among Quebec's intellectual bourgeoisie, where for one very ecumenical Gilles Pellerin, there are a hundred who pride themselves on what they don't want to know, and who will tell you with a smile that they have read the not-to-be-missed Garcia Marquez but not the equally not-to-be-missed Davies.

Here we see in action the national correctness that enjoins us not only to refuse knowledge of the Other, but also to let him see how much we don't want to know him, so we can show him how much we don't need him. We must express no interest in the films of Atom Egoyan, in the Group of Seven, in Ondaatje's novels, for fear of seeming to collaborate with the enemy. Otherwise we risk the penalty reserved for those guilty of favouring, through their degenerate inclinations, Canadian unity, a crime harshly punished behind the nationalist palisade. I mean, who knows? Someone might not greet you at the bistro l'Express, or the person at the next table in the Café Laurier might ask to be reseated. It's no laughing matter.

No, above all don't read the Other. He's the conqueror, after all. Even if Rohinton Mistry and Emily Carr had nothing to do with the American rangers who laid waste to Charlevoix in 1759. We must hang on to the status quo at all costs: you are the master, I'm still the vanquished, and the day will dawn when you will no long be master but I will. Meanwhile I'll be the orphan who self-colonizes his mind with references and aspirations made in France.

The most cartoonesque intellectual in Quebec, Pierre Falardeau, who has received grants from both the NFB and Telefilm Canada, refused to present his film at the Toronto Film Festival because, he said, the dice were loaded. As he wasn't going to be given a prize for his film *October,* three-quarters financed by Canadian taxpayers, he wouldn't go to Toronto. An intrepid man, this, who shuns risk and criticism to wall himself in behind the logic of self-aggrandizing martyrdom. We understand. One must never miss an opportunity to pose as a victim, martyr, loser. On the other hand, Falardeau, true to form in his colonized fashion, was tickled pink with his little prize at the Festival of Quebec Cinema in Blois.

The intellectual bourgeoisie, saving a few notable exceptions to whom I would gladly pay tribute were I not afraid of bringing them to the attention of the palisade's watchdogs, live in horror of Canada. For ideological reasons, of course, which have everything to do with a false, Memmi-inspired psychology (there are days when poor Albert must tell himself that these unfortunate souls have understood nothing . . .), and have nothing at all to do with open-mindedness. Let's have a look at a passage from Jean Larose, author of *La Petite Noirceur.*

Jean Larose is to my mind one of the most courageous intellectuals within the nationalist palisade, a learned iconoclast of which there are too few. He has, for instance, denounced that ideology of resentment that corrupts the idea of Quebec independence. And he's right. To want to found a country on imaginary or outdated grievances is to march into history backwards.

Here is his argument. For him, Canada represents dullness and mediocrity. The only exception is Glenn Gould, but even his genius cannot compensate for our appalling stupidity. This country is fine for refugees and others who are the wretched of the earth, but it is drab and devoid of imagination. English Canadians? Poor folk who are like the Québécois, only worse, and who are like that in English to boot. And the poor Québécois, with their "Latino-Iroquois blood," who have to put up with it all . . . Listen to him: "We must be ashamed to be Canadian, and we must keep faith with our loathing . . . It is up to us to ensure that the word 'Canada' (what an unsavoury collection of syllables, don't you find?) becomes synonymous in every land with complacent obtuseness." Larose seems to have gone to the same school as Pierre Falardeau.

"Latino-Iroquois blood," no less! Larose too refuses to know Canada and advocates ignorance and scorn. No argument could be more nationally correct than his. When the best minds of Quebec indulge in a demagogy so low, so simplistic, they betray the vocation of the intellectual—a vocation whose mission, if we are to believe de Gaulle, is to fight prejudice. No wonder Lucien Bouchard has had such a brilliant career.

Bouchard too makes hay with an English Canada about which he knows nothing. This man, who learned English at forty, and let it be said very well, first came into contact with his fellow citizens at the same age. And again, it was through the glass of a ministerial limousine. He too believes that the English are still there. He doesn't know that English Canada, in the ethnic sense of the word, is no more, and that if Canada is predominantly English-speaking, its culture no longer has anything to do with sliced white bread, overcooked roast beef, potatoes, and Yorkshire pudding.

Bouchard didn't get out of his limousine any more than Parizeau got off the train. He too requires this fiction for his demagogic arsenal. Parizeau and his circle claim that the English, who are people who know perfectly well what's good for them (still and always the cartoonesque view that here conjures a Briton with a cold, calculating, and materialist heart, devoid of emotion, doubtless with a frigid but rich wife), will negotiate a new economic relationship with Quebec, and the question of the national debt, among other minutiae, will be resolved in three weeks. That is exactly what Parizeau said to a hall full of students, and to the great astonishment of Mordecai Richler, they seemed to take him at his word. Bouchard says virtually the same thing. "We will vote yes," he proclaimed in 1995, "and at last negotiate people to people!" But with what people? There is no Canadian people, there are peoples in Canada, and they don't all talk with the same voice.

Quebec leaders and intellectuals, with their cartoonesque picture of the world, make some dubious and surprising errors in judgement for people whose task is to make sense of life's complexities. To achieve their short-term political goals, they prefer—and in this they are acting like demagogues—to ignore all diversity and throw everything into one conceptual basket. They are applying to the Other what Proust called a "Hindu vision," endowing English Canadians with the virtues of a superior caste. Once again they are turning human beings into inanimate monoliths with no heterogeneity, no free will. The Québécois will do this, the English Canadians will think that, and so on. It is an intellectualized, abstract view of the world, condescending where human beings are concerned, and above all wonderfully convenient. It makes everything so simple! And puerile. Nationalism, again, as the political embodiment of adolescence.

~ The Village

"CANADA" IS A Huron word that means "village." That's something I will never forget.

One day I found myself in a Kingston restaurant with my good friend, the writer and translator Wayne Grady. We were talking about literature, as usual. Among other things, Jacques Cabot's clever thesis concerning the American novel: that it was a Miltonian fable of *Paradise Lost* where the good sheriff always gets the better of the bad guys. I then asked him how he would define the Canadian novel (about which I knew nothing.) His reply: the Canadian novel is the story of a village.

I decided to check it out. I read the Canadian novel. Wayne was right. One of the first Canadian poems, by Oliver Goldsmith, has for its subject the construction of a village: "While now the Rising Village claims a name / Its limits still increase and still its fame . . ." The first English-language novel written in America is the work of Frances Brooke, *The History of Emily Montague*. Here are recounted the joys and sorrows of the village called Quebec. (The author was the wife of a pastor who had followed Wolfe's army to Quebec, and who, like so many founders and eminent citizens, went back to the mother country to die.)

But Wayne was only half right. The story of a village, yes, but told by only one voice. The entire Canadian novel is the chronicle of an inert village, where the narrator carries on a dialectical relationship with a restrictive world: the pastor covets in vain the doctor's wife, the butcher dreams of seeking his fortune elsewhere without ever bringing himself to do so, and all the great struggles are silent or underground. It's the humorous tales set in Stephen Leacock's Mariposa, Margaret Laurence's Manawaka novels, Matt Cohen's Salem, Davies's Deptford, the yuppie Toronto of Atwood. It's a village where everyone is in everyone else's pocket, and where the stifling atmosphere plays on the mind and blocks the way to the prospect of another life. One survives only because the wide open spaces are close at hand. Sinclair Ross's brilliant novel *As For Me and My House* is essential reading, as it anticipates all the others.

Fortunately and unfortunately, Canadians have not left the village behind. They have of course retained their pioneer culture, receptive to new initiatives and the outside world, but that hemmed-in feeling that makes them uneasy leads them at times to long for an American future that would supplant their British past. And so they are always, to one degree or another, vulnerable to colonization.

That said, to be Canadian is to come to terms with a precarious situation. To accept, for example, that the lure of elsewhere will always be a strong magnet for our talents. The Bells, Pickfords, and Neil Youngs will depart, that's the way it is. The Riopelles, Leclercs, and Héberts leave us for a long time too, and come back when they are old, their work done. Researchers and artists find in exile a more promising outlet for their gifts. The urge to move on is a powerful one, it has always been so, yet this siren song does not preclude great accomplishments.

On the contrary. The pioneer culture of the village, which was an outgrowth of the State, led Canadians to cultivate a communalism unknown in the United States. It is without doubt our most distinguishing feature. The cold and the isolation generated a creative approach to community that has almost no equivalent elsewhere. One need only look at our health insurance, the State monopoly on alcohol, State television, the universality of education and old-age pensions. It is a solidarity that counterbalances the precariousness that expatriates our old people and our best and brightest to Florida and California. Thus I accept that my old aunt lives in Miami with her son the astrophysicist; but I also accept that the State takes care of me without charge and subsidizes the books I read. So there.

But this Canadian, who is heir to an Anglo-Saxon, rum-running libertarianism that goes way back, no longer tolerates anyone telling him what to think, and in this respect the dictatorship of the village has met its match in the individual's private domain. There are inviolable zones where this sometimes onerous solidarity cannot penetrate: the voting booth, the bedroom, the non-conformist thinker's inkwell . . .

One thing is sure, the Canadian village does not care for the individualist, America's invisible monarch. By individualist I mean the neighbourhood nuisance with the cottage down the road who pollutes the lake with his big vulgar pink yacht and empties it of its fish with a net, and then goes on to destroy the silence with his bloody lawnmower and his radio going full blast, and I forgot to mention his uncouth, marauding dog that barks at the neighbours' children. And if you offer the slightest rebuke to this odious character, he retorts in his ropy voice that he lives in a free country, that he is sole master in his own house, and that he doesn't owe anybody anything. No, that sort of individualist violates our community rules, and he would be better off emigrating to the States.

The communal spirit that gave rise to affordable hospitals and universities also created Ontario Hydro. Electricity was nationalized in Ontario because we didn't want this natural resource to fall into the hands of private interests that cared nothing for the common good, as happened in the United States. Therefore it had to belong to everyone. This was in 1906. Note that the operation took place without the injection of any nationalist fervour, unlike sixty years later with Hydro-Québec. Today, unfortunately, under Mike Harris, the dominant free-market ideology has given private interests carte blanche.

This village has its charms, it goes without saying. With its shaded streets named after forgotten political figures, its mani-cured lawns richly bordered with flowers, its brick houses lined up one next to the other. Whether in the city or the countryside, people are friendly, and they willingly help each other out, pushing a car out of the snow or looking for a lost dog. Every-one is polite, as foreign visitors will confirm, polite to the point of hypocrisy: the same neighbour who has denounced you to the police because your cat is howling at night will not hesitate to give you a helping hand.

This instinctive solidarity is not just English Canadian—we find it in Quebec as well. English and French villages share an ingrained conviviality which is rooted on both sides in a long-standing northernness and rural heritage. The isolation our ancestors experienced for so long consolidated not only our traditions of community cooperation, but also modes of behav-iour that are remarkably similar on both sides of the linguistic divide.

Thus, I have often heard English Canadians refer to them-selves as "hewers of wood and drawers of water," when deploring the arrogance of American big business. It always surprised me, as I had assumed those words belonged only to the Québécois and to Miron. I was also struck by the tradition of English-Canadian politeness, which can be traced back to a long history in the countryside. These are people who do not complain when the food is bad in a restaurant; they hold their tongue because otherwise the place might close down, and then there would be no other place to dine. At the theatre we applaud even if the play is wretched; to boo is not Canadian, nor Québécois. At the movies, when the film breaks, we protest for form's sake and then line up in silence to be reimbursed. We don't gripe when the train is late; we rage inside, but on the outside we make allowances for the company, which does what it can. We remain polite even when we have no choice but to complain. We don't take up too much space, we do not disturb.

Pierre Bourgault, playing at being a sociologist in the tradition of Memmi, has described the colonized behaviour of the Québécois in the following terms: "Our attitudes are colonized. When a film breaks, we wait. In a restaurant, we wait to be served. The Québécois are fearful and lack self-confidence." He didn't know it, but he was describing a typical Torontonian, who, like the Montrealer, is a country boy transplanted to the city. Only a very old-stock Montrealer will storm out of a restaurant in the middle of a meal, yelling back at the head waiter that he will never again set foot in that dump; a fourth-generation Torontonian might do the same, the difference being that he would also ask to be reimbursed.

This village has its unpleasant aspects, of course. I don't like its outspoken trumpeting of the "community," where it finds its quiet little creature comforts and its family values, always favourably compared with those of others who are different. "We live in such a nice community and we want to keep it that way . . ." When I hear that, I want to climb the walls. Just as I shuddered while watching Atom Egoyan's *The Sweet Hereafter,* when one of the characters, unhappy with an overly intrusive lawyer, murmurs "We have to go back to what we were: a community . . ." This "community," both country village and city neighbourhood, which is silent on incest and censures the poor, is the one that for so long excluded Native people, hounded homosexuals, and refused French schools; it also forced painters into exile and accused the great Margaret Laurence of immorality. No, if there is one English usage that I actively dislike, it's that connotation of "community."

Fortunately, the "community" has changed, it's learned to adapt. It now sends its children to French immersion classes, it keeps its hands off gays, and it tolerates more abortion clinics. More and more the private person, in the words of Madame de Sévigné, is able to live in balance with the collectivity. We call that a "Canadian compromise," the marriage of individual rights and collective obligations.

But Canada has not completed its cultural decolonization. Hollywood and Wall Street will be powers to contend with for a long time, while ideological continentalism continues to make gains. We saw it only recently in Ontario, with Mike Harris and electricity. Soon he will be taking aim at medicine, like his friend Ralph Klein in Alberta. After that it will be free schooling. Harris dreams even of privatizing correctional services, which is to my mind the height of madness. He has already succeeded in setting up moral boot camps for young offenders, just like in the United States. One wonders when the American kowtowing will stop.

Not tomorrow. Big money, English yesterday and American today, has always favoured the implantation of a branch-plant ideology that considers it normal for major decisions affecting Chicoutimi and Oshawa to be taken in Pittsburgh or Atlanta. In that light, Stockwell Day and Lucien Bouchard go down on their knees together, the difference being that Bouchard boasts about it.

There are parallels to be drawn in any case between the Alliance in the West and Quebec nationalism, in the sense that the two ideologies share a supremely calcified conservatism, plus boundless admiration for the United States. Nationalism has always called for the *statu quo ante,* whether it be the re-establishment of French freedoms at the time of the Patriotes in the eighteenth century, or a return to the Confederation wanted by René Lévesque or more recently Jean-François Lisée. At their end, Canadian conservatives also want to turn back the clock, to the time when mama sent us off to school with a good warm bowl of porridge in our belly (in the words of Mike Harris . . .). When you come down to it, Day and Bouchard are fighting the same fight. Their future consists essentially of memories.

The branch-plant ideology hastens continentalization, as Brian Mulroney's Free Trade Agreement showed so well. Here, the Alliance Party is in the vanguard. It is a political organization shot through with individuals colonized by, and in awe of, the United States. Their arguments are overrun with Americanisms, as though they've never consumed anything but Californian radio and tv. For them, the Holiday Inn took over from the Empire Hotel a long time ago. It's not surprising, given the West's porous border. Cross-border exchanges in the region were common long before Confederation. And for years educators in Saskatchewan and British Columbia found it more practical and less costly to get their training in Saint Louis or Seattle. It was to be expected. Then radio and television came along, and the West continued its Americanization.

Today the Alliance supporters, former Reformers, call for the Senate to be elected and equal, and demand parliamentary hearings for Cabinet nominations—two quintessentially American procedures. Two senators for Alberta and two for Newfoundland, and on television members of Parliament grilling an aspirant to the Supreme Court, free to vote against her if she comes out in favour of abortion and French schools. These good people are in thrall to the American model.

Their branch-plant fires are stoked by the press of Conrad Black, who wouldn't hesitate, should the moment come, to lend his newspapers to the cause of annexation. That said, the prospect of a voluntary merger doesn't frighten many people, and there are few now among us so naïve as to contend that a commonality of language would suffice to facilitate such a coming together. No more than Guatemala would wish to be attached to Mexico just because the two countries are Spanish-speaking. Canadian culture is a more powerful antidote than one may think to the annexationist yearnings of our most influential and least patriotic citizens.

Certainly, the free-market ideologues will continue their fight as long as Canada is not totally Americanized. Their only obstacle: a population that is obscurely aware of its uniqueness, and that will refuse total amalgamation. It may love American movies, just as we do in Quebec, but it will hang on to its communal, pioneer origins, because that's what is in its best interests.

Fragile, more livable today than yesterday, and always uneasy, the village is holding its ground.

~ The Palisade

OPEN THE *Jesuit Relations*. On the night of May 19 or 20, 1656, three hundred Iroquois attacked the Hurons who had taken refuge on the Île d'Orléans:

> [The Iroquois] approached noiselessly, passing in front of Quebec without being noticed. They reached land below the Huron village before daylight. They spread out on all sides along the earthen avenues where corn was sown. In the morning, after all the Christian Hurons had attended mass, as was their custom, and had fortunately confessed, a part of them went off to work. The enemy, waiting in ambush, threw themselves upon them, massacred some on the spot, and led others off as captives, the rest fleeing into our house, which was surrounded by a good defensive palisade, fortified for just such eventualities.

The nationalist village differs from the Canadian village in that it dreams of a palisade.

It was Malraux who said that we often forget we are the children of our past. And our past was, in the beginning, marked by fear.

The first French colonizers were met with a hard land.

Cold that inflicted pain, sickness that killed. Around them the unknown forest, a vast wild solitude. And along with those uncertain beginnings, the constant fear of the Iroquois, who had no intention of letting themselves be despoiled. Fortunately the palisade was there, reassuring.

Some among us inherited from that time a siege mentality. Formerly, the intendants ordered the population to clear their land so that the Iroquois marauders could not hide in the underbrush. Today still, when you travel by canoe on the Ottawa River or the Gatineau, you can instantly distinguish the French properties from the English: the former are empty lawns, the latter retain the natural growth reminiscent of romantic, Byronic English gardens. Two cultures: on the one side a deterrent emptiness, on the other, artfully neglected greenery.

But not everyone felt insecure. Along with the settler came the coureur des bois. He embraced the wilderness, and refused to obey the directives exhorting colonists not to stray from home. Vagabonds with an often swaggering take on life, these irrepressible travellers and smugglers spread the French name far and wide, and performed a carefree vanishing act into other peoples.

Two equal but opposite breeds: one who reconstituted a gracious France, the other who Americanized himself utterly. We will always be torn between the homeland and the continent, a bit like Jack Kerouac, who roamed the roads of the United States only to come home each time to his mother's meat stew and sugar pie. I love my country, but I keep my knapsack close at hand. Just in case . . .

The dangers at the beginning were very real. You have to read the letters of Mother Marie de l'Incarnation, who kept a record of what the Iroquois wrought: the destruction of the

Hurons can "serve to impress on the French what will happen to us, if prompt help does not arrive ... If, therefore, France fails us, we must, in short, either leave or die." Over and over she confides to her correspondents that a return to France is perhaps imminent. To the end of her life the feeling of insecurity remained. When Dollard and his sixteen companions died at Long Sault in 1660, the population of Montreal was no more than 160. The oldest was thirty-one years of age. All that takes its toll. On must reread in this light the *Jesuit Relations,* which describes a Ville-Marie terrorized by the spectacle of Iroquois warriors who, August 29, 1661, having severed the head of the Sulpician Jacques Le Maistre, donned his cassock to parody the Catholic liturgy under the noses of the inhabitants. Tales of torture, sneak attacks, violent counter-attacks, kidnappings of young people, between two burned harvests and two supply ships that never made it to port. An insecurity, in other words, that had nothing imaginary about it and that lasted half a century.

There is the fear of death, that of the body, and that of the soul as well. Take for example this passage from the *Relations* of 1642, where the Iroquois captain Onagan arrives to return to Governor Montmagny two young Frenchmen captured the previous year, François Margerie and Thomas Godefroy: "These two young men whom you see are Iroquois, they are no longer French. The laws of war have made them ours ... We have learned how to transform the French into Iroquois." Assimilation so soon.

After the Iroquois threat came the English. The palisade now had to fend off not just arrows, but cannon. Sixty more years of uncertainty, and then the fall of New France. All this time the palisade was essential. No wonder it became solidly implanted in certain minds.

But nothing is simple. There are not two kinds of French Canadians, one Apollonian and a coureur des bois, and the other Dionysian and a colonist. The two tendencies are there in each of us, as they were in Kerouac. Always, there have been explorers nostalgic for the wood stove and farmers with an entrepreneurial spirit. The call of the wild is as much a part of us as the memory of the hearth.

One thing is undeniable. This composite personality is free. One could say that the French who came here found independence and freedom without looking for it. A certain predisposition must have been operative: it's not serfs who emigrated, but artisans, soldiers, small farmers, and women seeking to establish a home. Each left of his own volition, unlike Australia's convict colonists. Emigration was a first act of liberation on the part of our ancestors at a time when the idea of freedom was not widespread.

Having barely hit land, this quasi-proletarian found himself a property owner. Crossing the Atlantic entailed a guaranteed step up in life for whoever wanted to take advantage of it. There was an authority, of course, the paternal power of the French king. But the king was far away, and although one would gladly read the directives of his intendants, well, one didn't know how to read ... One was pious, of course, but there were so few priests. Slowly, the subject became a settler. He didn't pay tithes, and he grumbled when called on to do tasks for his superiors.

It's instructive to read the accounts of Pehr Kalm, Bigot, and Bougainville, who realized on the eve of the conquest that these men and women were French in name only, because they had fifty years of American freedom under their belts. We can imagine the astonishment of the noble Bougainville, who grew up in a France where hunting was the prerogative of aristocrats, and horseback riding that of the well-to-do. Here he saw eleven-year-old sons of settlers riding horses and peasants hunting bear and moose whenever they liked. He couldn't get over it. These same farmers stole from the French State, practised contraband in the midst of war with New England, and were often deaf to the call to arms. Here is Captain William Pote, prisoner in Quebec from the autumn of 1746 to July 1747: "Many farmers let us know, without embarrassment, that they would go over to the English were they to attack, rather than lose their land, as they have no interest in Old France and cannot count on their Indians, for they have often told me that if the English came they would side with whoever was strongest." In other words it was every man for himself, and to hell with "gentle France."

The conquest complete, when martial law was lifted and it was clear that one could work with the new authorities, people settled down in peace, with no regrets. They did business with the Scottish merchant and dealt with the English provost, and all was for the best. When the Americans arrived in 1775, they considered taking the side of the American Republic, equivocated, and then for the most part opted for the English crown. Note that such hesitations, followed by an eventual commitment, are the sign of a free people.

In fact, the Conquest only began to weigh heavily after the War of 1812, when the French ruling class saw itself refused advancement in business and in the public service. That led to the legitimate revolt of the Patriotes, too few in number, unfortunately, even among their own people. Already, as Durham observed, the exodus of French Canadians towards the New England mills had begun. We are hungry, we've got to leave, and as one settler said to Crémazie, your native land is the land that feeds you.

With Confederation, the clergy assumed power in Quebec, and Monseigneur de Laval's old dream became a reality. In the thirty years that followed, a fifth of the population abandoned the territory. They went óff to earn their daily bread in the United States just as the agricultural ideology was being firmly implanted in books, newspapers, and official pronouncements. Those who could afford to stay listened quietly, or at least gave that appearance. The press and the Quebec novel promoted a *reconquista* of French lands, but clearly they were little read. The ideology glorified by Gérin-Lajoie and Groulx, of a return to the land, timidity hallowed as a virtue, the spectre of Louis Riel on the gallows, none of that seemed to have much impact on this recalcitrant people. As proof, we now count more than fifteen million Americans across the border who are descended from French Canadians—men and women who, as Victor-Lévy Beaulieu has said, are American twice over. No, the people weren't listening.

Rather, they went off to reinvent their French homeland elsewhere on American soil. They colonized the West, and Northern Ontario. French parishes sprang up in foreign places that have since become familiar. I am myself a product of this exodus. My maternal grandparents, fleeing the poverty of a land that would benefit only the eldest of the family, the son of his father, settled in Ottawa in the 1920s. They found a church, and later schools for their children.

I grew up in Ottawa's Sandy Hill, where they had rebuilt their waterside village. I knew the sheltered warmth of this French Catholic household with its Christmas charity, Lent, Palm Sunday, compulsory Mass for the entire school on the first Friday of the month, the Easter vigil, the three hours of fasting before communion on Sunday. I was a choir boy and my brothers were Scouts. There was no village more Québécois than this neighbourhood, with its large families, the corner store, and the milkman and butcher who delivered to your house, and where everyone spoke French. I was fourteen years old before I began to speak English with ease.

The Sandy Hill I knew is no more. The large families have disappeared, the church has burned down, the school was demolished to make way for the University of Ottawa library. The streets where I delivered the newspaper *Le Droit,* populated then by immigrants and French-Canadian working-class families, have been gentrified. Sandy Hill now lives on only in my books and my memories.

Am I in mourning? Not on your life. Such changes have taken place everywhere. Quebec villages have emptied out at the same rhythm as Anglican churches. French Quebec has moved to the big city, just as yesterday's rural Ontario has become urbanized.

It's in the wake of this revolution, which did not always unfold happily, that nationalism has become an active and compensatory agent of nostalgia. The closer the Quebec of yore comes to drawing its last breath, the more it is glorified. The more fiercely one clings to the palisade, the less protection it is able to offer. Infiltrated everywhere by American television and by the Internet, it is more than ever extolled for its redemptive virtues.

Appalled by the legalized murder of Louis Riel and the demographic hemorrhaging, the intellectuals at the beginning of the twentieth century began to preach the reinstatement of New France's palisade. Which led to the apocalyptic demagogy that in 1925 prophesied the extinction of the Quebec people. Quick, we must gather in the herd and shut the doors. Let no one escape, everyone down on your knees! This was the first blossoming of Lionel Groulx's nationalism. That early movement petered out on the right, compromised by its flirtation with Pétain's and Mussolini's totalitarianism and its collusion with Duplessis. In the 1960s it came to life again on the left under the aegis of Albert Memmi, only to dissipate once more, done in this time by sectarianism.

But neither the language nor the methods have changed. Here is the nub of the argument, worthy of a defrocked Lionel Groulx: French language and culture will survive only if Quebec is independent. Otherwise death is imminent. Which enables the new clergy, obviously, to justify extreme measures at every turn. Just as the Church legitimized its hobbling of people's minds by invoking the salvation of their souls, the nationalist government excuses the bludgeoning of its citizens robbed blind by the taxman, the Liquor Board, and Hydro-Québec. We need a Quebec State, so we have to pay. And through the nose.

All that, of course, with the endorsement of the intellectuals who, on the right as on the left, strive to harness the population to an ideology that privileges the collective over the individual. "The collective takes precedence over the individual," wrote Gérard Dagenais, high priest of the French language and ardent separatist, with his customary limpidity. He perhaps wasn't aware of it, but he had just given voice to the sum and substance of Quebec nationalism. The right was already used to ruling with a strong hand; the left would exalt the iron grip of the collective.

HERE IS A LITTLE anecdote that I am sure everyone in French Canada has heard in one form or another.

In my neighbourhood there was a gentleman who dropped by from time to time to chat with my father. A good fellow, not very gifted for work, but . . . a talker. This is what he said, and I don't think I have it wrong, as I heard it a thousand times.

"If we all got together, ten of us with only three hundred bucks each, we could buy a little store, hire a manager, some employees, sell cheap to other French Canadians, then jack up the prices for all the rest. We'd make money in no time. After that we'd buy some apartment blocks, we'd collect the rent, no problem there. I tell you that in twenty years we'd all be rich. I've worked for someone else all my life, and I've had it up to here! It's not because we're French Canadian that we can't make money like the Jews, for God's sake! We could all do like Jos Lévesque! Look at him, he's forty years old, and he doesn't have to work. He collects his rent, he drinks his beer on his doorstep, he's laughing! We only have to do like him. But for that, we have to pull together. Me, I'm ready!"

Not surprisingly, his Sunday morning sermons after mass never got further than four or five beers. The more he drank, the more rich we would be, and the more angry he was that we did nothing about it. He must have come up with a thousand plans like that, without ever leaving his little job as a civil servant. He never had the three hundred dollars of seed money he prescribed. He also said that we didn't listen to him because we were jealous of his ideas. He wasn't too bitter, all the same, except when someone he knew made the mistake of succeeding on his own. Then he said that the other had done well because he was dishonest, an egoist who only thought of himself, and that one day he would come a cropper as he deserved.

For him the collectivity was a sacred, parental entity, and there could be no salvation without it. He never deviated from his collective ideal, he always dreamed of his never-ending crusade and of that Florida that would do such wonders for the French Canadians who would have the backbone to make common cause. His argument was a popular variant of the collective gospel preached by Bouchard and Bourgault. One guy on his own didn't have the right to succeed, but as a gang it was okay. As though the collective nature of the enterprise made up for the materialism associated with success.

It goes without saying that the fellow was anti-Semitic as well. Not because he hated Jews, he would have sworn up and down that he did not. He just couldn't forgive them for sticking together, an old nationalist fantasy. No need to tell you either that he was a tiresome individual who harangued everyone in sight once he'd had a few drinks.

Let's now take an older example, more to the tastes of Abbé Groulx: my compatriot Jean Éthier-Blais. In the book he devotes to the canon, Blais comes to the rescue of a Maurras he considers to have been unfairly treated. On the subject of the Dreyfus Affair, he begins by acknowledging, with a generosity that seems somehow half-hearted, that modern historians concur as to the captain's innocence. (A wondrously advanced individual, Jean Éthier-Blais, for whom that universal value called justice meant very little.) Taking up Maurras's argument, Blais asks indignantly: "Was the individual then more important than the State?" Which implies that one should have let the innocent Captain Dreyfus rot on Devil's Island so as to protect the French army from the Masonic Lodges, and the French State cowed by this "rich and active minority." Blais concludes: "Perhaps the Franco-Québécois civilization will vanish for want of having asserted the primacy of its own State, and for having knuckled under to the propaganda that places the self before all the rest." This says it all. In nationalist thought, in Quebec, man is nothing next to the collective. He yields to the greater number, and it is only within the group that he can fulfil himself and move forward, sure of himself and affluent, like my neighbour daydreaming over his beer. A legitimate State is not founded on the individual; on the contrary, the individual is made free by the collective.

It will be said: "Don't pay any attention, Blais was on the right." But we hear the same thought echoed by Pierre Bourgault. He too wanted us to join with others, and had we done so, we would have had ourselves a country. Like, for instance, the Jews.

You will tell me that Pierre Bourgault is not a Fascist like Blais. Falardeau neither. Both are dumbfounded every time someone throws that word their way, a word they're never shy to unleash when talking about their detractors. We can understand their indignation. They both support the workers, shed tears for truck drivers, are in favour of the emancipation of women and gays, and, aristocratic antimaterialists that they are, disdain the power vested in money. I'm no Fascist, they'll say, you're the Fascist!

The difference between the Blais and the Bourgaults stems from the fact that with the latter the subjugation of the individual to the collective comes from the left and not the right. They're inspired by the real world, not a dream world. But in their left-wing nationalist vision, the individual must still submit. In all his arguments Bourgault glorifies this knuckling under of the individual to the collective. We can now see how Hydro-Québec, with such a seal of approval, can impose whatever rates it wants. It's ours, and so we shouldn't complain . . .

Even today, nationalism canonizes Hydro-Québec as the greatest triumph of *Homo quebecensis* and the first accomplishment of the nation's father, René Lévesque. Hydro-Québec forces the issue with a constant stream of propaganda, allowing it to brush aside all public criticism. Thus it commissioned a television series with the ridiculous title *Les Bâtisseurs d'eau*

(The Builders of Water), wherein the good Québécois squared off against the nasty English exploiters, and both national and emotional buttons were pushed to the hilt.

It's not hard to see why the State corporation goes to such pains to exploit its myth. The reality, after all, includes elevated prices, virtual monopolies that throttle the consumer, the devastation of James Bay, floods, the ice storm, the scandalous forced buy-out of the St. François Valley farmers, its thirty-seven vice-presidents with their exorbitant salaries, and so on. Hydro-Québec, a state within the state, a taxman on top of the taxman, has every reason to soften up public opinion well in advance, just in case the Quebec Provincial Police should have some Cree hunters shot down who got it into their heads to dynamite pylons in order to protect their heritage. Hydro-Québec is extremely deft in making electricity an ideological issue. It muzzles the press and television by purchasing an enormous amount of advertising. When was the last time you saw a series of articles denouncing that corporation in *Le Devoir?* Let's not be naïve . . . And it gets whatever it wants from the provincial government, including, with utter contempt for justice, the most arbitrary and illegal edicts, and this in the name of a supposed collective interest. It's enough to make you ill, and to induce you to swear off all community spirit.

The overweening behaviour of Hydro-Québec is the most striking manifestation of Quebec nationalism's ideological excesses, all of whose benefits go to the privileged class. If the Canadian village is exposed to all the winds that blow across the Prairies and along the Great Lakes, the Quebec palisade is often a worm-eaten fort whose air is unbreathable. Try criticizing Hydro-Québec and you will be told that you are a bad Québécois. Monsieur Lesieur will say that after all it's ours, and he'll keep saying it even if his bill is higher than mine. It will refuse to buy ads in your paper if your reporter is too inquisitive. It will discredit the researcher who has proved mercury pollution is due to ecological disturbances triggered by the company. Historians will be paid to give the lie to Native demands affecting its territory. You will be hauled into court, if necessary. And if Hydro-Québec has its edicts adopted illegally, and they are later invalidated by a Canadian court, no problem, it will immediately arrange to have the PQ government pass legislation in due form to sanction what is arbitrary, immoral, and illegal.

To sum up. Quebec nationalism favours the collective over the individual. If it accepts in lukewarm fashion individual freedoms, it exalts at the top of its voice an import that is patently artificial, a collective liberation borrowed from foreign, Third World struggles. Thus it remains profoundly colonized. Reread Michèle Lalonde's *Le Dernier recours de Baptiste à Catherine* (Baptiste's Last Appeal to Catherine), which says, essentially, that to deprive a nation of its cohesiveness, all you have to do is to give people individual freedoms. It has the effect of drowning the fish in a "great democratic whole," a devilish prospect indeed.

This is a long-standing criticism of Canada on the part of the nationalists, always wary of personal happiness and more than ready to sacrifice it on the altar of collective salvation. Only it would appear that the Québécois have, up to the present, preferred individual liberty to a liberation that is artificial, borrowed, and forced. And the Quebec intelligentsia responds by denigrating this bad people that refuses to listen. It's sad indeed. To the right-thinking bourgeois readers of *Le Devoir,* all we can do is murmur the dictum of Bertold Brecht: the people having lost the support of its leaders, we must dissolve the people . . .

This entire comedy is worthy of late Sartre, who in his dotage swore only by the group as a whole, and condemned *habeus corpus,* the right to vote, tolerance, and those "formal freedoms that serve only to alienate all the more the proletariat." That same Sartre, the submissive fellow traveller, banned his own play *Dirty Hands* in Vienna so as not to offend the Communists. A sentence taken from *On a raison de se révolter* says it all: "I think that an individual in the group, even if he is a little bit terrorized, is still better than an individual alone and thinking in terms of separation." Or should we just say that Sartre, glorifying this human individual blended into the nation, would have made a good Quebec nationalist?

Thus, what will be at stake in the next referendum will not be the question of whether Quebec wants to be independent or to live in association with Canada according to the model borrowed from Jean Monnet and ridiculed by Charles de Gaulle. The Québécois will decide, rather, whether they want to preserve the equilibrium between their individual rights and their collective obligations, or to accept the subjection of the particular to the general. It should be a good fight: me against us, the free individual in a big country that is his or the palisade circling the dutiful settler under the stern eye of the father.

You will already have guessed that my choice is made. I've been suspicious of collective primacy ever since I was a militant for Franco-Ontario. In those days there was, in a small mid-northern Ontario town, a nice man who had succeeded in making important gains on behalf of his French-speaking fellow citizens. He claimed he was fighting for justice, not just for language, and he was a skilled negotiator, respectful of his neighbour, practical in his approach.

He was a school administrator by profession. I learned at about that time that he practised sexual harassment on a grand scale. Almost all the young female teachers he hired were invited, if they were pretty, to step into his office after class. We never knew if he went so far as to rape, but he certainly took full advantage of his "droit de seigneur." You had to have a strong character to resist him, he could become violent, and the teachers were well advised to keep mum if they wanted to hold on to their jobs. I saw him again some years later at a conference: grand as a bishop, basking in everyone's high regard, yet modest. Doubtless he died in his bed surrounded by his seven children and his twenty grandchildren.

He was never brought to justice. The few women who had the courage to complain were told that they must have been running after him. Or else were sniggered at. "When you have seven children, you're a going concern, eh, you have to understand . . ." And when things got serious, French-Canadian solidarity was invoked to protect the gentleman. "He's a pillar of the community . . . He's accomplished so much for us, we're not going to, all the same . . . We might do ourselves damage . . . What will they think of us elsewhere? No, our best weapon is silence. Let's turn the page."

The collectivity represents, of course, mutual aid, local festivals, the credit union, school, surroundings in which one may realize one's potential. But it's also collusion and muzzling, the refusal to accept criticism, the stifling of free will. It pains me to say so, but this gentleman's name was Riverain.

THERE ARE DAYS when the whole debate leaves me with a bad taste in my mouth, and like everyone else I want it to be over. On those days, I go for a walk.

I live in the Italian part of Ottawa. At the corner grocery store they sell olive oil by the gallon, braids of garlic, a thousand kinds of pasta, hard-crusted bread, anchovies, dry and fragrant cheeses, and in season, fresh olives and crates of grapes for making wine. I stroll there among the *mammas* who are shopping for Sunday supper. The store is in a small commercial centre in the middle of which is the reconstituted village where the old people gather. Sicilians, Calabrians, natives of Piedmont who speak an old-fashioned Italian, quarrel sometimes, laugh a lot. They have recreated here their marketplace from old Italy. They are retired workers who only yesterday made and remade the streets of Ottawa, and whose speech and dress we unfairly mocked.

Many have returned to Italy like Maisonneuve to France, but most have stayed here. Their children have naturalized them. They have remained attached to their nationality and they profit from their citizenship. Each is Canadian, but together they are other; I am their fellow citizen, but among themselves they are compatriots.

I sometimes go to their festivals. On Saint Anthony's Day, for instance, a joyful celebration that turns Preston Street, for a while, into Via Marconi in Little Italy. There is first of all mass in the church of the eponymous saint, where a French-Canadian priest officiates in Italian. Everyone is there, and you have to arrive early to find a seat. The ambassador is present, along with all those who have become successful and made a name for themselves. The most beautiful sight is the procession of veterans wearing their coloured costumes: the *bersaglieri* with their helmets at an angle and their long pheasant's feather, the *carabinieri* with the cocked hat topped with a red frond, all gussied up like Bolivian admirals. They are touching to see, these old men who lost wars in Abyssinia, Albania, Libya, so proud you'd have thought they had won them all. Beautiful losers, as Leonard Cohen would say, totally at ease in this country settled by the excluded, and whose true moral victory is a successful transplantation.

The banquet afterwards is a must. The food is good. Everyone is dressed up, the children, the adults, the elderly. All the beautiful dialects of the old country can be heard, but the young, of course, speak mainly English among themselves. Their grandmothers chide them for this, but embrace them immediately afterwards. Some even talk French together, since the Ottawa region boasts its share of French-speaking Italians. It's a wonderful family party where everyone talks at once around the table, mainly about hockey.

Suddenly I'm reminded of Michel Seymour, a Montreal academic whose thinking is generous and honest, and who is the author of *La Nation en question*. Would he see the diversity around me the way I do? I suspect he would. He would certainly understand these men who are Neapolitans or Piedmontese more than they are Italians, and who feel a peninsular solidarity only when their soccer players take on those of Brazil. But nationalist thinker that he is, Seymour practises the religion of the collectivity and places the people above all. He sees peoples where I see individuals. We will never perceive things in the same way. For me and for many others, the nation is contingent, it weighs less heavily in the scales than does my citizenship. My nationality imposes obligations that I willingly assume, but my citizenship gives me tangible rights. Michel Seymour, along with many like him, dreams of fusing nationality and citizenship, whereas I see a river and a bridge between the two. He wants a homeland and a country in one, I make a distinction between the two. He is wary of individual freedoms, I do not want his paternal collectivity. That's all, it's not serious, and one day the popular will will perhaps decide between us. Enough thinking, let's go back to the party.

Walking about aimlessly, I come upon a little group apart from the rest. Young people, all very beautiful, richly dressed, who speak an Italian I can actually understand. They're part of the ambassador's entourage, real Italians with no intention of settling here, who came to the festival because they had no choice. They are sniggering. I eavesdrop. They are making fun of the beautiful old warriors. They've decided that the Italians here are not attractive, nor very well dressed. Their tastes are kitschy, what with their plastic Roman fountains, paper vines, the Caesarian laurels in the restaurant's neon signs, and the great names, Dante and d'Annunzio, sullied by their inclusion on the menu! "And then," they all say at once, "these peasants speak so badly. That isn't Italian . . ."

I walk away. Disgusted? Not at all. I understand these young people, who when you come down to it are no different from so many of the French and English who, newly arrived on these shores, are astonished to find themselves not at home. Of course they criticize, and we, the vulnerable, are hurt. Centuries and a sea separate us; will we never one day, on either side, understand that?

I like the Italian village, I feel at ease there. But the party's over, the tables and the trestles are being taken down, so-called anonymous Ottawa is reasserting itself, everyone heads home. We'll see each other again on San Roccol's Day, or perhaps at my place, on St. Jean Baptiste.

I'm about to leave when an old gentleman whom I know calls out to me. He's an Eritrean who took refuge in Canada with his family ten years ago. Since his birthplace was for a long time an Italian colony, as a young man he learned the language being spoken on Saint Anthony's Day. He never misses this festival, where he meets the friends of his age that he's met since his arrival. He loves talking Italian with them, especially since it's the only European language spoken in Canada that he knows. Today he's brought along his granddaughter, lovely as a pearl, all dressed in white as though she were on her way to communion. She has such a beautiful smile that I can't help raising my hand to her.

Suddenly I remember that I've forgotten my two protagonists, Lesieur and Labine, at the entrance to the Mount Royal subway station. I bet they haven't budged an inch. Let's go find them.

What did I tell you? They're there, indeed, thick as thieves. On this November night, a blustery wind huffs through the city. His hand on his Basque beret, Monsieur Lesieur shakes one hand of Monsieur Labine, who holds his other to his Scotch cap. Deafened by the wind, the two shout kind words at each other: good night, thanks for everything, we'll have to get together soon! They separate.

I'm not sure what will become of them. There will be no cartoonesque ending to my colonial novel, certainly, with father Lesieur seeing the light and altering his views. No, he's fine the way he is, I don't want him to change. I'd just be happy if he could only understand why his friend Labine thinks and acts differently. I'm not pressuring him, he can do what he likes, and should he experience any doubts or disquieting moods, I'd be the last to know, because he would keep them to himself like the good bourgeois of the palisade that he is. That's his prerogative, as we all know. And I don't see myself, believe me, consoling my friend Lesieur with an "It's all right, don't be upset, anyone could have got things wrong all his life!" Really . . .

They'll probably play bridge together a while more, long enough for each to find himself a soulmate. One evening the two of them will again be matched against Madame Laramée and Mademoiselle Laplante, two players not to be taken lightly.

Lesieur will end up with Laramée, Labine will go off with Laplante, and they will all go on with their lives with no help from me. No news of the beautiful Irène, other than that her indispensable friend Nussbaum introduced her to the owner of a travel agency, a good-looking bachelor, not too confirmed, and he promised to show her some of the wonders of the world. She has apparently followed her guide to Rome. All I know is that she will have no regrets if she misses the next referendum.

For my part, I only wish for my friends facing me there a separatism more on the light side that will have dispensed with its victimist obsessions, and that will offer the Québécois an option that is truly new. In other words, a separatism that is not nationalist and that is free of its old fears, its obsolete complexes, and its old-hat pet hates. Then it will be up to us to choose between a Canadian space that we know and an imagined City. The choice will be clear, and the outcome of the referendum will be beyond question on both sides. But I'm dreaming, of course. Don't hold it against me. That's my vocation.

One thing is undeniable, the time will come when I'll have no more to say about any of that. The colonial novel will go on alone. And out of all this pondering, the only enduring image will be that of my little African girl in white, lovely as night and day. In her smile I saw all the indifference on which happiness thrives, and that will one day supersede, I'm sure, my often uneasy lucidity.